ALEXANDER WILSON was a writer, spy and secret service officer. He served in the First World War before moving to India to teach as a Professor of English Literature and eventually became Principal of Islamia College at the University of Punjab in Lahore. He began writing spy novels whilst in India and he enjoyed great success in the 1930s with reviews in the *Telegraph*, *Observer* and the *Times Literary Supplement* amongst others. Wilson also worked as an intelligence agent and his characters are based on his own fascinating and largely unknown career in the Secret Intelligence Service. He passed away in 1963.

*By Alexander Wilson*

# Chronicles of the Secret Service

## ALEXANDER WILSON

Allison & Busby Limited
12 Fitzroy Mews
London W1T 6DW
*allisonandbusby.com*

First published in 1940.
This edition published by Allison & Busby in 2016.

A CIP catalogue record for this book is available from
the British Library.

10 9 8 7 6 5 4 3 2 1

ISBN 978-0-7490-1845-0

Typeset in 11/16 pt Adobe Garamond Pro by
Allison & Busby Ltd.

The paper used for this Allison & Busby publication
has been produced from trees that have been legally sourced
from well-managed and credibly certified forests.

Printed and bound by
CPI Group (UK) Ltd, Croydon, CR0 4YY

# CONTENTS

# THE CHINA DOLL

'Have you ever read the fable of the wolf and the lamb, Carter?' asked Sir Leonard Wallace, leaning back in his chair, and looking up at his assistant.

The tall, good-looking young man with the wavy hair and bronzed complexion smiled.

'Well, yes, sir,' he replied. 'I suppose everyone has.'

He wondered what was in his chief's mind. Sir Leonard did not ask such questions, as a rule, unless there was reason behind them.

'Not everyone,' disagreed Wallace. 'That is rather an exaggerated statement to make. Still, Aesop's Fables are probably as widely read as anything written or told ever has been. It is pretty evident, however, that the powers that be in Japan know all about the wolf and the lamb. Japan has cast herself for the part of wolf and a play neatly arranged, to be produced and directed by herself.'

'Who plays the part of the lamb, sir?' asked Carter.

'China, of course. Poor helpless China, with her internal troubles, her disruption, her family quarrels is an easy prey for the voracious wolf. Japan has had her eyes on China for years. The time has now come when she thinks she is powerful enough to strike the blow. It will not happen all at once. She is too cute for that. Besides the Oriental method of torture indicates a gradual process. China will be annexed in a succession of cuts – eaten up slice by slice so to speak. And as she has commenced over Manchuria and Jehol so she will continue. China is held responsible for provocation just as the wolf put the blame on the poor lamb before devouring her. I've sent warning after warning to London. America has suggested a joint action which Japan would not dare face, but we are not ready to take any steps just now. Think of it! It makes me feel blasphemous. Of course I must admit to a feeling of admiration for the Japs. They have chosen their time well, and with amazing nerve and skill, when Europe is staggering about like a drunken man from one crisis to another. Well, I've done my best to point out what should be done and the necessity for quick action. I can do no more than that. There is one thing I can do and will do, though, before I leave this colony. I shall rout out, lock, stock and barrel, the nest of the Japanese spies here.'

'But I thought—' commenced Carter.

'So did I,' interrupted the other grimly; tapped a document lying before him on his desk with a shapely forefinger. 'This proves otherwise. It was brought to me this morning by a messenger from Winstanley. As you were out I opened it myself.' He held it up to Carter. 'Read it!'

The young man, who appeared greatly interested now, took

the sheets of foolscap covered with typescript, displaying the stamp of the Inspector-General of Police on each page, and commenced eagerly to peruse them. Sir Leonard removed the lid of the large tobacco bowl standing before him on the desk; proceeded to fill his pipe, making use of his artificial hand with amazing celerity and adroitness. When the tobacco was lit and burning to his satisfaction, he sat puffing away contentedly as though he had not a care in the world, watching with approval the keen, interested expression on the face of his young assistant as the latter stood by his side reading.

Sir Leonard Wallace and Carter were in Hong Kong; had been there for some months. At the earnest request of the British governor, Sir Leonard had accepted the appointment of acting governor in order to investigate with the fullest authority and on the spot a gigantic plot to defraud the government of Hong Kong. He had taken with him Carter as his private secretary while Cousins had been sent to the colony to act independently. His investigations and those of his colleagues had been entirely successful and, at the time this narrative opens, Wallace's periods of office as governor was drawing to a close. To be exact, there were but three weeks to run.

The conspirators had planned not only to deplete the Treasury, by means of forged government bonds, fictitious loans, and fraudulent contracts, but had been handing over to a Japanese consul secret information of a naval and military character concerning the defences of Hong Kong. It appeared that an agent of Japan had obtained possession of information regarding the conspiracy and a list of all concerned in it. This had been used as a lever to force the principals to supply the Japanese consul with the details he demanded. Naturally, when Sir Leonard Wallace had brought all this to light, a strongly-worded protest had been sent by the British government to Japan. As a result of this the consul had been relieved of his appointment, and ordered to return to Japan, while the Japanese government, as was only to be expected, denied all knowledge of any espionage activities in Hong Kong. Sir Leonard Wallace, however, had not been prepared to allow the consul to depart so easily. Directly information reached him that the official had been relieved of his appointment, and was, therefore, no longer a privileged person, he had given instructions for him to be subpoenaed as a witness against the ringleaders of the conspiracy. The Japanese had attempted to evade this and sail for his own country, whereupon he had been promptly arrested. His evidence had proved valuable at the trial but he had also been forced to part with information about his own activities. Wallace possessed methods of his own of exacting items of that kind from recalcitrant spies. Yumasaki, the ex-consul, discovered that fact to his sorrow. Afterwards he had been escorted to a ship and not left until she sailed for Japan.

Carter finished his perusal of the sheets of paper with a soft but prolonged whistle. He placed them on the desk in front of Sir Leonard.

'Then we couldn't have cleared them all out, sir,' he commented.

'Obviously not,' replied the governor, removing the pipe from his mouth, and tapping out the ashes into a tray. 'There must have been others hidden away somewhere. Yet I could have sworn Yumasaki had told me all. There's no getting completely inside an Oriental mind, though,' he added with a sigh. 'Well, we start again, Carter, and we have three weeks to make a clean sweep.'

'I wonder how Ransome found all this out. It's pretty good work on his part.'

'Very good work,' agreed Sir Leonard. 'He's a splendid man, but I think his popularity as a policeman has a lot to do with it. Those Chinese detectives under him would go through fire and water for him. It's what I've always contended. Treat a Chinaman well, and you can trust him up to the hilt; he'll do anything for you.'

'I can't quite see why these spies are remaining here,' observed Carter. 'After the manner in which you descended on the others, sir, followed by that rigid scrutiny of the papers of every Jap in the colony, I should have thought they would have waited a bit before commencing again; at least, until your term of office was over. They must know you will soon be leaving.'

Sir Leonard smiled.

'They probably thought I would not expect their activities to recommence so soon. They didn't anticipate Ransome and his sleuths being kept on the watch.'

'But what can they hope to discover now?'

'You must remember Yumasaki only received the plans of the fortifications from Collinson. He badly wanted the chart, promised him, showing the exact position of the minefields, lists of the number and calibre of the big guns, and a plan depicting the location of all magazines and other military and naval stores. He never received those. We ascertained that. Thank God he didn't. Collinson and Ferguson have run Great Britain into an expenditure of millions of dollars, as it is, by handing over plans of the fortifications. If every defensive scheme in the colony had to be altered, as well as the fortifications, the expense would be colossal. Besides, Japan naturally is anxious to keep watch, if she can, on the new scheme of fortifying the island. The more I think of it,' he added, lying back in his chair, and regarding the young man by his side, 'the more bothered I feel. This desperate anxiety to know all there is to know about our defences, taken in conjunction with Japan's operations in China, can only mean one thing: she anticipates a continuation of trouble in Europe and eventually a war into which Great Britain will be drawn. When that time comes, she will sail her warships into Hong Kong having, as she hopes, made herself perfectly acquainted with all defensive measures, and annex the colony confident that we shall be too heavily engaged elsewhere to offer resistance. The same, I imagine, applies to Singapore, but that's not my pidgin – at the moment. In the meantime, she will continue with her policy of slicing off bits of China as a punishment for pretended affronts gradually consolidating herself in that country.'

He suddenly sprang to his feet, and began to pace to and fro in the large, well-furnished apartment.

'Heavens!' he exclaimed. 'Were there ever such blind, inept fools as those at home? When I get back, Carter, I'll have so much to say about their lack of vision and dilatoriness that they'll – they'll want to make me Governor of the South Pole or somewhere as far away as possible to get rid of me.'

Carter smiled. He knew how caustic Sir Leonard could be and his opinion of certain statesmen. He imagined the bad time his chief would give them when he did return to England. The young man had seldom seen Wallace so deeply moved. It was a rarity for the Chief of the British Secret Service to display his feelings in such a manner; an eloquent proof of how seriously he regarded the Japanese menace.

Wallace continued his pacing for some time, his chin sunk on his breast, his artificial hand pushed deep into his coat pocket, the other firmly gripping his pipe. Carter remained by the desk watching him, making no attempt to speak. He knew the signs. Sir Leonard was deep in thought; that astute mind of his turning over the fresh problem that confronted him, and the young man, acting as secretary, knew better than to interrupt the brain that had once been described as the most brilliant in England. At length, Wallace returned to his chair, and sat down.

'What a pity Cousins went back to England!' he remarked. 'He would have been extremely useful now. Still, it's no use bothering about that.' He became silent again, his hand caressing his determined, well-shaped chin as his mind continued to grapple with the news that had caused him such perturbation. Presently he picked up the report from the Inspector-General of Police and read it through for perhaps the twentieth time. Occasionally he murmured fragments aloud as though they in particular impressed themselves upon him. '"A Japanese sailor from a *Maru* boat drunk with *samsui* was taken to the central police station and, in the ordinary course of routine, searched. Among the articles found on him was a document which Superintendant Ransome decided was in Japanese cipher . . . Mr Ransome, who knows the language well, set to work to get at its meaning, being convinced that such a letter in the possession of an illiterate seaman must have some particular significance." Bright of Ransome,' approved Sir Leonard, 'and brighter still that he succeeded in deciphering the document.

I should rather like to have that young man in the Intelligence Service.' He continued to read on, again murmuring certain parts of the report aloud. At last he threw down the sheets of paper, and looked up at Carter. 'In short,' he declared, 'a drunken Japanese seaman is found to possess a coded document which turns out to be a message obviously from Japanese espionage agents in this colony to a central headquarters in Tokyo. It contains nothing very significant except the fact that difficulties are great, more agents are required, and great care must be taken in smuggling them into the colony. Neither the address of the Tokyo headquarters is given nor, and this is more important, is that of the agents in Hong Kong. The fact that the seaman, on recovering from his drunkenness, seemed so appalled when he found his precious letter had been taken from him, and committed *hara kiri* directly he was questioned and realised it had been decoded, proves that he was acting under very stringent orders. It's a great pity that knife of his was lying within his reach when they were examining him. Still, I suppose we can't blame them; they could hardly have anticipated such an action on his part, and he must have been extraordinarily quick. Clever of the Japs, you know, Carter, to use common seamen as messengers. Who would be likely to suspect them? If this fellow hadn't slipped up and got drunk, we might have continued comfortably to believe Hong Kong was quite free of the spy menace. Poor chap, he took the only possible way out for him. The trouble is, his masters in this colony will know all about his arrest, death and, of course, guess the reason why he committed suicide. In other words, they will know we are wise to them again.'

'Ransome's investigations will already have told them that, sir, won't they?'

'Not necessarily. According to this' – he tapped the report – 'the superintendent's Chinese detectives did all the tracing of the sailor's movements from the time he left the ship until he was picked up drunk. Chinese are the craftiest people in the world, and obviously Ransome's bunch are particularly gifted. The pity of it is that such good work should have had such a negative result. Ring up Sir Masterson Winstanley, Carter, and ask him to come along to see me directly after tiffin. I can't manage it this morning owing to the visit of the arts and crafts deputation and my appointment at the Happy Valley to open the new sports club. Lord!' he sighed. 'How glad I shall be when I can shed all this ceremonial nonsense.'

Sir Leonard had all along found the role of acting governor of a colony, with its continuous succession of public duties, extremely irksome. That type of appointment did not appeal to him at all; nevertheless, although he had kept always foremost in mind the real reason for his presence in Hong Kong, he had not in any way neglected his multifarious social and official obligations. He had, in fact, proved himself an ideal governor. The manner in which he had handled a terrible situation, with murder stalking grimly any who threatened to prove of danger to the conspirators, had won the admiration and respect of everyone. There was a general desire that he should continue to hold his appointment for, at least, the usual period of five years; the Legislative Council had asked his permission to send a strongly-worded request to Westminster that his services be retained. Sir Leonard, however, quickly put an end to all hopes in that direction. While thanking the council for the confidence shown in him, he made it quite clear that he himself had no intention of remaining in the colony as governor.

As usual, he and Lady Wallace entertained several guests to luncheon but, directly afterwards, he went to his study, where he found the Inspector-General of Police, Sir Masterson Winstanley, already awaiting him. Without preamble, except to invite the Chief of Police to take a chair, he plunged into the matter which was uppermost in his mind.

'Thanks for the detailed and clearly-worded report concerning this Japanese affair, Winstanley,' he acknowledged. 'That young man of yours, Ransome, is to be highly commended for his enterprise and zeal.'

'I am glad to hear you say that, sir,' returned the IG. 'At the same time, I am deeply sorry all his work was allowed to go for nought, owing to the stupidity of the inspector in allowing the sailor's belongings to lie within the man's reach. There was no intention of making a charge. The Jap was only arrested to allow him to sober up. He'd been making a nuisance of himself. His belongings, with the exception of the letter, had been placed on the desk ready to be handed back to him. Nobody anticipated his taking the action he did.'

'Of course not,' agreed Wallace. 'I think you are being rather unfair to the inspector in calling him stupid. And, in any case, if the Jap had been stopped from committing *hara kiri*, I don't suppose we'd ever have obtained any useful information out of him.'

'I'm pretty certain you would have done,' replied Sir Masterson. 'I haven't forgotten how you made Yumasaki speak!'

'H'm,' grunted Sir Leonard. 'It appears I failed to get him to say anything. The fellow was cleverer than I thought. Tell me exactly what happened at the police station.'

'Superintendent Ransome was sitting at the desk, the

Japanese letter before him with its decoded translation. The inspector was standing by his side, a European sergeant a couple of yards away, and two Indian constables behind the seaman, who was, of course, standing facing Ransome. The fellow got into a terrible state of panic when he realised the letter was in the hands of the police. Then as soon as Ransome made him aware he knew the contents, and began questioning him, he suddenly sprang forward, grasped the knife and, before hands could be laid on him, had plunged it to the hilt into his abdomen. Ransome tells me it was a ghastly sight.'

'It must have been. And was nothing of any significance discovered at all while the superintendent's detectives were engaged in tracing the fellow's movements?'

Winstanley shook his head, his stern, dark face expressing his regret.

'You have seen the report, sir,' he remarked. 'Nothing has been left out.'

'I realise that. I was merely anxious to know if there was some little action, a movement, anything in fact, that may have been remarked by those who saw the sailor, mentioned to your men but thought too insignificant to note.'

Again the IG shook his head.

'The detectives spent the whole night at the job,' he declared, 'and you have read of the success that attended their efforts. As far as we know, everything he did and everywhere he went from the time he left his ship until his arrest, was discovered and noted.'

'Splendidly efficient work that, Winstanley,' approved Sir Leonard. 'It couldn't have been easy especially as he seemed always on his own.'

'Those men of Ransome's *are* efficient, sir. I take a great deal of pride in them.'

'And in him,' smiled the governor. 'Well, there is to my mind one very significant fact which you have all apparently overlooked.'

'What is that?'

'The seaman went from one drinking den to another, and he was always alone! It doesn't seem to have occurred to anyone that there was anything curious in that. And yet it strikes me as being most interesting. Sailors all the world over are congenial souls and fond of company. If they don't go ashore in port with their mates, they very soon pick up companions. This man did neither. He was all the time by himself, as far as your men have been able to ascertain.'

'He was probably acting under orders.'

'Of course he was. That's obvious. But don't you see my point? His instructions were that he was to meet someone who would give him a communication. Now a man entrusted with a mission of such importance would not ordinarily go and get drunk. In fact, he would be chosen for his reliability, wouldn't he?' Winstanley nodded, wondering what was coming. 'The last thing,' went on Sir Leonard, 'he would do, one would imagine, would be to make a round of drinking dens. Now a sailor on his own, without any mission but to enjoy himself, who went pub crawling would pick up companions. This fellow did not – we presume his orders debarred that – but apparently his orders did not prohibit him from going to those drinking places. Your investigations show that he came ashore at six or thereabouts, went straight to the Fan Tan saloon, where he stayed drinking for half an hour, sitting alone at one of the tables in the place. Leaving there, he went from one to another, remaining in each about the same period of time. In all, he visited six saloons. At twenty minutes past nine, he was arrested on the Praya, where he was found to be drunk. The fact that he was there indicates that he was not on his way to visit another den, but was returning to his ship. From all this, I gather that, although his instructions were to avoid companions, he was expected to visit drinking saloons. In other words, the person who gave him the letter was to meet him in one or other of those places. The regularity of the period he spent in each shows clearly that he was working to a timetable. In order not to be too conspicuous he had to have a drink or more in each. As it happens, the fact that he remained so steadfastly alone did make him conspicuous, for which we have reason to be grateful, because I doubt if his movements could have been traced otherwise. Obviously his employers did not anticipate the possibility of his getting drunk. Perhaps he hadn't a very strong head, or the fascination of *samsui* was too much for him and he was unable to resist taking more than he could hold. Anyhow that doesn't matter.'

'But,' objected Winstanley, 'the belief that he was met in one of those saloons doesn't help us much.'

'Oh, yes, it does,' disagreed Sir Leonard. 'We have narrowed the search down to one place. He undoubtedly received the letter in the last saloon he visited, otherwise the presumption is he would have gone to another. Had he received it in a previous one there would have been no point in his continuing his pilgrimage.'

'By Jove! I can see now what you've been driving at, sir. The last place he went to was that new dancing and drinking hall, the China Doll.'

'Exactly. That's where he was met and given the letter.'

'But why did he have to go to so many? Surely his appointment could have been made for one specific place.'

'There may have been a hundred and one reasons. You must remember we have been very severe on wiping out Japanese espionage in this colony, and the agents here now have found it necessary to be ultra-cautious. The man who eventually met the sailor may be known to your men and, as a police watch is always kept on these drinking dens, he was forced to be rigidly careful.'

Sir Masterson did not seem altogether satisfied with that.

'Ransome's Chinese are extraordinarily thorough,' he remarked, 'and have the patience of their race almost to an exaggerated degree. I don't know myself how they did it, but they seem to have traced every movement of the sailor's. Not once in their report, as you will have read in the transcription from my office, is there the suggestion that he may have met someone who passed something to him. It seems certain that he remained alone always.'

'That means nothing,' returned Sir Leonard. 'It is perfectly easy to transfer an object like a letter from hand to hand unobserved when two persons are in the act of passing each other, or even from table to table – underneath, of course – when contiguous as they are in those places.'

'Not so easy, when one of the parties as drunk as the Jap must have been by the time he got to the China Doll.'

'There's a good deal in that,' nodded Wallace, rubbing his chin thoughtfully.

'Isn't it likely,' hazarded the Chief of Police, 'that the agent who gave him the letter was an employee? A bartender or a waiter would entirely escape notice, if he passed it to him in the act of serving him.'

'In that case, the man would be in one saloon only. There wouldn't have been any reason for the seaman to visit six.'

'No; that's true.'

They discussed the matter for some time longer, the Inspector-General leaving with the promise that he would order Ransome to concentrate his men on obtaining a complete list of everyone, as far as possible, who had been on the premises of the China Doll between eight-thirty and nine-fifteen the previous night. Special attention was to be paid to Japanese patrons and, if there had been any, their places of residence were to be immediately subjected to a visitation and intensive search.

'I'm afraid I haven't a great deal of hope that anything will come of that,' remarked Sir Leonard, as the two men shook hands. 'Still I can think of nothing more promising at the moment. I have a feeling that something very significant has eluded your men, probably because it is too obvious to have been noticed. I haven't the faintest idea what it may be or how the notion got into my head, but I have been puzzling it out ever since I first read your report. Tell Ransome to set his men investigating everything of which they previously took no notice, because it was part of the scheme of things. You get my meaning?'

Sir Masterson Winstanley did, and departed with his own mind in a state of extreme perplexity. He had had so much to do with Sir Leonard Wallace and seen such evidences of the cleverness of a brain that seldom missed anything, and seemed capable of thinking several moves ahead of that of an ordinary individual, that he felt now the governor, without at the moment knowing what it was, had hit on the one point that would probably mean success in the investigations. It was perhaps only natural that the Inspector-General of Police should be anxious to fathom the elusive item upon which the governor was placing so much importance. As his rickshaw took him speedily to police headquarters, the uniformed coolies trotting along with rhythmic leg and arm movements, he continually muttered to himself: 'Too obvious to have been noticed! Now what the devil could fit in that was so much in the scheme of things that it might have been overlooked by observant fellows like Ransome's Chinese detectives?'

In the meantime, Sir Leonard had taken to pacing his study again, puffing clouds of smoke from his pipe as he strove to fathom that which was eluding him. For half an hour he tramped to and fro, quite forgetful that he needed rest in view of the fact that there was a garden party to attend later in the afternoon, that he afterwards was to receive the two unofficial Chinese members of the Legislative Council, Sir T'so Lin Tao and Sir Peter Hing Kee in audience, and that he and Lady Wallace were giving a great dinner and ball that night. For the time being his mind was devoted, to the exclusion of all else, to chasing something which he was certain would provide him with a very valuable clue. All at once he stopped dead. His steel-grey eyes gleaming triumphantly, he gave vent to a little chuckle.

'Of course,' he murmured. 'Fancy taking all this time to remember a fact like that.'

He did not remind himself that that which he had recollected, and connected with the present certainty, that Japanese agents were again busy in Hong Kong, had been the merest passing mention of something lacking, at the time, any interest whatever. It is a tribute to that retentive mind of his that an item so small should have been stored away and now resurrected. He left his study, walking along the corridor to his secretary's office. Carter was engaged in perusing, and signing, a pile of official-looking documents. He looked up as Sir Leonard entered the room; immediately rose to his feet.

'Carter,' commenced the governor, 'do you remember that Yumasaki was said to be rather keen on a Chinese dancing girl?'

The young man's brow wrinkled in thought for a moment or two; then:

'Yes, sir,' he asserted; 'I do vaguely remember something of the sort. Wasn't she called—?'

He paused frowning, as he strove to recollect the name. Sir Leonard watched him with a smile on his face. Presently, as Carter's memory failed to respond, the chief prompted it.

'She was called the "China Doll",' he declared. 'Am I not right?'

Carter whistled softly; his eyes gleamed.

'You are, sir – not a doubt of it. And the last place the Japanese sailor was known to visit last night is called the China Doll!'

'Ah! You have caught the significance. Leave those papers for a while, and set to work to find out all you can about the dancing girl – who she is, what she's doing, and so on; also if there's any connection between that drinking den and her. Go warily, and don't let it be thought the inquiries are coming from Government House. When you have your information, come along to me. I'll probably be dressing for the garden party.'

He turned, and walked out of the room, leaving Carter to start his inquiries at once.

Sir Leonard was on the point of leaving Government House for the fête before he saw his assistant again. In fact, he had come to the conclusion that Carter was having more difficulty in tracing the dancing girl than had been anticipated. Actually this was far from being the case, the young Secret Service man finding information flowing into his hands, so to speak. But, for the sake of precaution, he had taken a rickshaw to Queen's Road where, entering a cafe in which he knew he would not be recognised, had casually asked the Macanese proprietor questions over a pot of tea.

Resplendent in a morning suit that fitted him like a glove, a grey top hat on his head, Sir Leonard was about to enter his car when Carter arrived back. Lady Wallace was already seated, while an aide-de-camp, in full uniform, stood by ready to follow the governor. Servants in their official livery gave that touch of formal ceremony to the scene which Wallace disliked so much. The latter quickly read the signs in his secretary's face, and smiled.

'Got all you want?' he asked ambiguously.

'All, and more than I expected, sir,' was the reply.

'Excellent. You'll be at the garden party I suppose?'

'Well, I thought of missing it, sir. I have a good deal of work to do. But if you—'

'No,' interrupted Sir Leonard; 'I shall not want you there. There wouldn't be any opportunity of a private talk,' he added *sotto voce*. 'See me directly I return.'

He entered the car, the ADC following him in, and taking a seat opposite. Lady Wallace smiled at Carter, who thought he had never seen her looking more beautiful or happier. If Sir Leonard regarded the position of governor as something of a bore, his lovely wife had other views. This was due to the fact that probably during the whole course of their married life she had never had her husband so much to herself or been so assured of his safety as she was then. For the time being she was blissfully content. It meant nothing to her that he was governor of a British colony or that she occupied the position of first lady in the community; but it was a wonderful relief to be free from the feeling of deep anxiety which usually pervaded her on account of the dangerous duties he so often undertook at other times.

Carter waited until the car had gone, then entered Government House, and went off to his own office. He was no more enamoured of garden parties or functions of the kind than was his chief. Sir Leonard had often expressed his envy of him, for he, at least, could decline them. Carter's dislike of social engagements was greatly regretted by a number of the young ladies of Hong Kong society and by certain ambitious mammas as well. His position, his good looks, and the fact that he was generally reputed to be wealthy, caused many feminine hearts to beat a little quicker than usual and many feminine minds to dream hopefully at thought of him. Among his colleagues, he has the reputation of being a ladies' man; he admits himself to a weakness for falling in love. I am rather inclined to doubt the latter, or else he falls out of love as quickly as he falls into that trying state. At any rate, it is certain he avoids entanglements with remarkable dexterity. In Hong Kong he succeeded in keeping free from even the suspicion of an attachment. Perhaps that was because he knew the unmarried female of the species is more difficult to shake off in the colonies than at home and consequently more dangerous to a man who cherishes his state of singleness.

Sir Leonard left the garden party as soon as he could do so without causing conjecture or regret and, immediately on his return to Government House, sent for his secretary.

'I gathered from the expression on your face and your remark,' he observed, when Carter entered the study, 'that you had good news.'

'I certainly have, sir,' was the reply. 'I thought it better to make no attempt at inquiries from here, so I went to a cafe in Queen's Road where I knew I wouldn't be recognised.'

Wallace nodded his approval.

'Well?' he prompted.

'I discovered that the lady known as the China Doll is, in her way, quite a famous character. She is reputed to be beautiful and fascinating, and quite a severe competition is always going on for her services among the proprietors of the dancing saloons in the less salubrious parts of Victoria. The China Doll was built, and called after her, by a Macanese named Guttierez who presumably has the first call on her services. My informant, a man of the same race, told me, with much pretence of secrecy, that the money was actually supplied by Mr Yumasaki, the late Japanese consul in Hong Kong.'

'Ah!' exclaimed Sir Leonard in a tone of satisfaction. 'That sounds interesting. Go on!'

'Yumasaki was considered, at least among the circle that runs these dancing saloons, to be in love with the girl. She also was said to be heartbroken when he left Hong Kong. The piece of information that really matters, though, is this, sir. A short while ago she was engaged to dance in Kowloon with a troupe of Chinese girls from Shanghai. At once there was an organised attempt by the dance hall proprietors on this side to get her back. The money she demanded was a little beyond them individually, so they agreed to share her services. She, therefore, dances in eight different saloons every night and, six of them, the Fan Tan, Macao, Lotus, Cherry Blossom, Nanking, and China Doll are those visited by the Japanese sailor last night. Moreover, I was able to ascertain that her times for dancing in each corresponded with his presence in them.'

Sir Leonard's grey eyes gleamed.

'The obvious that was overlooked,' he murmured. 'Naturally the Chinese detectives knew of her engagement to dance in those places. To their minds it was just part of the scheme of things like the bars or the tables, the music or the waiters and, therefore, they overlooked a vital fact. Well done, Carter. We now know that the China Doll is in the pay of Japan. Obviously she it was who gave the seaman the letter. He was instructed to follow her from one place to another until she considered it safe to hand over the document to him. Had she still failed to find an opportunity in the China Doll, he would have gone on to the other two saloons after her. What are they called?'

'The Pearl and the Canton, sir. She does two circuits a night.'

'H'm. They work her hard enough. Now look here, Carter, an American liner is due in at seven. There's a case of diphtheria on board, and nobody will be allowed to land, at least for a day or two. I want you to impersonate a member of the crew and visit some of these saloons. You'd better be one of the mates. American sailors are always reputed to have plenty of money, and are, therefore, regarded by dancing girls and women of that type as their own particular prey. Pretend to become fascinated with this girl and follow her round. It may be as well to – er – appear to get somewhat intoxicated' – he smiled – 'in order that you may be considered an easy victim. There will be no danger of anyone disputing your assertion that you are from the liner – she is called the *Seattle*, by the way – as none of the passengers or crew will be ashore, but I shouldn't make too much of it. Get to know the China Doll – in common parlance, get off with her. There is no need for me to go into details concerning the information we want from her. You know all about that, and will have to be guided by circumstances on how to obtain it. But be tactful and wary, and it would be as well to go armed. Start your activities on her second circuit. You can slip away after dinner and make your preparations. If anything important transpires, ring me. I'll tell Batty to stand by in my study, until the ball is over and I can get there myself. Is all clear?'

Carter smiled cheerfully. That was the type of job he liked; something more in keeping with his real profession.

'Perfectly, sir,' he replied.

'I am sorry to be the cause of disappointing the many young ladies who, no doubt, are looking forward to dancing with you. Perhaps you'd prefer to remain for the ball and that I should delegate the job to someone else?'

A look of alarm showed for a moment in Carter's face as though he thought his chief was serious.

'Not on your life, sir!' he exclaimed.

Sir Leonard laughed.

'All right,' he observed, 'no need for anxiety lest I keep you here for the benefit of your many admirers. Be careful to alter your appearance sufficiently to make certain that no one who knows you will recognise you. And you'd better wear an American mercantile uniform. American officers don't change into civilian clothes as readily as do our people. They're more uniform-proud.'

Soon after ten-thirty that night, a tall, young American mercantile officer entered the Fan Tan Dancing Hall and, for a little while, stood at the door gazing round him. He was not unhandsome, but bore little resemblance to Tommy Carter. His hair was fair; he had rather high cheekbones, and a somewhat broad nose, while his underlip protruded slightly, features entirely unlike those of the young Englishman. Yet he was Carter. Rubber pads inside the cheeks, lower lip and nostrils, with dye on his hair, had worked the transformation. The nose pads also tended to give his speech a nasal twang, which was an advantage.

The Fan Tan was a large, garishly-decorated hall. At one side were half a dozen curtained alcoves in which it was possible to catch a glimpse of couples drinking, probably flirting – decorously enough, for the police of Hong Kong were strict. A bar ran the whole length of the wall opposite. Behind this, Chinese boys in blue smocks served drinks as fast as they could to the clamouring throng crowding by the counter, while others waited upon the people sitting at the many tables. A circular space in the centre of the polished teak floor was reserved for dancing, and several couples were deporting themselves there on Carter's entrance. In the background, on a small stage, flamboyantly coloured in the Far Eastern fashion, were five Chinese musicians playing an occidental dance tune with Oriental cacophony.

A greasy-looking gentleman in full evening dress, who would have declared, had he been asked, that he was a son of Portugal, hurried up to the pseudo-American. Everything about him was oily, while his dark almond-shaped eyes, yellow skin and thick nose suggested there was far more Chinese blood than pure Portuguese in him.

'You want the table, sare?' he asked. 'Very good table I get for you. You wise gentleman come here. Jose Fernandez run good show, much dancing, plenty girls. Come!'

Carter wondered where the fellow expected to find a vacant table. The place seemed full. However, Fernandez threaded his way across the room, dodging dancing couples with much agility, which the Englishman found it difficult to imitate. A table was discovered rather remote from the cleared space in the centre of the room, and Carter expressed himself as dissatisfied. It would be impossible, he reflected, to draw the China Doll's attention to himself from there.

'See here,' he protested; 'this table's not a bit of good to me. I guess I want to be near the fun. It don't matter if it costs more. I'm from the USA and I guess I'm not shy of dollars. Get me?'

Fernandez smiled expansively.

'Sure I get you,' he replied. 'I speak the American well. It will be difficult, but I will arrange. Come!'

He led the guest back to the centre of the room. Standing for a moment looking thoughtfully round him, he presently went to a table where sat a young compatriot with a Chinese girl. With much waving of arms, he explained the situation to them. They did not, at first, seem very much inclined to fall in with the suggestion he was apparently making; in fact, the young man scowled resentfully at Carter. A remark made by Fernandez, however, altered all that. The couple suddenly beamed, and nodded their heads, whereupon the proprietor hurried back to the supposed American sailor.

'They will move for ten dollars,' he announced, adding anxiously, and with conviction that he was speaking the American language: 'Is that all right by you, big boy?'

'Sure,' grinned Carter. He took a couple of American five-dollar bills from his pocket, having taken the precaution of well providing himself with United States currency. 'Here you are, buddy, give them to that guy and his sweetie with my compliments.'

Fernandez accepted the money with alacrity, and returned to the pair. Carter, with inward amusement, noticed the sleight of hand trick by which he pocketed one of the notes. The other was duly held out to the young Macanese but, before he could take it, the Chinese girl had snatched and pursed it, much to her escort's annoyance. The two rose from their seats; passed close to Carter on their way to the other table.

'I guess it's real nice of you,' he acknowledged, 'to let me have your place. Thanks a lot.'

The girl was inclined to linger, probably thinking a change of cavaliers would be of much pecuniary advantage to her, but her boyfriend read the signs, and hurried her away. Fernandez bowed low, as Carter took his seat.

'You want girl, yes?' he asked unctuously.

'I'll have a look round and select my own, I guess,' was the reply. 'Send me a highball, Fernandez, and make it snappy.'

The greasy proprietor hurried away, and gave the necessary orders. Carter was quickly supplied with the whisky, for which he found he had to pay more than double the usual price. Thereafter he surveyed the motley crowd round him with interest. The great majority of the patrons were, like the proprietor, of mixed Portuguese and Chinese descent. There were also a number of obvious sailors of diverse nationalities and English, American, French, and German inhabitants of Hong Kong of a somewhat low stratum of society. The dance hostesses were nearly all Chinese girls, with a sprinkling of Europeans and Americans in tawdry evening frocks. Carter noticed Fernandez having a prolonged conversation with an unattached group of the women and, from the glances cast in his direction, concluded he was telling them that the American officer was a splendid prey for their gold-digging propensities; that he would expect a good percentage of the spoils obtained by the one chosen.

'I rather think,' murmured Carter to himself, 'that you are in for a profound disappointment, my friend.'

He had been there about ten minutes when the band ceased its noisy clamour, the dancing couples returned to their seats, and Fernandez sprang on to the stage.

'Ladies and gentlemen,' he announced, 'the moment have arrive that we all are wait for. With great pleasure I now introduce to you – the China Doll.'

There was a storm of clapping. The lights were dimmed, a spotlight suddenly flashing into brilliance, and focusing the cleared space in the centre of the room. The five musicians, having supplied themselves with native instruments, commenced to play weird Chinese music. A slim little figure in gorgeous Chinese raiment appeared from a curtained doorway to the right of the stage, and sped to the centre of the room, amidst a renewed burst of applause. Carter, with a feeling of intense surprise, became aware that his previous conception of the China Doll had been entirely wrong.

Both he and Sir Leonard Wallace had taken it for granted that she, in common with most women of her type, was of the gold-digging and easy virtue variety. It needed only one cumulative look at this girl to feel convinced that her virtue, at least, was unassailable. Her face, despite the delicately-applied cosmetics, was that of a well-bred, refined, and pure woman. She seemed so much out of place in that *galère* as a gazelle in a cage of baboons. Carter understood now why she was known as the China Doll. The designation was entirely appropriate. Very small, very slim, and very chic, she was entrancingly doll-like. In addition, she was beautiful. Tiny expressive hands, dainty twinkling feet were but adjuncts to a lovely oval face, in which her large, almond-shaped eyes, shaded by long curling lashes, a small sensitive nose, a perfect little rosebud of a mouth were entirely fascinating. There was nothing flamboyant or theatrical about her silken garments or the fan she wielded with such dexterity as she danced. Carter thought the music barbarous; he could not understand the meaning of the dance. But he was not blind to the self-evident fact that every movement she made contained the utmost grace and charm, was the very poetry of motion. The more he watched, the more astounded he felt that she should be dancing in such a saloon for the entertainment of the uncouth, loud-voiced, sensual clientele it boasted. It also dawned on him that it was not going to be so easy to become acquainted with her as he and Sir Leonard Wallace had supposed.

During her gyrations, she came close to him on several occasions, the blinding limelight, following her round, included him in its glare. Each time they were in juxtaposition he smiled at her, but without any sign from her that she had noticed his interest until, towards the end of the dance, he thought to catch the faintest of responses from her lips. That encouraged him a little. He also felt that her eyes had studied him questioningly, rather as though she wondered what he was doing there.

The finale came with a clamour from the orchestra that grated unpleasantly on his unaccustomed ears. The tiny figure twirled to a standstill; sank in a graceful curtsy, and was up and had sped through the exit almost before he realised the dance was over. A deafening crescendo of applause broke out, the spotlight faded, and the house lights returned to full force. She did not give an encore, neither did she take a call. Before long, the five musicians had reverted to European instruments, and were playing a foxtrot. The floor was soon crowded with dancers. Carter noticed Fernandez eyeing him hopefully; beckoned the man across. The proprietor of the place hurried up to him.

'You want a girl now?' he asked. 'I find you very good one, very pretty, very loving.'

'Who's the dame that just danced?' demanded Carter.

'You not know of her?' exclaimed Fernandez. 'Everyone, I think, know of the China Doll.'

'How could I know anything about her? Only arrived this evening on the *Seattle*. So she's called the China Doll, is she? Well, get this, Fernandez; I want to become acquainted with her. She's sure an eyeful. Ask her to come along and have a drink with me.'

Fernandez looked vaguely troubled.

'It is impossible, sare,' he remarked regretfully. 'She not speaking or drinking with anyone. Every night she dance two times in eight dance halls. To this one she come at between six o'clock and half past and between half past ten and eleven. Now she go to the Macao; after that to Lotus, Cherry Blossom, Nanking, China Doll, Pearl, and Canton. Then she go home. She will not meet with men. Better you forget her, and have one of my lovely ladies – yes?'

'No. Go and tell the China Doll I admire her a whole lot, and I am anxious to get acquainted, and mean her no harm. Beat it! What are you hanging round for?'

Fernandez sighed.

'Sare, I tell you, it cannot be. With much regret I assure you—'

'Don't assure me of anything. I guess I've just got to meet this China Doll, and I'm not taking no for an answer. Get me? Now scram. And say, look here; I'll hand you a twenty-dollar bill when you bring her right along.'

The promise of a bribe of twenty dollars proved too much for the Macanese to resist. He hurried away without another word. Five minutes went by; then he appeared at the door through which the dancer had come and gone. Long before he reached Carter's table, the supposed American officer knew that he had failed to persuade the China Doll to emerge. His face expressed the most doleful disappointment, due entirely no doubt to the loss of the twenty dollars.

'She won't, not come,' he announced sadly. 'I try every way I know, but it no good. She look at you through the curtain, and I think she is coming, but the head she shake very no. Forget her, sare. I get you better girl – more fun, more everything – and you give me only five dollars.'

Carter rose to his feet.

'I'll try at the next place,' he declared. 'What did you say it is called? The Macao, isn't it?'

Fernandez was dismayed at the thought of losing such a promising customer. He pleaded, he argued, he even wept, but his supposed American guest was adamant. Carter strode to the door, followed by Fernandez begging him not to go. The last he saw, or heard, of the Macanese was a greasy-looking figure, under the glaring entrance lights, wringing his hands and bewailing his misfortune at the departure of a patron who had looked like being so profitable.

The Englishman found his way to the Macao. It was almost a replica of the Fan Tan, though perhaps slightly smaller, thronged with the same cosmopolitan types. The proprietor here was a Chinaman, whose narrow eyes, more like slits in his face than anything else, caused him to look more sinister than he actually was. Carter obtained a table by the same method as at the Fan Tan. He again watched the China Doll's dance through in close proximity to her; was gratified to note, from the slight uplifting of her daintily-pencilled eyebrows, that she recognised him. But his request to meet her met with the same negative result.

At the Lotus, the Cherry Blossom, and the Nanking, his failure was equally marked, though, when she danced by him at the last, his falling spirits were encouraged at receiving a definite, albeit somewhat perplexed, smile from her. He must have caused more pain and disappointment to the predatory instincts of five dancing saloon proprietors that night than they had experienced in the whole course of their previous careers. Carter felt he was up against it. Nothing he could do seemed capable of persuading the elusive little Chinese damsel to agree to make his acquaintance. At the Cherry Blossom and Nanking he sent her notes, but they were returned. Instead of as had been expected, accompanying her from place to place, sitting with her a while in each before or after her dance, spending every moment he could pumping her for information, he had not even been able to meet her. Between the Lotus and the Cherry Blossom, and the latter and the Nanking, he had thought to waylay her as she journeyed between them, but, perhaps suspecting some such attempt, she had eluded him. Before entering the Nanking, he had found a telephone booth; had rung up Government House, and given Batty a message for Sir Leonard Wallace describing his unexpected difficulties. He had long since abandoned the idea of pretending to appear intoxicated. It would not, he felt, aid him in any way to give her such an impression; on the contrary, his chances, if any, would be utterly ruined. She would certainly have nothing to do with a drunken man.

He entered the China Doll with the notion that, were any success to reward his efforts at all, it would be there. He could not tell why he should experience the feeling, unless it was because the Japanese sailor had there ended his pilgrimage. The very fact that the place was called after the name bestowed on her seemed to promise success at last. Also, she had certainly smiled at him in the Nanking.

The China Doll was more ornate though less garish than the others had been; gave the impression of greater affluence, and was certainly more luxurious. Larger, also, it contained a gallery, from which people, who had no intention of dancing, could look down on those who did. The place boasted two bands – one composed of half a dozen Macanese, who played jazz excellently; the other of a similar number of Chinese, who seemed reserved specially for the dance of the China Doll. At all events, they only performed for her while Carter was present.

The latter found Guttierez, the proprietor, less oily and more dignified than the others. He obtained a table for his supposed American guest close to the dancing floor by similar means to those adopted by Fernandez, but charged Carter twenty dollars for the privilege and pocketed the lot with an air of patronage as though it were his due.

The dance duly took place, and this time the China Doll showed no surprise at the presence of her very persistent follower. On the contrary, she gave him the impression that she had expected it, by the manner in which she looked at him. She caused him much elation also by smiling frankly at him just before the finale. The thunderous applause at the conclusion this time met with acknowledgment. She took a call, bowing jerkily from side to side of the room, to the huge delight of her enthusiastic audience. At length, she disappeared, and Carter looked round for Guttierez, prepared again to send the request which had almost become monotonous by repetition. For some minutes he was unable to locate the man, and was about to call to a waiter, when there arose a murmur of excited voices round him. Wondering what had caused the sudden interest, he was in the act of turning, when the swish of silken skirts caught his ear.

'I have saved you the bother this time,' came a delightfully soft voice that spoke English perfectly. 'I hope you are satisfied.'

Carter sprang to his feet in rank astonishment. Standing by his side was the China Doll, smiling at him, and obviously enjoying the surprise. He almost forgot the part he was playing in his amazement and elation that, at last, success had attended his efforts.

'Say,' he exclaimed, 'this sure is swell of you. I didn't think you'd come, but I meant to stick it out in the hope you would.'

He held the chair, while she seated herself. 'What will you have?' he inquired.

'Please a lemonade.'

He gave the order to a waiter who had hurried up, adding another of whisky and soda for himself. As he sat down, she regarded him with frank, curious eyes.

'You are very persistent,' she commented. 'Do you know I have only done this for one person before.'

'Then I guess I'm flattered,' was his reply. 'Who is – or was – the other guy?'

'He is the man I hope one day to wed.'

There was a little pause. Carter guessed she was referring to Yumasaki, but it was news to him that she and the Japanese ex-consul intended to marry.

'Gee,' he murmured, playing up to the role he had adopted. 'That's just too bad.'

'Why?' she asked.

The drinks were placed before them, and she began to sip hers. Carter noted with approval that she was dainty in everything she did.

'Can't you guess?' he asked. 'I suppose you thought I regarded you like any of those other girls. But you got me all wrong. I saw, first time you appeared, that you were different. It's kinda sudden, honey, but I guess I've fallen for you.'

'You mean – you have fallen in love with me?'

'You've said it.'

She half rose; then sank back into her chair, and laughed – a silvery cadence of sound that was wholly fascinating.

'How ridiculous!' she exclaimed. 'You must not talk like

that. But I am glad you did not think of me as you seem to think of those others. Please tell me about yourself. Soon I must go, for I have two more dancing halls to visit yet.'

'I know,' he nodded, 'and I'll be there.'

'Even though you now know I am one day to be married?' she questioned mockingly.

'Sure. What's the odds? There's nothing much to tell you about myself,' he went on, 'I'm a sailor – second mate of the *Seattle* – in tonight. Guess that's all there is to tell.'

'Quite a lot in very few words,' she commented with a smile.

She was deliciously alluring with the softest, most attractive voice he thought he had ever heard. Carter found himself wishing now that he was not forced by his profession to play the role of deceiver. She was so charming; such a dainty, enticing morsel of femininity. He had to force himself to remember that she was in some manner connected with the Japanese espionage system, since it was she, without doubt, who had conveyed to the sailor the letter which had proved secret agents were still active in Hong Kong. Very carefully, he commenced on his task of attempting to obtain information from her.

'You speak English remarkably well,' he observed. 'Where did you learn the lingo?'

'Lingo!' she repeated in puzzled tones. 'What is that, please?' He smiled.

'Sorry – I mean language.'

'I studied it in England. I was there, in college, for three years.'

'Were you really? Well, I guess that explains a whole lot. Say, can you dance European dances as well as that Chinese one you do?'

She nodded.

'Yes; but I think my value would decline if I danced anything but a native dance out here. So often good English and American dancers come to Shanghai and Hong Kong. I think, as a Chinese dancer, I am perhaps very good – yes? But, if I did the others, and wore European costume, I would lose my attraction – it would become grotesque.'

From which remark, he reflected, she certainly seemed to have her dainty head set wisely on her little shoulders.

'But why do you dance in places like this? I guess you deserve something better. You're too classy for a joint of this kind.'

She smiled; shrugged her shoulders slightly.

'I like it, and it pays me well. Besides—' She hesitated, as though rather afraid that she was being a little bit too confidential to this stranger. 'As you in America would say,' she went on a trifle lamely, 'it suits me.'

'Does your boyfriend like it?' he asked.

'Of course. It was he who—' Again she interrupted herself. 'I do not think he would like me to speak of him.'

'Why not?' he persisted. 'There's nothing secret about him, is there?'

'No – no; of course not, only—'

'I suppose he runs one of these joints, and doesn't want it to be known. Is that it? Of course!' he exclaimed, as though enlightenment had suddenly come to him. 'I get it. He owns this place. You're called the China Doll, and so is this dancing saloon. Guess I was a sap not to have connected the two before. It was called after you, wasn't it? Gee whiz!' he exclaimed again. 'Say, little girl, you're not telling me that Portuguese guy is your boyfriend! Why, he's old enough to be—'

'No, no,' she interrupted quickly. 'It is not Guttierez. My lover is not here. He does not come. He has other things to do. Please, you ask too many questions.' She forced a little laugh, but it was obvious that she was perturbed. 'I must go now. Already I am late.'

He rose with her.

'I'll see you to the Pearl,' he declared.

At that she looked positively startled.

'No; you must not. I have a rickshaw that takes me, and a servant to look after me. Please,' she pleaded, 'you will not come.'

'I won't come with you, if you'd rather I didn't,' he returned, 'but you'll sit with me there, won't you? Say yes!'

'It would be better I did not, but if you wish so much—'

'I do.'

'Very well. Afterwards you will go back to your ship, please. I do not wish you to come to the Canton.'

He managed to look thoroughly disappointed.

'Say, that's just too bad. I was looking forward to you and me having a good time together when you'd finished for the night. Won't you let me meet you and see you home?'

'No – please not.' Her soft, brown eyes looked pleadingly into his. 'My fiancé is jealous – he would not understand.'

'But there wouldn't be any harm in it. Besides, he wouldn't know, unless you told him.'

'He would, because always he takes me home from the Canton.' Her statement gave Carter a surprise that he had the greatest difficulty in controlling his features. 'I must hurry, please. For a little while I will sit with you in the Pearl.'

'Swell,' he murmured mechanically.

She was gone, and he resumed his seat, conscious that he was the cynosure of all eyes in his vicinity. Apparently the men in his neighbourhood regarded him with envy. But their feelings did not concern him. He was grappling with the surprising fact that Yumasaki was in Hong Kong. He must have returned secretly, and be the ruling spirit of the Japanese agents there. Carter felt that he had obtained one priceless item of information. There could be little doubt that the man to whom she alluded as her fiancé, who took her home at night, after her dancing was done, was Yumasaki. It had been a well-known fact that they were in love with each other, and she was not the sort to get herself engaged to another man directly the one she loved had left the colony. Besides, she had shown concern when he had pretended to guess that her fiancé had an interest in the China Doll, and had called it after her. Also she had made no denial. Carter decided that he had learnt something that Sir Leonard Wallace must know at once. He felt sorry for the girl. She was such an entrancing little thing, and he believed that, though she had acted with great secrecy as Yumasaki's messenger, she was not actually concerned herself in the Japanese espionage activities. Carter's impressionable heart had been touched. Everything about the China Doll delighted him, not the least being her fascinating repetition of the word 'please'.

He finished his drink which he had not previously touched, and strolled out of the place. At once he sought for a telephone booth. He had a certain amount of difficulty in locating one but, when he was beginning to grow a little anxious, success rewarded his efforts. This time he found himself talking to Sir Leonard. The ball was over. The governor was greatly interested in his disclosures; was equally certain that the girl could only have referred to Yumasaki. At once Wallace made up his mind.

'Tell her,' he directed, 'that you have just met a man who informed you her fiancé is a Japanese Secret Service agent called Yumasaki. Hint that there were other items of information about him as well, and appear mysterious. Say you can quite understand now why she didn't want to talk about him. You may as well pretend that your informant was a police officer. I think, after that, she will be only too anxious for you to go on to the Canton saloon and possibly see Yumasaki. If she still persists on your not going, ignore her request. Yumasaki is bound to want to meet you, anyway, once he is told what you have said. He might take you to his hiding place. I sincerely hope he does. Well, that's all, I think, Carter. Hurry, away. You mustn't miss her.'

Wondering what his chief had in mind, but believing he could hazard a pretty shrewd guess, Carter left the kiosk, and hastened to the Pearl Dancing Hall. He found it to be the smallest and perhaps the most tawdry. It was run by an obese Chinaman who greeted him as though he had been expecting him. The fellow was standing by the door, when he entered, and bowed as low as his corpulent proportions would permit.

'It is my great privilege, honoured sare,' he announced, 'to welcome you to my welly poor establishment. The illustrious China Doll has dilected your humble selvant to place at your disposal a table.'

'Say, that's real nice of her,' acknowledged Carter. 'Lead on.'

Treating him with every appearance of respect, the fat Chinaman took him to a table in an advantageous position; called up a boy to attend to his requirements. Carter sat down, and looked about him, wondering why the place was called the Pearl.

There was nothing pearly about it, while its patrons appeared even less engaging than those in the other halls. Most of them were Chinese of a low class. Carter thought they looked a lot of cut-throats, making the mental reservation that appearances are often deceptive. In any case he preferred Chinese cut-throats to oily dagoes. He had arrived only just in time; had hardly taken his seat, when the Chinese orchestra broke forth into its weird dance music, and the China Doll appeared.

By that time, he practically knew her dance by heart, had even begun to understand the rhythm of the music. Nevertheless, he was not bored. There was something so dainty and fresh about the little figure gyrating gracefully in the centre of the room. He knew well quite a number of English actresses and dancers, practically all of whom were sophisticated to a degree and extremely artificial. There was nothing of that about the Chinese girl. She appeared entirely natural; childlike in some ways, wise in others. The more he saw of her, the less he felt it possible to believe she herself was an espionage agent of Japan, though no one knew better than he that her type was very successful in Secret Service work, mainly because of its entirely innocent appearance. However, he believed he could swear he had not been mistaken in her. Yumasaki was probably using the girl without her understanding the nature of the work upon which he was engaged.

She smiled quite frankly and in most friendly fashion now, as she danced by him. He, on the other hand, contrived to wear a puzzled and somewhat worried expression on his face every time she glanced in his direction. She proved that she had noticed this when, the dance over, she again caused a good deal of comment and interest by approaching him, and accepting the chair he held for her.

'You see,' she observed, 'I have kept my promise. What is the matter, please? You look troubled.'

He pretended to evade the question.

'This is mighty nice of you,' he told her. 'Shall I order a lemonade again for you?'

She nodded.

'With much ice, please.' The order was given to an attentive waiter. As soon as the boy had hurried away. 'You have not answered my question,' she reminded him.

'Oh, it's nothing,' Carter replied with an appearance of reluctance. 'Say, what is your name – your proper name, I mean.'

'Does it matter? After tonight we will not meet again.'

'Don't say that,' he protested. 'I want to be friends, and I'm coining right along to see you every night while my ship's in port.'

'You must not, please. It would not be wise.'

'Gee! That's real unkind of you. You seem mighty mysterious. I shall begin to believe that what I've heard is true, if you won't let me see you again.'

He found her big brown eyes fixed on his face with an expression of trepidation in them.

'What is it you have heard?' she asked anxiously. 'Tell me, please.'

'I'll think about it, if you let me know your name. I can't call you Miss China Doll, can I?'

'You would not be able to pronounce the Chinese words. It means in English the Dove of Gladness.'

'Say, that's pretty. Suppose I call you Dove?'

She smiled.

'In England I was called Joy. It is the same, you see, as gladness.'

'Then Joy's good enough for me.'

The lemonade, pleasantly tinkling with ice, was placed before her. Carter paid its excessive price, adding a generous tip, and they were alone again. She drank a little; then again her anxious eyes regarded him.

'You do not wish to tell me that which was troubling you,' she persisted. 'I feel it is connected with the things you say you have heard.'

He laughed.

'You're like all your sex, Joy; a whole heap inquisitive. Guess it's nothing much, but I sure felt a bit worried. Say,' he looked her straight in the face, 'is your boyfriend's name Yumasaki?'

There was a crash. The glass which she had been holding in her hand had dropped to the floor, smashing in hundreds of pieces, while a pool of lemonade spread round her feet. Carter immediately sprang up, producing his handkerchief, and expressing concern for her silken robe. It had luckily escaped being splashed, however, and a Chinese boy quickly mopped up the liquid, sweeping away the broken glass. Carter insisted on ordering her another drink, pretending not to notice the sudden pallor of her face and the fear in her eyes. He began to speak of trivial things, as though he had forgotten the question he had asked her; but she was not listening. When the second lemonade was before her, she turned to him; clutched his arm almost fiercely.

'What do you know of Yumasaki?' she asked in a low, tense voice.

'Nothing much,' he replied; 'anyhow, I guess it's none of my business.'

'Tell me, please.'

'Well, OK, if you insist. When I left the China Doll, I met a guy at the door who had a whole heap to say. He began by asking me if I knew you well. I told him to scram and try being fresh with somebody else. But he refused to be shaken off and I guess, when he told me he was a dick, I—'

'Dick!' she repeated. 'What is that, please?'

'A cop – a bull!' She looked exceedingly puzzled.

'I do not understand.'

'A police officer.'

'A police officer!' she gasped. 'Are you sure?'

'He said he was, and I guess he ought to know.'

'Please go on.'

'I told him, since he seemed so almighty anxious to know, that I had only met you tonight, and he sure got my goat by warning me to be careful. He said you were in love with a Japanese Secret Service agent called Yumasaki, who—'

'He said that?' she interrupted, adding almost to herself: 'Then they know!' There was a pause, while she stared at him with fear-stricken eyes. 'Was there anything else, please?' she asked.

'Yes; he said several things about this guy Yumasaki, but I was too anxious to get here to pay much attention; besides it had nix to do with me.'

'What were the other things?'

Carter looked uncomfortable.

'Say, girlie,' he begged, 'let's forget it. I can understand why you weren't too darned keen to speak to me, if you're mixed up in the Secret Service racket, but it means nothing in my life, I guess. I like you a lot, and I don't care a button if your boyfriend's a spy. Only take my advice, steer clear of that sorta thing if you can. I'd hate like hell if you got into trouble.'

She rose to her feet.

'Excuse me, please. I must go.'

'Oh, I say, don't go yet. Why, we've only been sitting here for ten minutes and, if you won't let me come to the next joint, I shan't be able to see—'

'I have changed my mind,' she told him. 'I think I would like to speak to you, please, after my last show.'

She was gone. Carter reflectively lit a cigarette.

'Sir Leonard right as usual,' he murmured to himself. 'I wish I had that uncanny ability of his of being able to anticipate how the other person's mind will work. To do it when the brain concerned is a woman's is sheer wizardry.'

The China Doll's final engagement for the night was at a dancing saloon in the very centre of Chinatown. The neighbourhood reeked of dried fish, roast pig and burning joss sticks. Although it was now half past one in the morning, everyone seemed wide awake and excessively noisy. It appeared that a wedding celebration was taking place nearby. Drums and strange shrill instruments were making the night, or rather early morning, hideous; crackers were continually exploding with startling suddenness. Carter was relieved to get inside the Canton. Even there, above the music of the Chinese dance band, could frequently be heard the sounds of festivity from without. The place was packed to suffocation. It seemed as though the revellers had overflowed from the streets into the saloon, for the majority were blue and black smocked Chinamen or Chinamen in European clothes dancing with Macanese Chinese and white girls with a verve that was entirely unoriental. The few men present of that indefinite race, generally known as dagoes, were of a particularly greasy species, while European sailors were in a minority. Carter, as an American mercantile officer looked, and felt, quite out of place.

The proprietor this time was a Filipino. He also had apparently been told to expect the supposed mate of the *Seattle* for, on Carter's appearance, he escorted him to a table that had obviously been reserved for him, unpleasantly close to the band. The heat was intense, the whirling fans making little difference to that stifling atmosphere. The Canton was much like the Pearl; as tawdry and as unwholesome. Carter saw things going on there that nauseated him, and made a mental note to advise the Commissioner of Police to tighten up the regulations governing dance halls.

The China Doll's dance was performed under immense difficulties, but she went through it with the same spirit she had displayed all along, not appearing to notice the mass of polyglot humanity threatening, by its congestion, to encroach on the space reserved for her. Carter had a clear view, but people pressed behind and on either side of him, while the wailing notes of the band deafened him. He was glad when the dance was over, and agreeably surprised to be told by the Filipino that the China Doll would receive him in her own room. The proprietor, an astonishingly savoury specimen compared with most of the others, and possessed of a really courteous manner, escorted him through a curtained doorway and along a bare, whitewashed passage. He knocked at the door and, on receiving an invitation from within, opened it and, standing back, motioned Carter to enter. The latter stood on the threshold astounded. Having come from the gaudy dance hall he felt, for a moment, that he was dreaming. The room to which he had been bidden was small, but exquisitely furnished in the Chinese style. It was a perfect picture, and invitingly restful. The China Doll, reclining on a long chair, smiled slightly at the astonishment, and invited him to sit at her side. He promptly crossed the apartment; sank with a sigh of pleasure into the depths of a luxurious chair. A small lacquer table, on which was a tray containing a decanter of whisky, soda siphon, and glasses, stood within easy reach. She begged him to help himself. Carter, who had been forced to drink more that night than he relished, refused; lay back, and allowed the whirling fan suspended from the ceiling to play on his overheated face.

'This is swell,' he remarked. 'It's real nice of you, Joy, to have me in here. Say,' he asked, 'what caused you to change your mind about my coming to this saloon?'

'After the information you gave me,' she explained, 'I thought it best you should meet my fiancé. In a moment, he will be here. I have told him what the policeman said to you.'

Carter contrived to look embarrassed.

'But I thought you said he was jealous and would not understand.'

She shrugged her shoulders, and smiled. The fear she had shown at the Pearl, when he had confided to her the supposititious remarks of an imaginary police officer, had apparently left her entirely. She seemed now quite at ease and unconcerned.

'Personal matters that appear important,' she remarked, 'become trifles before events of general urgency. My friend, I think, was a little displeased, but any foolish jealousy he may have felt faded at the importance of my tidings.'

'That is so,' observed a quiet voice, which pronounced the sibilant sounds as though hissing them. 'One cannot allow one's own feelings to take precedence of bad news affecting one's national activities.'

The stilted and precise English told Carter who the newcomer was, even before he turned to survey the man who had opened the door and entered the room so quietly. He had heard it before with its distinct hissing inflection. A short, stoutish man, wearing the costume and felt-soled shoes of a Chinese gentleman, stood eyeing the two through a pair of large, tinted spectacles. Carter recognised Yumasaki at once, despite this attire, a recently grown moustache, and the glasses which normally would have constituted quite an effective disguise. The Englishman had, on several occasions, had official dealings with the Japanese, when the latter had been consul in Hong Kong; had met him at social gatherings; had been present during Sir Leonard Wallace's severe cross-examination of him regarding Japanese espionage in Hong Kong. Carter had no fears that his own disguise would be penetrated, but he knew he would have to retain all his wits about him, if he were to prevent any suspicion arising in the mind of the spy.

Yumasaki closed the door softly behind him, advanced towards the pseudo-American, and bowed low. Carter rose from his chair; held out his hand in friendly manner.

'Glad to meet you, Mr – er—' he began.

'Shall we dispense with my name?' came from the other, as he barely touched the hand extended to him. 'It really does not matter.'

Carter shrugged his shoulders.

'As you like,' he returned. 'I guess you mean me to take the name for granted anyhow; otherwise I don't see that there'd be any point in you wanting to know what that police guy said to me.'

'Let us be seated,' suggested Yumasaki.

He waited until Carter had once again sunk into the comfortable depths of his chair; then followed suit in another directly opposite. The China Doll had not uttered a word since the appearance of the Japanese, but her soft eyes were watching him a trifle anxiously, Carter thought as he glanced at her, as though she sensed antagonism in the air. The Englishman himself felt this. Yumasaki's manner was suave, and contained all the excessive politeness of his race but, behind it, there seemed to be a suggestion of something that was certainly not friendliness. Possibly jealousy lurked there, despite his words. The British Secret Service man resolved to put an end to any feeling of that kind at once.

'Say,' he remarked, 'I want to tell you right now you've got no call to be jealous of me. I guess I fell for this lady all right, but I didn't know she was engaged to you, and I'm not the sorta guy to butt in where I'm not wanted. I'd sure like to be friends with Miss China Doll, though, if she's willing. You can't object to that?'

'My dear sir, I object to nothing,' came the reply. 'Shall we proceed to matters of greater moment? I understand a police officer interviewed you outside the dancing hall called the

China Doll. Will you kindly repeat to me exactly the statements he made to you?'

'I don't rightly know why I should,' demurred Carter. 'I guess I'm a bit muddled. The lady told me she was engaged to you – at least, I reckon it's you she meant. Is that so, sister?' he asked, turning to the girl. She nodded. 'Well, you look to me to be a Chinaman, while I kinda expected a Japanese, you see.'

'Since you appear in such difficulties, shall I admit that I am a Japanese wearing Chinese clothes?'

'I get you. All right, I'll spill the beans. First of all, though, you've got to know that I don't want to get mixed up in any Secret Service racket.' He thereupon repeated that which he had told the girl in the Pearl Dancing Hall, adding a few details to colour the recital. 'That's about all, I guess,' he concluded.

Yumasaki had listened attentively without interruption. He now began to question Carter cleverly in an effort apparently to discover if the police had any suspicions of his whereabouts. The young man answered with obliging frankness, declaring that they certainly seemed to know something judging from the manner of the man who spoke to him. The Japanese then turned to the girl and spoke rapidly in Chinese. Unfortunately Carter was not well acquainted with that language, and was able to understand only a phrase or a word here and there. He gathered, however, from the little he was able mentally to translate that among other matters, Yumasaki was referring to the affair of the letter found on the sailor who had committed suicide. Possibly he was blaming it for his present dangerous situation. Presently he turned to Carter.

'I am much obliged to you, sir,' he acknowledged, 'for the

information you have imparted. I regret that your interest in the China Doll has involved you in a matter that is, doubtless, distasteful to you. At the same time you have been of service to us and that I regard as fortunate. You are, I believe, an officer from the American liner, *Seattle*. Is that so?'

Carter nodded.

'Yes; I am second mate.'

'May I ask you to say nothing about meeting me here?'

'Sure. I guess that's easy.'

'Excuse me if you please. I will see if you can leave without any more police officers wishing to talk to you.'

He rose, and left the room in the same silent manner as he had entered it. Carter turned to the girl, who was looking distinctly perturbed again.

'So that's the man you're going to marry, Joy,' he commented. 'Can't say I'm impressed, but I guess I'm prejudiced. Say, what are you looking worried about?'

'The situation to us is rather worrying,' she replied. 'You would not understand. But let us forget it, please. It's not pleasant. This morning you will go back to your ship, and you and I will never meet again. I shall be sad.'

'Why shouldn't we meet sometimes? The *Seattle* won't be sailing for several days, and I guess you'll find me around.'

'You must not, please. I really mean it when I say we shall not meet any more. Promise me you will not come here again to the saloons.'

He spent some minutes protesting, but she remained firm in her determination. At length, with an appearance of intense disappointment, which was not very much alien to his actual feelings, he acquiesced, giving the required promise. Womanlike, she then began to express her regret, which he believed to be entirely sincere. Yumasaki made his appearance in the same unheralded, quiet fashion, shut the door behind him and, crossing the room, stood before Carter, his hands hidden, in typically Chinese fashion, in the voluminous sleeves of his garments.

'It is evident,' he announced, 'that there is much police activity tonight. Always these halls are kept under strict surveillance, but there are certainly more officers about than is usual. I think it will be wise if you remain here.'

Carter gave the appearance of considering the situation.

'Well, that suits me,' he declared presently, 'so long as I can get back to my ship by six.'

Yumasaki shook his head slowly. The Englishman could see his eyes narrow behind the tinted lenses of his spectacles and, at once, prepared for trouble. The Japanese agent began to assume a sinister aspect, as he stood there facing the man who had made no secret of his interest in the China Doll.

'I do not think you will reach your ship by six o'clock,' came in the sibilant tones. 'I do not think you will ever again see her.'

Carter clutched the arms of his chair; the China Doll slid from the couch with a little cry.

'What the heck do you mean?' demanded Carter.

Yumasaki shrugged his shoulders.

'It is a matter of the greatest regret to me,' he remarked politely, and as though he were discussing the weather, 'but I have reached the conclusion that you know too much. Consequently, it would be the height of unwisdom to allow you to live.'

'Don't be a sap!' growled Carter. 'Your ideas of a joke don't appeal to me.'

'I am not joking, my dear friend. There are great issues at stake and, under such circumstances, one life more or less makes little difference. You forced yourself upon the China Doll who, I should like to remind you, is my property. Incidentally, you have become mixed up with affairs of which you most certainly should know nothing. You will, doubtless, agree that you have only yourself to blame, and be prepared, I hope, to meet your death with the fortitude of a gentleman who recognises the necessity of it.'

The girl's face had turned white beneath her make-up, with the result that she looked rather ghastly. She grasped Yumasaki's arm, and spoke to him pleadingly in rapid Chinese. Carter realised he was in a desperate position. However, he had been in others even more dangerous, and his cheerful spirits were in no way dampened. On the contrary, he rather gloried in the situation, and laughed quite naturally. The China Doll stopped talking; turned to regard him with wonder. Yumasaki's cold, threatening assurance received something of a setback. He had not anticipated this extraordinary young man receiving sentence of death in such a manner.

'You are amused,' he commented frigidly. 'I am glad. Such disregard of dying will enable you to face the transition to another existence with equanimity.'

'I have not the slightest intention of dying, Mr Yumasaki,' replied Carter coolly. 'I guess I enjoy living a whole heap too much to feel any hankering after that other existence you speak of.'

At the use of his name, the Japanese scowled ominously, but made no comment on it.

'I very much regret your attitude,' he remarked smoothly, as though reproaching a child for being unreasonable. 'I am sorry to say I entirely disagree with you concerning your expressed intention of not dying. As I have said, it is a necessity.'

'Look here,' remonstrated Carter, 'you asked me to say nothing about meeting you here and, I guess, I said I wouldn't. Isn't that enough for you?'

Yumasaki shook his head.

'There is too much at stake,' he pronounced. 'You have also forfeited your life,' he added, his tone becoming harsh for the first time, 'because you have dared to cast eyes of desire on this lady who belongs to me. That, in itself, deserves execution.' At that, the China Doll once again broke into vehement protests. He silenced her with a gesture. 'Your pleading for him,' he declared, still speaking in English, 'but proves that he has roused your interest, which I will not tolerate. You will go. I cannot escort you to your abode this morning, for reasons you will appreciate. T'so Lin Tao will afford you the protection necessary. Go!'

The China Doll turned her eyes, full of misery and compassion, on Carter, who grinned cheerfully at her and rose from his chair.

'So long, Joy,' he cried. 'Say, there's nothing to look down in the mouth about. I'll be seeing you.'

'You are a brave man, Mr – er—'

'Call me Tommy,' he invited. 'I guess it'll sound kinda cute coming from you.'

His good spirits actually brought a smile to her lips.

'Goodbye Tommy,' she murmured softly. 'Forgive me, please, for bringing you to – this.'

'Oh, shucks! You've brought me to nothing. Yumasaki here *will* have his little joke.'

The Japanese turned savagely on the girl.

'Go!' he thundered. Without another word she went, closing the door gently behind her. Yumasaki swung back to Carter. 'You persist in regarding this affair as a joke?' he asked, resuming his suave manner.

'Sure,' was the reply. 'And nothing you can say will make me alter my opinion. So I suggest we stop playing games; shall we? I kinda feel it's time I hit the hay.'

Yumasaki ignored his remarks.

'You will observe,' he stated, 'that this room possesses no windows, the door is very powerful. I am now going to leave you to spend a few minutes in reflection. You will be locked in and, therefore, cannot escape. Presently some men will come to speed your soul on its last journey. There will be a little discomfort, but I can promise you no pain. I will not see you again alive, so I will bid you farewell – Tommy.'

He pronounced the name with mocking intonation, and turned to leave the room.

'Just a minute, Mr Wise Guy,' called Carter. 'Guess I have a word or two to say myself about this little party you're arranging. Do you think that, if I'd reckoned I was in any real danger, I'd let you leave this room? Why, you poor Japanese mutt, I could break you in two with my hands.'

Yumasaki stepped softly back to him, a sneering smile curving his thick lips. His hands were still tucked in his sleeves.

'I am quite well aware,' he conceded, 'that, as far as brute strength is concerned, you have much the advantage of me.

I am, however, an exponent of the art of ju-jutsu, and could render you helpless in a few seconds. I possess another big argument in my favour.' He drew his right hand from the sleeve in which it had been concealed and Carter saw he was grasping a long Japanese dagger. 'I am also,' proclaimed Yumasaki, 'very expert in the use of this weapon. Before you could grasp me, you would be impaled. Have I convinced you I am not a fool?'

'On the contrary, you have convinced me you are. I've been wondering all the time what kind of weapon you were holding inside that sleeve. That's why I spoke of breaking you in two. I wanted you to supply me with the information. You see, I figured it out you might be holding a gun pointed at me, which would go off, if I made any aggressive movement.'

'A revolver would make too much noise, my dear friend. Besides, I am so much more efficient with a dagger. I fail to see why you consider me a fool because I have shown you I possess this admirable weapon.'

'Oh, I didn't say you were a fool because of that. You are a darned fool, though, to let me know you aren't packing a gun, *because I am*. Get me?' As he spoke, he whipped out his revolver, immediately covering Yumasaki, who shrank back with a gasp of sheer consternation. 'I see you realise yourself now,' commented Carter, 'that you are, or were, a fool.' Swiftly he placed himself between the Japanese and the door. 'Now get this, Yumasaki. I am not afraid of a revolver making too much noise. In fact, it would be all to my advantage to fire, especially now those infernal fireworks outside seem to have stopped going off. Any attempt on your part to call for help, or any aggressive movement and you get yours. Savvy? Now sit down in that chair.' He indicated the one he had vacated. Yumasaki hesitated a moment then obeyed. 'Drop that dagger on the floor at your feet and kick it towards me. Come on; get a move on!' as the Japanese again showed hesitation. Carter was reluctantly obeyed. The knife came slithering across the carpet. He bent, still keeping his eyes on the other; picked it up with his left hand. 'This will make a nice little curio to take home, I guess. I wanted one of these.'

Putting the dagger under his right arm, he backed towards the door. Not for one moment did he take his eyes off Yumasaki as with his left hand behind him, he felt for the key, which he had already noticed in the lock, and turned it.

'Now,' he observed, 'you're going to talk, and talk fast.' He returned to his prisoner; sat down opposite him. 'Take those glasses off. I don't like them.' He was obeyed. 'Place your hands on your knees. That's fine.'

Yumasaki's face was a paler yellow than usual. He looked a very much frightened man.

'Who are you?' he muttered.

'Shall we dispense with my name?' suggested Carter, in the exact words previously used by the Japanese. 'It really does not matter. You made a pretty bad blunder in not reckoning that I might be armed, didn't you? I guess you're mighty sore about that now. Well, let us get on. You're going to spill the beans about this secret service racket, get me? If you refuse, or I think you're not coming clean, I'll shoot. I can do it without the slightest trouble coming my way. In fact, I'll probably earn the thanks of the government for removing a pest. Commence right at the beginning, and get a move on.'

Yumasaki was cornered, and he knew it. The dice was heavily loaded against him. Moreover, he felt quite certain the other would not hesitate to shoot, were the slightest excuse given him and, unlike most Japanese, Yumasaki regarded his life as his most precious possession. He must have long since decided that the man who had so completely turned the tables on him was not merely an American mercantile officer but, if he still wondered who he was, he refrained from making further attempts to find out. The expression on his captor's face warned him that questions might be decidedly injudicious.

At first, in response to Carter's demand, he strove to temporise, but as he became aware, to his vast astonishment and increased dismay, of that young man's knowledge, for Carter let him know the full extent of his information regarding Yumasaki's previous activities, he apparently came to the conclusion that it would be safer and wiser to open out completely. Perhaps he still nursed a hope that his opponent might be destroyed and himself rescued before the former could divulge the facts he was forcing from him. Whether that was the case or not, Carter learnt all Sir Leonard Wallace was so anxious to discover. Of course, it remained to be verified, but the British Secret Service agent had little doubt that it would prove entirely correct. Suggestive movements of his revolver every now and again brought vehement assertions from Yumasaki that he was telling the truth – as well as beads of perspiration to his brow, despite the fan, at fear of his imminent end.

He had returned from Japan on a steamer with half a dozen compatriots of the Secret Service. They had been smuggled ashore in bales of merchandise, and had spread themselves among the dancing saloons, five of which – the Fan Tan, Macao, Nanking, China Doll, and Canton were actually owned by Yumasaki, having been bought with money supplied by his superiors in Japan. The China Doll had been his actual headquarters but, aware that his connection with that establishment had become known, he had transferred his residence and all articles or papers of an incriminating nature to the Canton. A suite of rooms above the actual dancing hall had been transformed into a flat, which included a secret chamber in which he worked and kept confidential documents. The acting proprietors of the China Doll, Fan Tan, the Macao, the Nanking and the Canton were all in the pay of Japan, each of them having been compelled to work on his behalf by threat of the revelations of unsavoury incidents in their past lives of which he possessed proof.

'Very nice too,' commented Carter when he had forced all this from the reluctant spy. 'So the address you gave as your headquarters, when you were first found out, was just a blind, and the papers discovered there phoney!'

Yumasaki nodded.

'How is it,' he ventured, 'you are so well informed?'

'Ah! How am I?' mocked Carter. 'You sure would like to know, wouldn't you?'

The Japanese clasped his hands beseechingly.

'Please do not give me away. After all, if you are in truth an American ship's officer, it is no concern of yours what is happening in Hong Kong, which is British.'

'I kinda like the British,' replied Carter, 'and I guess I've no time for the Japs. And don't you think I'm some sore about that nice little execution you planned for me?'

'That was only – only a joke,' Yumasaki told him hurriedly. 'Surely, sir, you could not think I would seriously intend any harm to you.'

Carter laughed outright at that.

'Fruity,' he chuckled, 'distinctly fruity! And, of course, this dagger was really meant as a little surprise present for a guest you held in high regard?'

'How was I to know whether you were trustworthy or not? When the China Doll told me about you, I thought I had better see you, since the information she conveyed to me sounded most ominous. There was the suspicion that you might be a public spy. The dagger was for my own protection.'

'Sez you,' jeered the pseudo-American. 'There's just one thing more I'd like to know. Did you make inquiries to substantiate my statement that I was the second officer of the *Seattle*?'

Yumasaki inclined his head.

'Directly the China Doll told me about you,' he acknowledged, 'I caused Guttierez to telephone the customs office. He was informed that the *Seattle* was in, and that in spite of the fact that there was diphtheria on board, one of the officers had come on shore. Guttierez was even able to obtain a description which tallied with you.'

Carter smiled. He could trace the forethought of Sir Leonard Wallace in that.

'Very accommodating customs they must have here,' he murmured. 'No doubt, they are anxious to find a man who broke quarantine. Naughty me!'

Yumasaki could not understand this flippancy. He eyed Carter doubtfully.

'You will get into severe trouble,' he declared in a tone that implied a certain amount of satisfaction.

'I will, won't I?' agreed the other cheerfully. Then he became stern once more. 'Look here,' he demanded, 'what has the China Doll got to do with this racket of yours? I'm darn sure you haven't any hold over her to force her to fall into step like Guttierez and the rest.'

'She is to be my wife,' explained Yumasaki, as though that in itself was complete reason for the girl to take part in his espionage activities. Suddenly an idea seemed to occur to him. He leant forward, his eyes alight with renewed hope. 'Listen, my friend,' he begged, 'I will make a bargain with you. Forget all you have learnt tonight, give me my freedom, and you can have the China Doll. I will abandon all claim to her.'

Carter shot to his feet, the dagger falling from beneath his arm as he did so.

'Why, you miserable rat!' he cried, disgust and indignation mingling in his voice. 'You worm! I've a darn good mind to plug you offhand for that. So that's the kind of noble lover you are!'

He raised the revolver threateningly. Yumasaki apparently thought he actually meant shooting him without further ado and, either in a desperate attempt to escape the bullet, or with the intention of making a bid for life and liberty, launched himself forward from the chair at Carter's legs. His action was so apparently unpremeditated and sudden that the Englishman was taken by surprise. He was unacquainted with the tricks of ju-jutsu. Before he could step aside, his ankles were grasped, and the next moment he found himself flying over the prone form of the Japanese, to land with a crash behind him. Immediately,

Yumasaki had grasped the dagger, jumped to his feet, and darted to the door. Carter had been badly shaken by his fall, but he had not relinquished his hold on the revolver. He struggled into a sitting position as the Japanese was turning the key.

'It's no use, Yumasaki,' he cried. 'If you don't come back, I swear I'll shoot.'

For answer, the fellow flung the dagger at him. Carter threw himself aside only just in time, and the weapon stuck quivering in the wall beside him. At the same time he fired. Yumasaki screamed with agony; collapsed to the floor with a smashed leg. Carter rose to his feet, shook himself, and hastened across the room. He locked the door again, as excited cries reached his ears from outside.

'You brought this upon yourself,' he observed severely, looking down at the groaning man, writhing with pain at his feet. 'If you had behaved yourself, you wouldn't have been shot.'

He pocketed the revolver, dragged Yumasaki to the couch, lifted him upon it, and set to work to do what he could to ease his leg. There came a deafening clamour – fists beating upon the door, voices raised in Chinese and other languages, and other noisy sounds expressive of consternation and anger. Apparently it was known by his henchmen that the Japanese did not carry a revolver, and they had rightly conjectured that the man who was to be killed did, and had used it. Carter took little notice of the row. He had torn a strip of material from Yumasaki's garments and was temporarily bandaging the wound, making a mental resolution at the same time, to learn ju-jutsu. Presently he was surprised to hear the shouts outside change to cries of consternation. The drumming on the door suddenly ceased.

Then the handle was turned, followed by a loud, authoritative knock.

'Open this door,' came a command in English, 'or we break it down. The game is up, Yumasaki.'

Carter grinned.

'You hear that, Jap?' he asked of the groaning man. 'I guess the police are here.'

'Are you there, Carter?'

The young man recognised the anxious voice of Sir Leonard Wallace, and grinned more broadly than ever.

'Coming, sir,' he called.

The next moment he had unlocked, and thrown open the door. Several police, headed by Sir Leonard and Superintendent Ransome, poured in. Behind them, Carter caught a glimpse of the pale, troubled face of the China Doll. He smiled reassuringly at her, and joined Wallace, who was standing by the couch, regarding Yumasaki with deep satisfaction.

'I'm afraid I had to shoot him, sir,' he announced regretfully. 'But he would play about with daggers.'

'Thank God, you're safe,' observed Sir Leonard. 'The little lady almost caused me to believe we'd find you dead, though I must admit, knowing you, I had more confidence in your ability to remain alive. Still, there were anxious moments.'

'Did she fetch the police, sir?' asked Carter.

'She did, and at a good deal of risk to herself, I should imagine. All right, Ransome, Yumasaki is quite helpless. Carter and I will take care of him. You had better carry on the good work.'

The Superintendent of Police saluted, and hastened out of

the room with his men. Sir Leonard proceeded to tell Carter that, directly after their telephone conversation, he had got in touch with the Commissioner of Police, with the result that Superintendent Ransome immediately proceeded to the Canton with a dozen men, and surrounded the place. Sir Leonard had joined him there. The China Doll was seen to emerge and had gone off in a sedan chair, accompanied by a gigantic Chinaman, who appeared to be more of a guard than an attendant. They had been followed. When a quiet spot had been reached, the China Doll had ordered her conveyance to be put down. Then before her custodian could stop her, she had slipped out, and had started running along the road. She was chased, but the police tracking her had cut off her guardian, and had arrested him. She had been conducted to Sir Leonard and Ransome. It had been her intent, it transpired, to run to the Central Police Station, a courageous notion that could hardly have succeeded. When they gathered from her story that a young American was in deadly danger, they had broken in. Carter noticed the girl standing by the door, went to her, and took her hand.

'It was fine of you to think of helping me,' he acknowledged. 'I'm terribly sorry I had to shoot Yumasaki, but—'

'I am very glad,' she interrupted surprisingly.

'You're glad?' he echoed in amazement. 'But I thought you loved him.'

'I hate him!'

She said this so vehemently that Sir Leonard heard, and turned to regard her curiously.

'Thereby seems to hang a tale,' he commented. 'Come and sit down,' he invited her. She approached him shyly; accepted the seat he indicated. He turned back to the still groaning Japanese who had been too much concerned with his own troubles to listen to the conversation going on round him. 'I'm afraid I can't let your injury put me off, Yumasaki,' he pronounced sternly. 'If you expect any consideration from me you must confess everything – and now. You know who I am?'

The spy raised pain-stricken eyes to his.

'Yes, Your Excellency,' he groaned. 'You are the governor.'

'The governor?' cried the China Doll in tones in which awe blended equally with surprise.

'Yes,' smiled Carter. 'Didn't you know?'

She shook her head, and was about to rise out of respect but he stayed her.

'Then – then who are you, sir?' she asked.

'I am his very inadequate secretary,' he answered; then, addressing Sir Leonard: 'There is no need for you to question Yumasaki, sir. I have made him confess.'

'Everything?'

'The whole woicks,' Carter assured him with a grin.

Sir Leonard smiled.

'I think you can dispense with the disguise now,' he remarked.

'Thank the Lord for that.'

The young man promptly removed the rubber pads which had so altered the shape of his face. The China Doll watched the transformation with amazement, and gasped audibly.

'I regret your American sailor friend has gone for good, Joy,' he remarked in his normal attractive voice. 'Except for my hair, which is dyed, you see me as myself.'

'Then everything – your desire to know me – was for the

purpose of trapping Yumasaki and the other Japanese espionage agents?'

He nodded.

'I'm terribly sorry to have had to deceive you,' he apologised, 'but please believe that it has been a very sincere pleasure to have made your acquaintance.'

'I understand,' she murmured. 'There is no necessity to explain, please. But, had I been aware of this before, I could have been of great assistance to you. I know so much.'

'You are not a Japanese agent yourself, are you?'

She smiled, and shook her head. Sir Leonard interrupted the conversation to demand from Carter a recital of all he had learnt. Greater activity than ever prevailed on the part of the police as soon as Wallace was acquainted with the facts. Ransome sent for reinforcements. The dancing saloons, with which Yumasaki had been in any way connected, were raided, and searched from their roofs to cellars; the managers (or acting proprietors) and all employees were arrested, and removed to the cells of the Central Police Station. A good many of these were afterwards, of course, released, when it was ascertained that they had no connection with the Japanese spy system. The secret room at the Canton was a cleverly-constructed apartment which, when opened, proved a veritable gold mine of information. It contained not only the Japanese plans for espionage activities in Hong Kong, but proved to be a clearing house for the information gained by the agents throughout China. Japan's activities in Hong Kong would henceforth be completely crushed. Further, she would receive a bad setback throughout the Far East, for not only had secret codebooks, orders, and plans come to light, but also a list of agents operating in China Proper. When the China Doll heard of these discoveries from Carter – he had returned to the room in which Yumasaki lay under guard to find her still sitting where he and Sir Leonard had left her – she asked to be taken to the governor. The Japanese held up a protesting hand. He had been attended by a doctor, and was able now to think of other matters besides his wound.

'It is useless,' he remarked in his precise but sibilant English, 'to hope to obtain from the governor the slightest consideration for me by pleading to him. He is made, I think, of steel.'

To his utter astonishment, and that of Carter as well, the girl turned on him like a veritable spitfire. For five minutes, she spoke in rapid, angry Chinese, until the man on the couch positively wilted and, into his face, came an expression of such utter consternation that it was comical. The two Chinese policemen guarding him, grinned broadly, and nodded approval. Carter wondered what it was all about. When, at last, she ceased speaking, she turned her back on the prone and livid Yumasaki.

'Will you,' she asked Carter, 'be so kind as to take me to His Excellency, please?'

'Of course.'

He led her up to the secret room in which Sir Leonard was still engaged with the Commissioner of Police, who had joined him, and a couple of interpreters.

'This lady has requested to see you, sir,' announced Carter.

Sir Leonard smiled kindly at her.

'What can I do for you?' he asked.

She dropped a graceful little curtsy.

'Will you be kind enough, Your Excellency,' she begged, 'to give me complete copies of all you have found in this room. I wish to send them to my government in Nanking.'

'Copies will, in any case, be despatched to Nanking,' Sir Leonard assured her. 'Why do you particularly wish to send them?'

She smiled.

'I do not particularly wish to send them myself, please. So long as my government receives them, I am satisfied.'

The five men were regarding her curiously.

'You have my word for that,' declared Wallace. 'I gather, young lady, that you are not simply a dancer?'

She smiled again, and shook her head.

'I am of the Chinese Counter Espionage Service,' she confided. 'Dancing was merely a blind for my other work. Also my pretended love for Yumasaki, and the fact that I allowed him to make love to me, was only a means to an end, please. I had obtained his confidence – he even permitted me to carry out small functions for him. I, for instance, gave the letter to the Japanese sailor who had been sent from the ship. I also,' she added, 'delayed him and made him drunk so that he would fall into the hands of the police.' A little murmur of admiration and approval broke from the men. 'I had discovered everything,' she went on, 'but the contents of the secret room of Yumasaki – first it was in the China Doll, before he thought it safer to come here. My work is now finished. I return to my home in Nanking after sixteen months' absence.'

'By Jove!' exclaimed Carter. 'To think we almost considered arresting you as one of Yumasaki's accomplices. And I made a bet with myself that you were only mixed up in Secret Service work as a cat's paw! Ah, well, Joy, I'm jolly glad we're allies.'

She smiled very sweetly at him. Sir Leonard rose, and extended his hand to her, which she took very timidly.

'You deserve well of your country,' he declared. 'I will see that you convey the copies you spoke of to Nanking yourself. And Mr Carter will escort you.'

'Oh, Your Excellency,' she cried, 'how kind you are. Thank you so much.'

Carter chuckled softly to himself.

'Sir Leonard,' he whispered to Sir Masterson Winstanley, 'is taking an awful risk of losing a bright young assistant.'

The dour commissioner entirely lacked a sense of humour.

'Good God!' he exclaimed *sotto voce*. 'You are not thinking of marrying the girl, are you?'

The young man's eyes twinkled, but he sighed.

'For the first time in my life,' he muttered, 'I find myself wishing I was a Chinaman!'

# NOUGHTS AND CROSSES

## Part One

Anthony Anstruther felt intolerably bored. For weeks he had wandered through London searching for excitement and adventure; anything to give a zest to life. But from north to south, east to west, nowhere in the metropolis had he found anything that was even calculated to raise his interest above the ordinary level. A city that newspapers and novels had persuaded him to believe was full of glamour, of thrills, had turned out to be entirely humdrum, commonplace to the last degree. It was most disappointing. He had found that strolling through the environs of Soho at dead of night was very nearly like walking through a graveyard. Visions of crooks, assassins, members of foreign anarchistic organisations had faded woefully at the deserted appearance of Greek Street, the apparent respectability of Old Compton Street, the peacefulness of Dean Street. It was the same down amidst the unsalubrious highways and byways of the East End and Dockland. All the excitement produced by the latter was a dog fight and the spectacle of a drunken sailor resisting arrest.

Anstruther was one of those fortunate young men with far more money than he could possibly spend in a lifetime. He had been in the army, but had resigned his commission because he found the life dull. Yet now he was regretting his action. There were certain interests in a peacetime military career; one had an occupation and, even if it were not exactly congenial, it gave one something to do. Civilian life was sheer ennui. The trouble with Anthony Anstruther was that he had been brought up wrongly. Ever since he was a child, he had been pampered and petted. In addition, he possessed an ultra-vivid imagination. Now at the age of twenty-six, he had become blasé to the last degree. That was why, thoroughly tired of the ceaseless round of useless gaiety indulged in by his circle of friends, he was feverishly searching for the excitement he craved. And, as is the way of anything for which one sets out assiduously to find in this world, it eluded him.

Eventually he gave it up, having reached the conclusion that there is no adventure or romance in modern England. It was then, of course, that he found himself suddenly plunged into more excitement, not to mention danger, than even he, in his most imaginative moments, had dreamt. Fate delights in playing that kind of trick.

He had taken a girl friend to the theatre; afterwards, at her request, had escorted her to a nightclub in Greek Street. She had never been to a place of that type and, possessing something of his imagination and romanticism, had expected to find herself amidst glamorous and thrilling people, quite unlike those of the circles in which she moved and had her being. He had warned her that she would be disappointed, but she had not listened to him, probably thinking his attempt at discussion was prompted by a belief that a girl of her breeding and refinement would be shocked by the ultra-Bohemianism of the denizens of a Soho nightclub. They had not been there more than a quarter of an hour before she reached the conclusion that she had been cheated. Everything fell so tremendously below expectations that she felt she had never been more disillusioned in her life. The patrons were mostly respectable-looking men and women in correct evening attire who danced together quite decorously, the proprietor was a dignified individual who might have been a retired naval officer; the band was composed of half a dozen bored musicians completely lacking anything in the nature of verve or fire. Only the three or four dance hostesses appeared in any way interesting, mainly because of their queer profession and the stories she had heard of the gold-digging propensities of their type. They were all extremely young girls, very much made-up, but well dressed, with that hard expression on their otherwise pretty faces that comes from preying upon impressionable men. The club itself consisted solely of a long room lined with tables and divans, the walls crudely painted with designs that suggested the artist was probably drunk when he executed them. Sonia Hardinge wondered why people attended such places; what interest or excitement they obtained from it. Others have pondered over the same problem. Human beings are queer creatures.

She and Anstruther danced a little; drank a little; nibbled at the sandwiches without which liquid refreshment could not be obtained. Then she rose.

'I am utterly bored, Tony,' she confessed. 'Let me go.'

He picked up her wrap, which she threw over her arm, for it was a warm night in June, and they walked out of the place.

'I told you you would be disappointed,' he reminded her. 'I have been searching for something exciting for ages, until I know London like a book, but there's nothing in the whole of this city to raise even a thrill. It's sickening.'

'All nightclubs can't be like this,' she decided.

'They're all just as uninteresting. Some are more sordid and tawdry than others; that's all.'

They walked towards Soho Square, where his car had been parked. Sonia was a pretty girl of the athletic type so typical of post-war femininity. She was tall and straight with a graceful carriage, fair hair, frank blue eyes, and aquiline features. She and Tony Anstruther, with his strong, good-looking face, and military bearing, made an attractive couple. They had almost reached the square, when she laughed softly.

'You and I are both looking for something which life seems to deny us,' she observed. 'I almost think I shall be forced to accept one of your numerous proposals one of these days, in the hope that we shall be able to find a thrill in marriage.'

'I wish you would,' he murmured. 'After all, I love you, Sonia, and you say you are fond of me. Why do you keep putting it off?'

'Tony, you know very well, that we're built all wrong for wedding bells just yet. If we were married now, we'd probably get bored with each other in a few months. When I marry you, my dear, I want to be sure of our happiness.'

'Does that mean,' he asked eagerly, 'that you will marry me some day?'

'I suppose so,' she returned lightly; adding, with a little laugh, 'unless I meet and fall in love with a fascinatingly glamorous international crook or something of that kind.'

'I don't believe there are any crooks,' he grunted. 'I've become convinced that the world is composed of commonplace, unattractive creatures who are as pure as driven snow. Good Lord! What a damned nerve!'

She glanced at him quickly on hearing his sudden exclamation; then her eyes followed his. They had reached the square were almost opposite his car, which was standing close to the railings of the little garden in the centre. A small tattered individual, who looked like a tramp, appeared to be busily engaged in covering the bodywork of the dark blue Bentley with chalk marks. Giving a snort of indignation, Anstruther hurried across the road, closely followed by Sonia. He pulled up dead and swore softly to himself as his eyes took in numbers of parallel lines drawn at right angles to each other. The car seemed to be covered with them. In the spaces between were sometimes noughts, sometimes crosses. The fact that a tramp had committed the sacrilege of playing the game, beloved of children, called Noughts and Crosses on his beloved car, for a few seconds caused Anstruther to lose all power of expression. Then he found his voice in grim earnest.

'Here, you!' he cried. 'What the devil do you think you're doing?'

The small man looked up, and leered drunkenly.

''Lo,' he greeted Tony. 'Can't yer see wha' I'm doin'? Playin' Noughts an' Crosses, tha's wha' I'm doin'. Go 'way!' He turned back to the car; made an erratic cross, and chuckled. 'Tha's done yer, m'beauty,' he exclaimed. 'See'f yer c'n beat tha'.'

Sonia's sense of humour rose uppermost. A peal of delighted laughter rang out. The tramp straightened himself, turned, and regarded her with tipsy solemnity. He was a strange little man, not more than five feet in height, clothed in garments that had lost all right to individual terms. In fact, they looked like a heap of rags pinned and sewn together. Several days' growth of beard adorned his face that was amazingly wrinkled and almost unbelievably dirty. His brown eyes, despite the heaviness that an overindulgence in strong liquor had caused, were extraordinarily sharp.

'I've a jolly good mind to hand you over to the police,' declared the indignant Anstruther. 'Those blessed chalk marks will probably leave scratches. Hang it all! What on earth possessed you, you little worm, to select my car for your rotten game?'

'Is't your car, mate?'

'Of course it is.'

'Good. Then let's play 'gether. You c'n be th'noughts; I'll do cross – crosses. See?'

From among his rags, he produced a second piece of chalk, which he held out to Anstruther. The latter knocked it out of his hand and, striding forward, pulled open a door, rummaged under a seat, and produced a chamois leather.

'Here,' he ordered, pushing it into the tramp's hand; 'set to work and clean that car at once.'

The little man threw it on the ground; kicked it away with such violence that he staggered and almost fell.

'Shan't clean car,' he hiccoughed. 'Wanna play Noughts an' Cr – Crosses.'

Anstruther became thoroughly exasperated. Retrieving the

chamois from the road, he proceeded to rub off the chalk marks himself. At once a most unholy clamour of drunken protest rose from the tramp. Two or three people had already stopped to watch events. Now a crowd began to collect; windows of adjoining houses opened, and curious heads protruded. When the assembled throng gathered what all the fuss was about a great roar of laughter rent the air. Anstruther felt himself turning crimson, Sonia dived into the interior of the car, and stopped there. The tramp struggled desperately to prevent Tony from rubbing off the chalk marks.

''S not fair,' he protested. 'Jus' 'cos y'know yer couldn' beat me at Noughts an' Crosses, yer won' play.'

A man detached himself from the crowd, and strolled forward. He was a hunchback whose deformity reduced him to a height no greater than that of the tramp. His clean-shaven face was sallow and drawn, as though he habitually suffered much pain; his hair was jet black and rather unruly – he wore no hat. His features were nondescript and not unpleasant, with the exception of the eyes, which were dark, glittering, and restless, seeming to contain in their depths a suggestion of evil. Despite his unfortunate figure, his clothes fitted well and were of excellent material. He watched, for a few moments, the struggle still going on between Anstruther and the tramp; then he intervened.

'Pardon me,' he apologised to the former, in passable English but a thickness of utterance that was rather ugly, 'I have not the intention of butt in for the curiosity. I t'ink I can manage the leetle man for you.'

Tony stood away from the tramp, and regarded the newcomer with interest.

'I shall be very grateful if you can,' he acknowledged, wiping his brow with a silk handkerchief. 'He is beyond me.'

The hunchback stepped up to the little man, and touched him lightly on the arm. The latter swung round with a grunt.

'Wha' more of 'em,' he grumbled. 'It's a trap, tha's wharrit is. It's a trap to gemme' 'way fr'm my lit game.'

'The motor car is not the place for to play the game. I have the slate. Come! I will show you how properly to play heem.'

'D'you mean ter say yer think yer can play better'n me?'

'I am the expert. No one have yet beat me.'

'Garn! I'll show yer. No one's beat yer!' He spat contemptuously in the road. 'C'm on. I'll show yer.' He linked his arm in that of the hunchback; leered up at Anstruther. 'Yer c'n have yer ole car,' he remarked. 'I don' wannit.'

'That's all very well,' grumbled Tony unwisely. 'I think the little beast ought to clean away those marks before he goes. I can't drive the car through London looking like that, and it will take me ages to do it.'

'Do yer goo', yer swine of a naris'crat,' hiccoughed the tramp. 'Your sor's no goo' – no goo' 't all.'

The hunchback shook his arm free; walked to the car, and peered in at the girl sitting there.

'Madame,' he observed, 'if you and your frien' will come to my house and wait for the leetle time, my servant will clean the car.'

'It is very nice of you,' she replied hesitantly, and her eyes met Tony's inquiringly. Her instincts were naturally to refuse such an invitation, but here, she thought, was a chance of experiencing something a little out of the ordinary. She gathered from the expression in Tony's eyes that he was thinking the same, but was leaving the decision to her. At once she made up her mind. 'If you are sure it won't be any trouble to you,' she decided, 'we shall be glad to accept, won't we, Tony?'

'Rather,' he agreed heartily. 'Of course,' he added, 'I shall insist on paying your man for doing the job.'

'Do not mention it,' protested the other. 'And it will be no trouble for me to have you in my home, Madame. It will be the great honour.'

Anstruther helped the girl from the car. The hunchback, with a flourish of a long arm, indicated a house across the square, and began to lead the way.

'Here, mister,' called the tramp, 'I don' wanna play with aris'crats.'

'You are going to make the play with me, my frien'. Come!'

Grumbling drunkenly to himself, the little man fell in behind. The crowd, amused still, began to disperse. It was mostly composed of people living in that district; southern Europeans, to whom laughter came easily. They considered they had been afforded a free and very entertaining show; turned their steps homeward with increased happiness.

Sonia and Anstruther were approaching the house, indicated as his residence by the hunchback, who was two or three yards ahead, when they were astonished to hear a voice behind them whisper urgently and without any sign of intoxication in it.

'Don't go into that house, as you value your lives. Make some excuse, return to the car, and drive away.'

They glanced over their shoulders, to see the tramp almost on their heels. He still continued to leer drunkenly, and was staggering in his gait. A whiff of his drink-perfumed breath reached their nostrils, and caused the girl to shudder with disgust. But only he could have uttered the warning. They were extremely puzzled; were quite unable to fathom such a mystery.

'Did you speak?' asked Sonia frigidly.

'Wha'sat?' with a loud hiccough from the man. 'Don' speak temme – yah, aris'crats! Of course I spoke,' came immediately afterwards in a whisper. 'Take my advice! You're going into danger.'

Such a warning in their state of mind was calculated to have the opposite effect to that intended. The tramp was not to know this, however, and he grunted a remark that sounded like 'Pig-headed fools', as they continued on their way. Anstruther had reached the conclusion that he and the girl had unconsciously become involved in something of the nature of that for which he had so long been in search, and he meant to see it through. He regretted the fact that Sonia was present, but did not believe that any real danger could threaten them. However, as a concession to his conscience, he asked if she would rather not enter the hunchback's house.

'Of course we're going in,' she whispered. 'I feel quite thrilled. The tramp man must be only pretending to be drunk, though he smells as though he's swallowed a public house. Perhaps he's a detective in disguise, Tony.'

'Detective be blowed,' muttered Anstruther contemptuously. 'Detectives don't play Noughts and Crosses on cars.'

The hunchback unlocked the door of a three-storied house and threw it open for them to enter. Sonia had had an idea that the buildings in that district were mostly devoted to tenements and flats; wondered what the hunchback wanted with a whole house. From the little she had seen of it, before entering a narrow, musty hall, she had concluded that, by daylight, it would look very dilapidated. The passage was in darkness.

'Wait,' came in the hunchback's thick accents. 'I will put the light. So!'

A single electric bulb flared into life, rendering visible the hall in all its nakedness. Except for linoleum under foot, it was completely devoid of furniture. A door on their right was opened, and Sonia and Anstruther shown into a room, which rather surprised them, after the appearance of the hall. It was not exactly luxurious, but it was comfortable-looking. The two easy chairs, the couch, were by no means new, but they were upholstered in good quality material that must have once appeared impressive. An oak bookcase filled the whole of one wall and was crammed with books, a sideboard was placed against another. A large table in the centre of the room with three chairs on each side and one at either end was covered with a red cloth. The carpet was attractive and thick while, on the huge old-fashioned mantelshelf, was a valuable clock, also vases of flowers.

'This my sit-room,' announced the hunchback. 'I am landlord,' he went on to explain, 'that let the rooms to my countrypeoples.'

'Are you French?' inquired Tony.

'No, no, no,' was the emphatic reply. 'Me I am Roosian. You like the Roosian?' he asked Sonia.

'Oh – er – yes, of course,' she hastened to assure him, though she did not remember having ever met one before then.

'I am please. Will you sit? I will send my servant Ivan to clean the car at once.'

'I say,' acknowledged Anstruther, 'it's jolly good of you to take all this trouble.'

'It is the pleasure.' He clicked his tongue as though annoyed with himself. 'Ah! I forget the leetle man. I have the weakness for Noughts and Crosses and, too sad, I cannot play them mooch because mos' people t'ink it is children's games. When to your help I come, I am a leetle selfish, for I t'ink at last I find a man who like the game wi' the passion of me.'

'But,' objected Tony, 'he is a tramp – and drunk.'

'What matter is that? Pardon, I mus' go find heem.'

He hastened from the room. Sonia looked at Tony and smiled.

'Noughts and Crosses!' she murmured. 'That tramp must have dreamt about there being danger here. A man who is keen on playing a kid's game like that can't be dangerous.'

'Unless he's mad,' hazarded Anstruther.

'O – oh!' Sonia's eyes opened wide. 'I never thought of that. Do you think he is, Tony?'

'I shouldn't think so. He looks sane enough.'

'He has queer eyes, though. Have you noticed them? There is something about them that seems – wicked. I can't tell what it is; but, when he looked at me just now, I felt like shuddering.'

Anstruther laughed softly.

'That little blighter of a tramp has made you imaginative,' he remarked. 'I wonder what happened to him. He followed us in, didn't he?'

'I don't know – I didn't notice. I should like to know why he was pretending to be drunk. He isn't a tramp either – really a tramp I mean; he had such a nice, well-bred sort of voice when he warned us not to come in here.'

Anstruther stroked his chin thoughtfully.

'You're right; so he had. I hadn't thought of that before. I hope there isn't any actual danger, Sonia. I should never forgive myself, if I were the cause of anything happening to you.'

'Don't be silly! What could happen to me? Besides, I accepted the invitation to come here – you didn't. Therefore, you wouldn't be to blame if something did go wrong.'

'I would. I backed you up.'

'You're not getting the wind up, old boy, are you?' she scoffed. 'After all, both you and I have been longing for a thrill. If we get one from the hunchback, we ought to be grateful.' She sighed. 'It's too much to hope for I'm afraid.'

'I say,' he observed suddenly, lowering his voice to a whisper, 'perhaps we shouldn't be talking aloud like this. Someone may be listening.'

She laughed.

'I believe you *have* got the jim-jams,' she bantered.

'I can't help feeling a bit uneasy about you,' he confessed. 'If I were alone, I'd be all for an adventure, preferably with a spice of danger in it. Goodness knows I've been hoping and searching for something of the sort long enough. It's a different matter to drag you in, though. The disappearance of the tramp has made me wonder, and I've had time to think. There must have been some reason for—'

The sound of voices outside the room interrupted him. The door opened, and the hunchback entered, escorting the ragged individual who had uttered the strange warning. Under the glare of the electric light, he looked more disreputable than he had done in the illumination diffused from the street lamps. His garments, if they could be dignified with such a description, were filthy, his hands and face repulsively dirty. Yet Sonia could not help feeling there was something attractive about him, despite the fact that he bestowed on Anstruther and her a most uncomplimentary and resentful scowl. The extraordinary number of wrinkles on his face and his magnetic brown eyes fascinated her. Apart from that, she was tremendously intrigued at the thought that his drunkenness was assumed. As he stood inside the room, swaying gently, she began to doubt if it was; he looked so completely intoxicated. Nevertheless, she could not forget the warning he had uttered in a completely sober voice.

'I find heem,' announced the hunchback unnecessarily. 'He go back himself to the car and start the play again. I am sorry, but he not seem to like you. I have mooch trouble persuade heem to come in.'

'Dir'y aris'crats,' mumbled the tramp. 'T' hell wi' all aris'crats – mo' cars an' jewels an' money an' food 'n'everythin'! Yah!'

He scowled again, hiccoughed loudly, and lapsed into silence.

'You mus' not mind heem,' insisted the hunchback. 'He do not mean the harm. I have send my servant to make clean the car. Soon it will be all right. Madame and sir, I regret I do not before introduce myself. I am Nicholas Karen, ver' mooch to your service.'

'We are greatly obliged to you, Mr Karen, for your kindness,' responded Anstruther. 'My name is Anthony Anstruther. This lady is Miss Hardinge.'

'So!' Karen bowed politely. 'We now know each other. Please be seat.' They sat side by side on the couch. 'Maybe you are honger or thirst? Will you take the refreshment? It will not make the trouble.' They thanked him, but declined. 'Ah! You do not mind if I wi' my frien' play the game?'

'Not at all,' Tony assured him. 'Go ahead! Miss Hardinge and I will watch.'

'T'ank you. I will go fetch the slate. Excuse for the moment.'

He left the room, closing the door behind him. Tony and Sonia sat looking at the tramp, who still stood swaying slightly, his eyes sometimes wide open, sometimes very nearly closed, the very picture of sullen inebriation. They both were anxious to speak to him, but were not sure whether it would be wise. He settled the point for them, by addressing them in a whisper they only just heard. His lips did not seem to move.

'Having got in,' he breathed, 'the question is how to get you out. Perhaps he means you no harm, but I can't imagine his going out of his way to do anyone a good turn. No; don't speak. This may be a trap. I don't think he suspects me, but one never knows. Whatever happens, don't by word or sign show that you think me anything but what I look. I've got to rely on you to that extent – can't help myself. If there's any trouble coming to you, I'll do my best to get you out of it.' Suddenly he raised his voice, and again spoke in thick, drunken accents. 'Wharrer yer thinkin' 'bout, you two, eh? Tha's wha' I wan' to know. I'm's good s'you 'ny day, an' don' yer forget it, see? If I wanter play Noughts an' Crosses on yer bloomin' car why shouldn' I, answer me tha' – why shouldn' I?' He waved his right arm in an emphatic gesture that almost caused him to overbalance. 'If I'd m'way, I'd drown all aris'crat babies a' birth, tha's wha' I'd do – s'truth I would, s'elp m'bob.'

The hunchback had returned during this drunken diatribe, and stood, for a moment, listening, a smile on his sallow face. He stepped forward as the little man showed signs of becoming violent; took him by the arm.

'You please don't mind heem,' he advised the others. 'He too mooch drunk to know what it is he say. Look,' he added to the tramp, 'I have the slate. We will play.'

He placed a large slate of the type used by small school children on the table, pulled out a chair, and sat down, inviting his ragged guest to take another. The latter did so after fumbling ineffectually for a while and eventually needing help. He took the piece of chalk handed to him with a grunt of satisfaction.

'Noughts me,' he enunciated. 'You c'n be cross-crosses.'

'As you like, my frien', but it would have been proper if first we have toss the coin.'

The tramp leered at him.

'Not on yer life,' he vowed. 'P'raps yer would 'a called noughts, an' I allus star's we' noughts – nev' lose then. Are yer ready, pal?'

'Yes, I am ready.'

'Then off we goes.'

To Sonia and Tony sitting there watching, the scene was fantastic, incredible. That two men – even though one appeared drunk and a tramp, and the other a foreigner, a hunchback and possibly rendered eccentric through his deformity – should solemnly sit at a table and play Noughts and Crosses on a slate was almost beyond belief. Anstruther could not rid himself of the feeling that he was dreaming. The whole affair – the drunk tramp playing the game on his car, the interposition of the hunchback, the warning from the inebriated man in anything but an uncouth or intoxicated voice, and now the two queer individuals playing Noughts and Crosses on a slate, both appearing in deadly earnest – was of the absurd stuff of which dreams are made. There was nothing real about the situation. Sonia did not regard it in quite the same light as Tony. She was most struck by the humour of the circumstances and badly wanted to giggle. They had been much impressed by the whispered remarks of the little man during the absence from the room of Nicholas Karen and, more than ever, Anstruther felt he had been extremely foolish in allowing Sonia to enter the house. It was obvious to them both now that the tramp was playing a part, that he was no more drunk than they were, even though he looked it and exuded such an unpleasant odour of strong liquor. They had become intensely interested in him; wondered who he was, and what was behind his extraordinary pretence. Tony would have been delighted at the prospect of becoming concerned at last in something that promised adventure, had it not been for the presence of the girl. She, for her part, was feeling delightfully thrilled. The prospect of danger did not frighten her; on the contrary, she welcomed it. Probably that was because she did not really feel in her heart that any actually existed.

The two men at the table played Noughts and Crosses with the seriousness of experts engaged in a game of chess. This was most marked in the case of Karen, whose dark eyes grew almost feverish as he found the tramp, despite his drunkenness, a foeman worthy of his steel. The onlookers began to realise that there was more in the game, as played by these two utterly dissimilar beings, than they had thought possible. At last, the concentration of each and the deliberation with which the noughts or crosses were inserted on the slate seemed to indicate this. Karen won the first game, and gave vent to a chuckle of glee. The tramp grunted with disgust; made a remark under his breath that was not audible. The Russian had provided himself with a little sponge with which he rubbed out the filled-in diagram, after he had indicated his win with a short line at the top of the slate. The figure was drawn again. This time the little man won, and a line was put to his credit. Thus it went on, sometimes one, sometimes the other winning; each game taking a considerable time to play, because of the thought each man gave to his moves. It became very monotonous to the watchers on the couch. They wondered uneasily why the servant had not entered the room to announce that he had cleaned the car. He seemed to be taking an unconscionable time about it. Both Karen and the tramp appeared totally to have forgotten their existence. At last, as the two finished their tenth game, and the Russian boasted six wins to four, Anstruther touched Sonia on the arm, and rose to his feet.

'I am sorry to interrupt, Mr Karen,' he observed, 'but it is time Miss Hardinge and I left. I am sure your servant must have removed the chalk marks from the car by now.'

The Russian looked up at them and, for the first time, they had actual indication that his friendliness had been assumed. The expression on his face was definitely antagonistic, and Tony became aware of the evil that lurked in his eyes of which Sonia had already spoken.

'There is not the hurry,' he remarked suavely. 'Ivan will come at the right time.'

He turned again to the tramp, who had given no sign of the slightest interest. Appreciating the fact that he and Sonia had been invited into the house for some sinister purpose, but having not the slightest idea what it could be, Anstruther was now deeply incensed with himself. He gripped the girl's hand protectively.

'I regret having to insist,' he declared firmly. 'It is getting late, though. Miss Hardinge and I can let ourselves out without interference with your game. We'll say goodnight, Mr Karen, and thank you very much for your hospitality.'

The Russian muttered something in his own language; rose from his chair.

'Wait,' he commanded harshly. 'I will go to see Ivan.'

'We'll come with you,' asserted Tony, showing quite plainly he objected to the other's tone.

For answer Karen walked quickly to the door, opened it, and called along the passage to someone. The tramp took the opportunity of leaning across the table. Again his words came in a whisper that only just reached their ears.

'I'm afraid you're for it. Don't know what the fellow wants with you, but you're going to find out. Of course you'll be indignant – who wouldn't – but take care to include me in your annoyance. And trust me to get you out of the hole.'

'How do you know we can trust you?' came from Sonia who, anxious not to be overheard by the man at the door, did little more than move her lips.

The tramp understood her, however, and grinned slightly.

'You haven't any choice,' he breathed; thereafter he took no further notice of them.

He was vigorously, though erratically, cleaning the slate, when Karen returned to them. Four men entered the room, and stood behind the hunchback. They formed a villainous-looking quartette and, for the first time, Sonia began to have qualms. One, big and burly, with a bushy fair beard, and hair that stuck up from his head like the quills on a porcupine, possessed the smallest and shiftiest eyes she had ever seen in a human face; another, of medium height, had a sallow face like Karen's, the chief feature of which was a broken nose; the third was as nondescript, and of similar build to the second, with large teeth protruding from a loose mouth, giving him the appearance of wearing a perpetual grin. The fourth was perhaps the most striking. There was not a vestige of hair on his head, his face was dead white, and he had large fish-like, unblinking eyes. These might have been redeemed by eyelashes or brows but, as he had neither, his appearance was startling. He was as tall as the bearded man, but extremely thin, with long arms and talon-like hands. Altogether he was a repulsive object.

Karen touched the tramp on the shoulder. The latter leered up at him; then blinked foolishly as he caught sight of the four newcomers. Apparently he had not previously been aware of their presence.

'S'truth!' he muttered, 'wha's all thish? Whereish the beau'y chorush c'm from?'

The Russian smiled. Anstruther and Sonia, watching anxiously, had no reason to think that he bore the little man anything but the friendliest feelings. In fact, there was something almost affectionate in the smile.

'You would like the drink – yes?' he inquired.

'Drink?' echoed the tramp in the eager tone of a dying man in a desert sighting an oasis. 'Mishter, you'll shave m'life 'f you gimme drink.'

'Good. After, we will resume the game.' He turned to the bearded man, spoke rapidly in Russian; looked back at the tramp. 'Go wi' heem, my frien'. He will give you all the drink you want.'

The little man struggled to his feet; patted Karen on the arm with drunken affection.

'You're pal tha's wha' yerrar – a pal,' he pronounced.

The Russian smiled again.

'I like you also,' he confessed. 'Nevaire have I meet any man can play the Noughts and Crosses like you. You play so well drunk, how great mus' you be not drunk!'

'Drunk! Who shays I'm drunk?' He paused, looked Karen in the face, and nodded solemnly. 'Tha's it,' he agreed. 'Knew some'ing was'h wrong. You're ri', pal, abs'lu'ly ri' – I'm drunk.'

He followed the bearded man from the room, chuckling hoarsely, as though at some great joke. Directly the door had closed behind him and his companion, Karen drew up a chair, and sat down. He subjected Anstruther and Sonia to a long, insolent look, and now there was no mistaking the evil in his eyes.

'Look here,' protested Tony angrily. 'What is the meaning of this? Who are these men? Am I to understand you intend keeping us here against our wills?'

'Oh! So many questions you ask,' returned Karen. 'Sit down at the table, and we will talk – yes?'

'I'll be damned if I will,' came violently from the young Englishman. 'Miss Hardinge and I are leaving at once, and you will attempt to stop us at your peril.'

'How fierce that is!' he laughed, and made a remark in his own language to his followers, which seemed to cause them much amusement. 'Well,' he went on to the two who realised now they were, to all intents and purposes, his prisoners, 'if you will not sit, you will stand. It makes no matter to me. The men wit' me are my frien's. I bring them to show you you will be mooch foolish to try run away. The leetle man I sent out of the room, because it is not wise he should hear what I say. It is true he is drunk; he also likes not the rich peoples, but he is English, and I do not take the risks. I like heem mooch, because he, the same as me, have the passion for the Noughts and Crosses game. Now listen, Monsieur, and you also, Madame. Tonight you will not go to the home. There is one leetle service from you I want. Two, three days maybe you are free. No harm is intended to you, if you are behave.'

'This is outrageous,' broke out Anstruther. 'You can't keep us here, do you understand?' He turned to Sonia. 'Come on, dear. We're going.'

He walked to the door, Sonia following him closely. Karen did not say a word, but turned in his chair to watch events. Tony strove to push between the three men barring their way to the door. At once he was grasped by two of them and, though he fought desperately, found they were possessed of enormous strength. Before long he was rendered helpless. Sonia had been grasped by the man with the fish-like eyes. A scream was stifled at its inception by one of the talon-like hands and, despite her frantic struggles and several well-planted kicks on the shins of her assailant, she was soon as helpless as her companion.

'How foolish!' commented Karen. 'I think it will be better you are tied.'

He spoke to the others, and left the room. Tony looked miserably at Sonia, whose eyes, practically the only part of her face visible, on account of the brutal hand covering her mouth, were horror-stricken.

'Forgive me for getting you into this, Sonia,' he pleaded. 'I'll never forgive myself. God! If I could only get my hands free! Let that lady go, you brute,' he suddenly shouted. 'Do you hear me? Take your filthy hand from her mouth.'

Fish-eyes grinned.

'Not do – she make row,' he replied. Apparently his knowledge of English was not very great.

Karen returned, carrying several lengths of rope. He assisted his followers to bind the two and, in a remarkably short space of time, they were trussed so tightly that they could neither move arms nor legs. They were unceremoniously dumped on the couch, from where Anstruther proceeded to give full vent to his outraged feelings. Karen stood over him listening; apparently much interested in the outburst.

'You are mos' stupid young man,' he declared, when Tony paused for breath. He bowed mockingly to Sonia. 'Madame, accept please the apology. I mooch regret that we are force to do this. Now maybe, you both listen. If you make the noise, you will be gag. Am I understand?'

'Go ahead!' snapped Tony. 'Tell us what you want with us.'

'Ah! That is better. Well, I tell you. I t'ink you are the ver' rich young man and the lady also. Her clothes are mooch beautiful – you have the ver' expensive motor car. I want from you five t'ousand pounds.'

'Five thousand pounds!' gasped Anstruther. 'So that's what you are; rotten bandit! Well, if you think you can bring your beastly foreign ideas into this country, and get away with it, you've made a mistake. Five thousand pounds, indeed! You can jolly well whistle for it, you swine.'

Karen bent over him, caught his nose between his thumb and forefinger, and gave it a cruel twist that brought involuntary tears to his eyes.

'I like not that kind of talk,' snarled the hunchback. 'It is better you are more polite. Next time you are speak in that manner, Madame will suffer.'

'You wouldn't dare,' stormed the young man.

'No? Then watch, please.'

He turned to Sonia, took hold of her nose, and was about to subject it to the same treatment, when Tony cried out:

'Don't! For God's sake, don't!'

Karen stood regarding him mockingly for a few moments, still grasping Sonia's nose. Then he released her.

'I t'ink we onderstand each other,' he observed, nodding his head, as though to confirm his own statement. 'I am not the bandit. I am the head of a mooch good society what have beeg ideal. We need money – plenty of money, because the funds are ver' low. Now, will you give me five t'ousand pounds?'

'No; I'll see you damned first.'

'Good for you, Tony,' applauded the girl.

She was very pale, but now that she had recovered from the first shock, there was the light of a great courage in her blue eyes. Karen shook his head slowly, almost, it appeared, sadly.

'How unwise!' he exclaimed. 'I am sorry.'

'Sorry!' snorted Tony; 'you'll be more sorry when I've done with you. You are the fool, Karen. Do you think you can do this sort of thing in England? Why, if Miss Hardinge is not released before morning, there'll be a search for her. The police will quickly find out where she is. You've forgotten the people who watched the fuss over the car, haven't you? They heard you invite us to come here, and saw us accompany you. What about that, my fine fellow? What about the car standing in the square which your servant Ivan was supposed to clean?'

'He clean it nice,' returned Karen casually. 'It look now ver' pretty, and it wait outside the door. Soon it will take us all away –

oh, so far from here. This house is only mine for the leetle while. One month more and my rent is finish. What matters one month? I have mooch better house. Tonight we go. Then what about the police? They mooch puzzle – huh?'

The faces of Sonia and Tony blanched. The trap into which they had fallen appeared to be closing tighter round them.

'What's the sense of taking us away?' demanded Anstruther desperately. 'Look here, let us go, and we will both promise to say nothing about what has happened.'

Karen laughed, turned, and explained what had been said to his three henchmen. They had been listening with interest, apparently finding great difficulty in following the conversation. When Tony's offer was translated, they joined heartily in their leader's laughter. The Englishman glared impotently at them.

'But we waste the time,' declared the hunchback. 'Once more I offer you the freedom for five t'ousand pounds.'

'How do you know I have so much money?'

'If you not have it, you first time would have told me. I t'ink you ver' rich young man, and Madame, also. I t'ink is rich. You will give – yes?'

'How the devil can I get it, if you keep us trussed up like this?'

'I will arrange. You have the cheque book?'

'Supposing I have?'

'Ah! That answer my question. It is evident you have it. You will write the cheque for five t'ousand pounds, and a letter also, to the bank for the manager to give money to bearer. You will say you and Madame go away for a leetle time, that is why you want the money. Then for four, five days you will be my guests, and no harm will come to you. After, you go to the home. Are you agree?'

'What happens if I refuse?'

The hunchback shrugged his deformed shoulders.

'Then I am mooch sorry. You and Madame will be dead.'

Sonia shrank back with a little cry; Anstruther laughed, albeit a trifle unsteadily.

'Of course you're joking,' he exclaimed.

'Me, I nevaire make the joke. You will see. Madame and you can fink of it while we take you safe from here. At ten o'clock I will once more ask you. If you again refuse the leetle request, then p'ff! It is all ovaire – just like that!'

Despite his casual manner of speaking, there was no mistaking the threat underlying his tone. It was evident he meant everything he said. The expression on his face was utterly merciless and cruel; his wicked eyes held a gloating quality that suggested that he would as gladly murder them as receive the five thousand pounds he demanded. Tony was about to break forth into a fierce and bitter denunciation of the fellow, but realised, in time, that no good could come of giving further vent to his feelings. Their only sensible course was to appear to accept the position in the hope that the man posing as a drunken tramp would be as good as his word. He had said they must trust him to get them out of the hole. They had no alternative now. Anstruther would gladly pay five thousand pounds to ensure the safety of Sonia, but he felt, deep in his heart, that it would do nothing of the sort. They were as likely to be murdered once the money was paid over as they would be if he refused to give the cheque and the letter for his manager. He did not bother to consider then what the latter would think at receiving a communication of such a nature. That, after all, was a trifle. All his thoughts must be concentrated on saving Sonia.

'What good would it do to murder us?' he demanded.

'Sooner or later the police would get on your track, and the inevitable end would be trial and execution.'

Karen laughed harshly.

'Many I have kill,' he stated. 'What matters two more? Pah! You talk the foolishness.'

'What guarantee have I,' asked Tony, 'that you will let us go if I arrange to get the money?'

'Have I not say you will be free after two, t'ree days? But we waste once more the time. I wish resume the game wit' my leetle frien'. You will be taken to another room until we ready to go away. Paul will watch you so you not make the noise. You like Paul – yes?' he asked Sonia, indicating the hairless man, with the horrible fish-like eyes. She shuddered, and he laughed with evil amusement. 'Paul do not like people shout for help. I t'ink he may do t'ings that hurt mooch. It better you keep ver' quiet in the othaire room.'

Speaking rapidly to the three men, he was answered by nods and grins. Sonia was picked up as though she had been a baby by the man she loathed so greatly. Tony was carried from the room by the other two. They were conveyed up a narrow staircase, into a back room on the first floor that contained nothing but a bedstead, on which was a heap of dirty linen and blankets, a couple of chairs and a cheap dressing table. They were deposited on the bed side by side, and Paul sat down to watch them. The other two men left the room.

# Part Two

The tramp had been escorted to a kitchen at the rear of the premises by the big, bearded man. He had been given a seat at a table; a glass and several bottles of beer placed before him. There seemed no doubt that Karen had developed a liking for the little man and had every intention of treating him well. The tramp's eyes had gleamed at sight of the bottles. Without waiting for an invitation he had opened one and had proceeded to drink from it without bothering to use the glass. His escort had been greatly amused at this, and had nodded with genial approval. Apparently he spoke no English at all. Nevertheless he and the little man, with whom he presented such a striking contrast, had contrived to become quite friendly over the drinking bout that followed. By the time Karen appeared, to inform his ragged guest that he was ready to resume their game, the bottles were empty. The tramp looked blissfully happy, though his drunkenness had not increased to any marked extent. He was obviously of the genre that, once intoxicated, can go on drinking without any appreciable difference to his degree of drunkenness. It is true his legs seemed inclined to refuse their function but, with the help of the hunchback and the other man, who turned out to be Ivan, hitherto described by Karen as his servant, he was taken back to the room where he and the Russian had already played the great game of Noughts and Crosses. Karen regarded him anxiously as he fell rather than sat in a chair.

'I hope you are not too mooch bad to again play?' he observed.

'Too bad – me?' returned the tramp. 'Not on y'r life. I'm all ri' – quite all ri'.' He cast a bleary look at the couch. 'Tha's goo',' he commented, 'dir'y aris'crats gone 'way. Goo' rid'nce bad rub'sh. Don' know wha' you wan' bring in tripe like tha' fer.'

'You're quite right, my frien'. They were no good. It was stupid for me to be kind to them. Well, they have go home. Come! We will forget them and play – huh?'

'Tha's ri – we'll play – an' wha's more, I'm goin' beat yer – see?'

The diagram was drawn on the slate, and the two settled down solemnly to continue their absurd game. An hour passed by, and still they were at it. They had hardly spoken, except to utter exclamations or grunts of pleasure or disgust, according to the manner in which the games went. Karen continued to win the greater number though, despite his condition, the tramp proved a doughty opponent until, at last, after mumbling drowsily and incoherently, he suddenly collapsed over the slate and fell asleep. The hunchback regarded his tousled head for a few moments then, with a sigh, rose to his feet. Crossing to the door, he summoned his confederates. They came, looking very much as though they themselves had been taking a nap. Karen addressed them in Russian.

'It is a long time since I have had an evening so pleasant,' he declared. 'The leetle man plays the game like an expert. He must be marvellous, amazing, when he is sober. At last I have found a worthy opponent, only to lose him again. It is a great pity. I wish it were possible always to keep him with me. Fools that you are; why cannot you have brains, and learn to play like him?'

'What are you going to do with him, Nicholas?' asked the man with the broken nose, who rejoiced (or otherwise) in the name of Ilitch Gortschakoff.

'Unfortunately, he must be returned to the streets. It would be too risky to make him a member of our brotherhood, although the sentiments he has expressed show him to be in sympathy with us. His kind talk a lot, but lack courage.'

'Perhaps the police will make him tell about the man and woman,' observed Ivan Keremsky. 'They are certain to find out about him and the car and how you invited the two to come in here.'

'He is too drunk to remember much, but what does it matter? We will not be here, and who can trace us? You will drive us to the Haven, Ivan. Afterwards, you will take the car to the other side of London, and hide it so that it cannot be found for a day or two. I would like to keep it, but alas! It would be dangerous even to alter it. The police of this country are very clever, and we must make no stupid mistakes.'

'What becomes of the man and woman?' asked Gortschakoff.

Karen's face twisted into an evil smile.

'When we have the money, we will kill them,' he replied. 'It is easy at the Haven – eh?'

The others grinned. The man with the protruding teeth, however, seemed uneasy.

'I do not quite understand this affair,' he confessed. 'How did you find these people and how did you know they have so much money?'

'Did I not explain, when I told Ivan to clean the car?' replied Karen impatiently. 'You, Leon Turgenev, have not the brains of a mouse. I was returning here, and saw the little man enjoying himself. You know the passion I have for Noughts and Crosses! I stood watching him. I was about to address him, when along came the man and the girl. They became angry, because he was using their beautiful car for such a purpose. I soon formed the opinion that they were wealthy – it is easy to tell – and I thought it would be good if I could lure them in here, and afterwards force them to assist our depleted funds. It was less difficult than I expected, the little man unconsciously assisting me by his attitude towards them. Him I brought in, because I saw that, at last, I could enjoy my beautiful game with a worthy opponent. I greatly regret the necessity of parting from him.'

'I think it would be safer to kill him also,' remarked Turgenev.

Karen suddenly flew into a rage.

'Kill that poor little man!' he snarled. 'Be careful, Turgenev.

I do not kill those who please me. Enough; it is time we went. Is everything packed and ready?'

He was answered in the affirmative, and ordered them to carry out to the car the baggage and other articles they intended taking with them. He also instructed them to keep a watch for the police constable on beat. Keremsky and Gortschakoff departed at once, but Leon Turgenev lingered behind.

'I am not easy in my mind over this scheme of yours, Nicholas,' he confided. 'In my opinion it is perilous. I do not see how you can expect to obtain such a large sum of money from a bank without trouble.'

'Will I not have a letter from the manager, fool? I shall represent myself as a hotel proprietor in the confidence of the young man. I will say he and the woman have run away to be married secretly, and they are hiding from their friends in my little hotel. The letter will support me. Is that not a simple plan?'

A slow smile exaggerated the perpetual grin on the other's face.

'You are clever, Nicholas,' he admitted. 'It is a good scheme.'

'Of course it is a good scheme. Always you are full of doubts of every plan. Never was there a greater pessimist than you, Leon Turgenev. Sometimes, I feel the brotherhood might do better without you. It is fortunate we are so few, and you are necessary to us.'

His words and the tone in which he uttered them caused Turgenev's sallow face to grow pallid. There was no mistaking the threat. Nicholas Karen, he knew, did not stop at half measures, even with his own comrades, if it suited his purpose to remove them. Without another word, Turgenev hurriedly left the room. The hunchback smiled sardonically at the door he had closed behind him; turned once again to the sleeping tramp. Had there been an onlooker acquainted with the cold-blooded nature of the man, he would have been astonished by the expression showing now on Karen's pain-twisted face. He regarded the dilapidated individual, snoring away in such drunken fashion, with extremely friendly, almost affectionate eyes. There was a note of genuine regret in his voice as he murmured:

'You have given me pleasure and, for that, deserve well of me. I shall always be very sorry I had to let you go.'

He sighed; turned away, and walked towards the door.

He stood there for some moments, reflectively looking back at the tramp; then, shrugging his shoulders, went out of the room. It is difficult to explain such matters, but it is quite within the bounds of reason that his very disability was responsibility for this love of a brutal scoundrel for the very childish game of Noughts and Crosses. Obviously he was not a normal human being; nobody with a character as cruel and ruthless as his could be. Who knows but that the gibes and sneers he received as a youngster, on account of that broken back of his, had resulted in a boy who, otherwise, might have grown into a decent and kindly man, becoming embittered, and consequently developing into the monster Nicholas Karen undoubtedly was? He had been thrown back upon himself for his own amusements, and one of those, the game of Noughts and Crosses, the delight of his childhood, had developed into the passion of the man. It seems ridiculous, but the fact remains. Possibly he found something deeper, more scientific, in the game than most people who try it. At all events, he invariably won with the greatest ease, against those whom he persuaded to match their wits against his. It is hardly to be wondered at, therefore, that, when he came upon a man who, though drunk, proved almost his equal, he conceived an affection for that man. Nicholas Karen was genuinely sorry to part from the tramp.

Several minutes went by after he had left the room, and the filthy, wretched-looking creature, sprawled in ungainly fashion over the table, continued to snore drunkenly. Then the ugly sounds ceased abruptly, the tramp raised his unkempt head, and gazed round him.

'They told me a lot,' he mused, 'but not enough. There's only one thing for it; I'll have to follow them to this place called the Haven. The question is how!' An expression of disgust caused the much wrinkled face to screw up ludicrously as he contemplated his ragged garments. '"If dirt were trumps",' he quoted, '"what a capital hand you would hold!"'

His sharp ears caught a sound outside the door, and promptly he resumed his former position, but this time did not snore. General Cousins, of the British Secret Service, was too experienced a hand to make such a mistake. Someone may have been listening, whereupon the sudden resumption of snoring would have been quite sufficient to rouse suspicion. Into the room stepped Leon Turgenev. He moved quietly, as though he were fearful of being heard. Regarding the sprawling form of the tramp for a moment, his grinning mouth looking even more repulsive than usual, on account of the sneer turning down the corners of the lips, he appeared to make up his mind. Softly crossing to the table, he caught hold of the apparently unconscious man by the hair and, lifting the head, gazed long and searchingly at the face. The little man moved uneasily, muttered something unintelligible, but did not open his eyes. Turgenev seemed satisfied; let the head drop back on to the arms. He then commenced a rapid search of the clothing. None of the pockets were intact, but receptacles had been fashioned by the simple expedient of using safety pins to repair the deficiency. From these came a weird conglomeration of articles that had obviously been taken from dustbins. There was nothing a tramp might not be expected to possess, but everything conceivable, from a piece of string to a broken and rusty table knife, of which such an individual would make use with the ingenuity of his kind.

Turgenev did not actually suspect him to be other than a thoroughly disreputable and drunken hobo, but the Russian was an extremely cautious fellow and not so ready to accept outward impressions as his comrades. He knew that the very fact of the little man being an exponent of Karen's beloved game was enough to unbalance the latter's judgement. It was for that reason he had taken it upon himself to search his leader's tattered guest. However, all he came upon was simply proof that the man was nothing more or less than his appearance proclaimed, and Turgenev was completely reassured. He replaced the articles he had taken from their receptacles, and presently departed from the room as quietly as he had come, but far more easy in mind. Nevertheless, although he never knew it, he had been within an ace of receiving most unpleasant confirmation that his search was justified. Pinned inside Cousin's left sleeve, underneath his upper arm, was a fully loaded automatic. With his arms thrown across the table, he was resting on it, but once when Turgenev was feeling in his garments, the Russian's fingers reached within an inch or so of its butt. Had he found it, his suspicions would have been completely roused, but the little Englishman would never have allowed him to give the alarm. It is certain he would have destroyed him rather than that the painstaking planning and searching of weeks should have been brought to naught.

Cousins remained as he was, waiting for events to shape themselves. He knew he would soon be dismissed, when he intended, by some means or other, to accompany or follow the Russians to their other hiding place, which Karen had called the Haven. He would have liked to have searched the house in which he then was, but that could be left to others; besides, he did not anticipate that anything of an incriminating nature would be found there. Karen and his associates would naturally remove everything that might help to condemn them. The minutes went by; then abruptly the door opened again, and he heard the entry of several people.

'There is nothing further to detain us,' observed Karen's voice. 'You, Ivan and also you, Ilitch, go to Paul and help him carry the man and woman out to the car. See that they are well gagged first. They are to be placed on the floor inside and covered with a rug. You will have to wedge them in as best you can – double them up if necessary.' He laughed cruelly. 'I am afraid it will spoil mademoiselle's dress, but that will not matter. Soon she will not need any dresses. Leon, go and make certain that nobody is about, then come back and help me carry the little man out to the square. It is better not to wake him. We will prop him up against the railings of the garden, and he can continue his sleep. If he remembers anything when he rouses and is sober, he will think he has been dreaming.'

Karen was left alone with the tramp, but this time was too much occupied to indulge in a repetition of his previous distress at parting from him. He carefully inspected the room to make certain there was nothing left about that might, in any way, afford a clue to the identity of him and his companions or reveal their purpose in London. He had rented the house in a fictitious name, and had described himself as a Frenchman from Bordeaux. The other four, with the help of forged passports, had entered England under various aliases and at ports widely apart.

Karen uttered an exclamation, as his eyes fell on Sonia Hardinge's vanity case lying on the floor near the couch. It had fallen there and been overlooked. Being an evening bag, it contained only a compact, lipstick, a handkerchief and a purse containing a couple of pound notes and some silver. The Russian poured the money into his hand, eyed it reflectively for a few moments, then, with a smile, crossed to the sleeping tramp and, searching among his filthy garments, pushed a pound note into one of the safety-pinned receptacles. This act seemed to afford him a great deal of satisfaction. The rest of the money he pocketed, as well as the purse and vanity case. Turgenev came back to inform him that all was clear. The two then lifted between them the man who was apparently in such a deep slumber, carried him from the room and the house. They paused at the front door for some time to assure themselves further that there was nobody about to observe them. Satisfied, they crossed the deserted square to the garden, propped him up against the railings, and left him there.

Cousins waited until he was certain he was alone; then opened his eyes. He had been placed at a point equidistant between two lamps and in the deeper darkness thrown by the shadow of a large tree. He grunted with satisfaction, knowing that it was impossible for him to be seen, unless someone approached within a couple of yards of him. He felt fairly certain neither Karen, Turgenev nor their comrades would pay any further attention to him. For his part, he could see the house and car quite well, there being a lamp in the vicinity. Watching intently, he saw Sonia Hardinge carried out, followed a little later by Anstruther. The Russians almost ran from the house with them, in their haste to get them stowed quickly in the car before a policeman, or a belated pedestrian arrived on the scene. Cousins swore under his breath. Knowing Russian, he had, of course, understood all that had been said, and could picture to himself the cramped and unnatural manner in which the girl and man would be forced to travel. However, the Secret Service agent could spare no time to sympathise with them in their plight. He had other matters occupying his mind, chief of which was the manner in which he was to track the car to its destination. Having discovered so much, he was not going to spoil his good work by losing touch with the Russians now. A taxi was out of the question; first because, unless he was extremely lucky, the car would have departed before he could find one at that hour of the morning; secondly, no taxi would be capable of keeping up with a powerful Bentley full out; thirdly, the Russians would be almost certain to discover they were being followed at a time when traffic was at its lowest ebb. There was also the fact to be considered that, even were a taxi found before the other car departed, the driver would naturally jib at accepting an individual so disreputable as a fare, and precious moments would be lost while Cousins convinced him that he was not quite the tramp he looked.

The little man had already practically decided upon his only possible means of keeping in touch with his quarry. It was risky, and would be supremely uncomfortable, but such considerations did not bother him. On the luggage grid at the back of the car had been strapped several bags, obviously the Russians' personal belongings. Cousins had made up his mind to add himself to them. The question that caused him anxiety was not the extreme precariousness of such a position, but whether, with his additional weight, the straps would hold. If they gave way, and he was left lying injured in the road surrounded by the bags, it would be small satisfaction for the loss of the men he was after. There was also the danger that he might be observed getting on or clinging there. However, that had to be risked.

The kidnapped couple had been jammed in with some trouble and doubtless much pain to themselves. Karen returned to the house. His distorted form was unmistakable. The lights were extinguished; the hunchback appeared again, carrying an object under his arm, which Cousins guessed, with a chuckle, to be the precious slate. He shut the front door, and entered the car. One of the others got in after him. The watcher reflected, muttering a curse on them, that they would be sitting with their legs resting on the prone and twisted forms of their victims. The remaining three crowded into the front seat. As they were settling themselves, the little Secret Service agent, as silently as a shadow, darted across the square. Fortunately the car was facing away from him; his chances of reaching it unobserved were, therefore, much greater than they otherwise would have been. No alarm was raised, and a little prayer of thanksgiving left his lips, as he clutched at the straps holding the bags in place. He had no time to test them for, at that moment, the car started. There was just sufficient space left on the grid for his feet. He sprang up, feeling, as he afterwards admitted, thoroughly scared for fear that everything would give way. However, the straps held, and he was there, clinging like a monkey, to a position that few monkeys would have relished.

As the Bentley gathered speed, he began to feel he would never be able to sustain such an attitude. The carrier jerked up and down, threatening every moment to dislodge his foothold, while his arms felt as though they were being torn from their sockets. He was forced to hang on in a stooping position for, had he straightened himself, his head would have appeared above the pile of suitcases, giving his presence away to any of the Russians who happened to glance through the little rear window of the car. It was an ordeal such as Cousins had never before suffered, and it is certain he will never forget it. The presence of an obvious tramp on the luggage carrier of a car, clinging precariously to a pile of suitcases, naturally excited great curiosity among the few people who saw him. It was extremely fortunate that it was an hour of the morning when London is at its quietest. The driver of a lorry, bringing his vehicle to a halt behind the Bentley at adverse traffic lights, called out warningly to him, one or two street cleaners further on flung ribald remarks at the grotesque figure, a policeman at Camden Town shouted. Whether the occupants of the car heard or not,

Cousins could not tell. If they did, it is certain they missed the significance of the cries. The little Secret Service man was greatly relieved when all active life was left behind, and they were on an open deserted road, even though, here, pace was increased, and his position became more dangerous than ever.

He never knew how he managed to hang on during that nightmare drive, but somehow he did. The car sped northwards along Tottenham Court Road and Hampstead Road to Camden Town, swung to the right there, speeding along Seven Sisters Road and Forest Road to Woodford, through which it passed at a very high speed. Forking to the right beyond Woodford, it ran through Loughton and took the Forest Road towards Epping. Cousins was extremely interested in the route, but the pain in his arms and the tremendous strain caused to his legs, in his desperate endeavour to keep his feet resting on the carrier, occupied his attention, giving him little time to spend in conjecture concerning their destination.

About a mile beyond Loughton, when the powerful car was negotiating the hill, as easily as though it were on the level, pace was suddenly slackened and, immediately afterwards, the Bentley swung dizzily to the left through an open gateway. The abruptness of the turn caught Cousins unprepared and, this time, despite a desperate effort to keep his ill-shod feet on the grid, they slipped off, and he found himself being dragged painfully along. It is a wonder the straps encircling the bags held under this increased strain. They must have been manufactured from very stout leather. The pace of the car now decreased, until it was moving very slowly. The little Englishman, having ascertained that it was running up the drive of a house, and had apparently reached its destination, let go with a grunt of relief. He promptly collapsed where he was, strained muscles of his legs utterly refusing to function. His arms also ached intolerably. However, he succeeded in crawling to the side of the drive and, taking shelter behind a rhododendron bush, set to work to restore life to his limbs, at the same time straining his eyes through the darkness in order to keep watch on events.

The outlines of a large, two-storyed house could just be discerned but, as was only to be expected, there was not a light to be seen anywhere. The Bentley came to a standstill before the front door. It was far too dark for Cousins to see more than that, but obviously one, or all, of the Russians would have descended, and summoned the occupants of the place unless, of course, there was nobody there, and Karen possessed a key. Watching intently, vigorously rubbing his legs the while, the Englishman's guess that there was somebody in the house was presently proved to be correct. Illumination suddenly blazed out from a window almost directly over the front door. A head looked out and a conversation took place with the men below. Cousins was not close enough to hear what was said. It could not have been more than a few words, however, for the man above quickly disappeared. A few minutes passed by, then the front door opened; a glow of bright light shone out from a spacious hall, and the watcher was now able clearly to see all that took place. The two unfortunate captives were carried in and up a staircase. A little while afterwards an attic window to the left of the house – he had not previously been able to notice the existence of attics – became illuminated, and he observed the shadows of men moving about. It was a definite advantage to know where the girl and Anstruther had been taken. Cousins expressed his satisfaction in a little exclamation. By that time, he felt that his legs and arms had sufficiently recovered to resume their normal functions, but he remained where he was keenly watching the movements of Karen and his associates. The man who had opened the door was joined by two others. From what the Englishman concluded, the conspirators, in all, totalled eight. Had there been any more in the house, they would undoubtedly have also appeared by then. Of course, there may have been others elsewhere, but he was fairly confident there were not. It was essential that all in that house, in any case, must be apprehended. He knew Ivan Keremsky had been instructed to drive the car to the other side of London before daybreak and hide it, and possibly would not have returned by the time the house was raided, but Cousins had already conceived a plan for the capture of the hairy Ivan and incidently the car.

The bags were unstrapped from the luggage rack and carried inside. Then the lights of the car were extinguished, the men gathered together in the hall, and presently the door was shut. Apparently Ivan was not to make his journey at once. Cousins waited a few minutes, after which he ran quietly across towards the house, taking advantage of all possible cover for, although the night was very dark, he knew it was conceivable that his form might be silhouetted at times in places where the background was less murky than was general. He reached the car, ascertained there was nobody standing by or within the vicinity, then cautiously began to circle the house. It was quite a large building of the villa type standing in, as far as he could see, well-kept grounds.

The scent reached him from near at hand, causing him to reflect grimly that the scoundrels had found, after so much difficulty, they were hardly in their correct environment. Turning a corner, he became aware of a thin ray of light shining from a window. At once he grew doubly careful, treading with painstaking caution, for a gravel path ran round the house. The warmth of the night was, no doubt, responsible for the window being partially open, though the curtains were drawn, the little stream of light coming from the centre where they did not quite meet. Approaching on hands and knees, Cousins heard the subdued murmur of voices from within. He crawled right under the window and raised his head until he could apply an eye to the aperture. He was enabled thus to see into the room while the voices reached his ears now quite distinctly. Karen was there, with Turgenev, Keremsky, and Gortschakoff. There was no sign of Vogel, who was doubtless guarding the captives, but a short, stout, florid-faced man in a dressing gown was talking to Karen and appeared to be perturbed. They all had glasses in their hands, and were standing.

'What you tell me sounds very well,' the stout man was saying in Russian, 'but I am not certain it is wise. It is true the funds are low, and I am not in a position to supply any more from my business. Five thousand pounds will certainly be of great help, but are you sure it will be handed over to you?'

'Bah!' replied Karen in a tone of disgust, 'you always were thin-skinned, Voronoff, even though you are thick-bodied. Of course, I am sure. With the letter and the cheque and my own story of the elopement, the bank manager will not hesitate.

Why should he? Perhaps he will give a wedding present,' he added with a laugh.

'Supposing the young man refuses to write the letter and sign the cheque?'

'Will he, do you think, when one of us holds a dagger to the breast of the girl?'

The fat man shrugged his shoulders.

'Under those circumstances,' he admitted, 'I daresay he will do what you require. But I am not satisfied that you are wise in coming here now. It was arranged you should hide here afterwards – not before. This kidnapping and your desertion of the house in Soho Square will bring in the police when we did not wish their interest to be roused. There will be a hue and cry for the man and girl and consequently for you, my dear Nicholas.'

'For Monsieur Felix Dorrien, not for me,' corrected Karen softly.

'Have you not forgotten a description will be circulated? Your figure is somewhat obvious, and easily recognised.'

The hunchback snarled; his face became livid. He stepped towards Voronoff and, for a moment, it looked as though it was his intention to strike him. The fat man started back hastily.

'Leave my figure alone,' snapped Karen harshly.

'My dear friend,' protested the other in conciliatory tones, 'I was not intending any disparagement. I was simply pointing out that you are rather conspicuous, owing to your unfortunate disability.'

'I can take care of myself,' growled Karen in no way consoled.

'Voronoff is right,' put in Turgenev, though with diffidence.

'Would it not be better that one of us went to the bank instead of you, Nicholas?'

'No,' snarled Karen. 'I will be there at ten. No report will have been made to the police by then or for some hours afterwards.'

'But what about the "afterwards",' murmured Gortschakoff.

'I will see to that. Once I am back here, there will be no need for me to go out again. You three and Vogel have the arrangements for the twentieth in hand.'

'Ah! So the twentieth is the date settled?' remarked Voronoff.

Karen nodded. He was beginning to recover from his spleen.

'All will be present at the ceremony. Two bombs will be thrown into the midst of them. Gortschakoff, Keremsky, Vogel and Turgenev will stand on the edge of the crowd ready to make certain if any escape, but none will escape. Our plans are too well formed for that and the bombs are the most powerful we have ever had. You have them in your own care, Voronoff?'

The man in the dressing gown nodded.

'They are in the cellar, packed in straw. You and I possess keys.'

'Excellent. This blow will shake the British Empire from end to end and bring about its disintegration. Chaos will result. It will be an historic day.' Karen's wicked eyes sparkled. His whole attitude was that of a fanatic. His enthusiasm infected the others. They became no less excited than he. 'It is a great, a marvellous scheme,' he went on, 'and I – I, Nicholas Karen, have conceived, and planned it all.'

For some moments the conversation continued on those emotional lines. Cousins shivered as though he had suddenly felt very chilly. It was Voronoff who brought his companions back to a more matter-of-fact level.

'The two men you have selected, Karen,' he remarked, 'they will not fail at the crucial moment?'

The hunchback shook his head confidently.

'They are zealots like us. They and their families have suffered wrongs since childhood. Their hatred is so great, it even startles me. No, they will not fail. Even if they do, our brave friends will be ready to act. They are prepared to sacrifice their lives, if need be, to render successful such a truly noble assassination.'

'How much have you promised the two men?'

'One thousand, five hundred pounds each. It will be handed to them the day before the great deed takes place. They will be able to send it to their families.'

'They will be wise to do so,' commented Turgenev dryly. 'Their chances of surviving will be small.'

The hunchback shrugged his shoulders.

'Perhaps, in the confusion, they will be able to get away. But it does not matter. If they die, they will die heroes of a great cause. From the time the money is handed to them, Gortschakoff and Keremsky will never leave their sides.' He paused thoughtfully, then went on: 'At present they live in the district called Deptford' – he pronounced it Dep-ti-for, but Cousins understood – 'I think it would be wise to bring them here one night, and keep them here. What say you, my friend?'

The idea did not appeal to Voronoff. He protested vigorously but, as Cousins had already discovered, once Karen made up his mind about anything, and insisted on it, the others fell into line like a lot of sheep. He insisted on this occasion and Voronoff, although antagonistic to the scheme, capitulated.

'We will now sleep,' pronounced Karen. 'There is no need for

Vogel to stay with the two upstairs. They can remain bound and gagged, and it is impossible for them to escape. Gortschakoff, go and tell him to come down – he will be thirsty.' The man with the broken nose nodded, and left the room. 'At eight I will see the young man,' he went on to the others, 'make him sign the cheque, and write the letter. When I return from the bank, and the money is safe in my hands, the two can die.'

'What is to be done with their bodies?' asked Voronoff anxiously.

Karen chuckled sneeringly.

'Always you are afraid, my friend. You need have no fear. The respectable Russian merchant of the City of London will not be compromised in any way. I guarantee that. We will remove the bodies far away from this house tomorrow night.'

Voronoff did not appear altogether at ease, even after that promise. He shook his head doubtfully.

'To me,' he confessed, 'there seem many flaws in this scheme for obtaining money and despatching this man and woman. I am—'

'Ah, bad!' snapped the hunchback. 'You are a fat fool.'

The tall, gaunt, hairless man with the repulsive eyes entered the room with Gortschakoff. He threw a notecase, some silver, a watch, and two or three rings on the table.

'I removed these from the two,' he announced.

Karen opened the case; took therefrom a bundle of notes and a cheque. The former, with the silver, were counted, after which they were stowed away in one of his pockets.

'Thirty-four pounds and seven shillings,' he stated with satisfaction. 'It is good. The watch and rings and the notecase can be buried with them. It will be safer. I will keep with me the cheque book for the present. It is time you departed, Keremsky. Soon dawn will break.'

Cousins waited to hear no more. Crawling, until he had left the gravel drive and was on a lawn, he straightened, and set off at a run for the entrance gates, keeping well amidst the trees. Owing to the fact that he had, for so long, been looking into a lighted room, his eyes had become unaccustomed to the darkness, with the result that he sustained several painful bumps. However, he made light of these, and reached his objective just as he heard the engine of the Bentley being started. He gave one of the open gates a push that caused it to swing across the drive. Keremsky would be forced to draw up, in order to clear the way for the car. When he got out, Cousins intended to enter the tonneau, prepared to act. His automatic had been removed from its hiding place; was now in his hand. Crouching behind a bush he waited.

The Bentley came down the drive with hardly any sound, apart from the rasping of the wheels over the gravel. Its brilliant headlights picked out the scene with startling clearness, giving a theatrical effect to the surroundings, but the Englishman had no fear of being observed. He was well hidden. The car stopped directly opposite him; the bearded Russian descended, and walked to the gate. Cousins heard his muttered exclamation of surprise. No doubt, he was wondering what had caused such a heavy, five-barred affair to swing across the drive, when there was no wind. Apparently his suspicions were in no way roused, however, since he merely strode to the gate, and pushed it back; returned at once, without hesitation, to the car. The

Secret Service agent had calculated upon the fellow's obvious obtuseness. An unerring judgement of men, as indeed all who are successful in such a profession must be, Cousins had quickly sized up the Russians, forming the opinion that, with the exception of Karen and Turgenev, their intelligence was not of a high order. Turgenev, he had decided, was actually the most dangerous, even though the hunchback had by far the cleverest brain. Karen, however, allowed himself to be influenced by personal considerations and was overconfident.

By the time Keremsky had resumed his seat at the wheel, Cousins was crouching inside the car. Like a shadow he had flitted from his hiding place, opened the door, and crept in. The Russian had heard no sound above the soft, rhythmic purring of the magnificent engine. Indeed, there had been no sound to hear. He slipped in his gears, and the Bentley glided away in the direction of Loughton. It had reached the village, when something cold touched his head just behind the left ear. At the same time, a voice, the tone of which was equally chilly, told him, in perfect Russian, that if he did not do exactly as directed the weapon, caressing the back of his head, would be fired, with an unfortunate result for Keremsky. There is no mistaking the feel of the business end of a pistol. Such an experience has a paralysing effect upon most people. It paralysed Ivan to such an extent that his hands fell from the wheel, and he stiffened as though he had suddenly congealed. Fortunately his foot also left the accelerator, otherwise the car would have swerved on to the pavement, and there might have been something of a crash. Instead it slowed down; presently came to a halt.

Being still in gear, the engine stopped. Cousins had timed

his action admirably. A few yards away was the police station. Ordering Keremsky to descend from the car, and hold his hands high above his head, he followed. The Russian might have been prepared to sacrifice his life 'to render successful a truly noble assassination', but he was obviously not eager to sacrifice it by making an attempt to turn the tables on the man who was now threatening him with death if he did not do exactly as he was told. He obeyed orders like an automaton, marching to the police station, his arms stretched heavenwards, without even daring to catch a glimpse at the person who had so abruptly and so rudely transformed him from a contented, optimistic being to a shocked, fear-stricken wretch. There was not a soul abroad to witness the amazing and diverting spectacle of a dirty little tramp shepherding a great, burly, bearded fellow into the arms of the law at the point of an automatic pistol. The officers on duty, however, received the surprise of their lives. Possibly they were, or had been, bemoaning the fact that nothing ever happened at Loughton. If so, something certainly happened now.

A sergeant, looking distinctly sleepy, sat at his high desk in the office, aimlessly turning over the pages of the uninteresting charge book. Opposite him, on a bench, dozed a constable. They came to their feet with astounded exclamations as a big man appeared, his hands raised high above his head, followed by perhaps the smallest and most disreputable tramp they had ever seen. For a perceptible period, neither of the officials on duty was able to utter a word; then the sergeant found his voice.

'What's all this?' he demanded in authoritative tones. 'Who are you?'

'Don't bother to ask questions now,' returned Cousins. '"Theirs not to question why; theirs but to do or die." Not that I am asking either of you to die, but I certainly want you to "do". Here, hold this,' he thrust his automatic into the bewildered constable's hand. 'Shoot him, if he so much as blinks an eyelid.'

Too much surprised to do anything else, the officer held the weapon pointed at the Russian, whose back was still turned to Cousins. The latter stooped down, and removed the dilapidated shoe from his right foot. The sergeant decided he was being made the victim of some outrageous practical joke.

'If you don't explain the meaning of this tomfoolery,' he stormed, 'I'll lock you both up until you become sober.'

Cousins straightened himself to his full stature – which meant that his eyes could just look over the top of the desk – and grinned cheerfully. His wrinkles, merging amazingly into myriads of happy little creases, overcame the sergeant's wrath. Despite himself, the latter chuckled, but he became deadly serious when he observed the symbol that the little tramp was holding towards him, cupped in his dirty hand. His eyes opened wide; a prolonged whistle pursed his lips. His manner underwent a marked transformation.

'I see you understand,' murmured Cousins. 'Excellent.'

'What do you want me to do, sir?' asked the sergeant.

The Secret Service man returned the emblem to its hiding place in his shoe, which was again donned. He then took the revolver from the policeman, who appeared more perplexed than ever at the sudden change in his superior.

'First of all,' directed Cousins, 'search him thoroughly.'

This was done by the bemused constable, under the watchful

eyes of the other two. During the process, Keremsky came face to face with his captor for the first time and, as he recognised the tramp who had played Noughts and Crosses with his leader, his little, pig-like eyes threatened to start from his head, his mouth dropped ludicrously open. For some time he could only stare stupidly; then a volley of abuse in choice Russian poured from his lips. Cousins listened, but did not bother to reply. Ivan ceased abruptly, however, when the pistol was raised threateningly, and his face paled at the thought that he was about to be shot. Nothing of interest was found on him, all articles being piled on the sergeant's desk. There was not a weapon of any sort amongst them, unless a large clasp knife could be given that designation.

'Now lock him up in your strongest cell, Sergeant,' ordered Cousins, 'and don't under any circumstances whatever, open the door until men of the Special Branch come for him.'

The three of them escorted the crestfallen Russian to a cell. He was locked in, and promptly despatched a further broadside of expletives when he was certain he was not to be shot. They could still hear his voice as they turned along the passage and re-entered the office. The sergeant jerked his thumb over his shoulder.

'What is he, sir?' he asked curiously.

'Just an anarchist of Russian nationality,' Cousins told him calmly.

The two policeman looked at each other and whistled. These were great events for Loughton. The constable's face actually paled with excitement. It could be easily seen that he was burning to know who the tramp was, but dared ask no questions. His superior's respectful demeanour towards the little man warned him it might be unwise. Cousins requested the use of the telephone. Asking for a certain number that is in no directory, he was immediately put through and, for ten minutes, perched on the sergeant's high stool spoke concisely and rapidly into the mouthpiece ending with detailed instructions and directions. The police officers pretended not to be listening, but they would not have been human had they closed their ears to that which was being said. Cousins was extremely clever at the manner in which he conveyed all information to the other end without divulging more to his hearers in the police station than he wished them to know. Nevertheless, they learnt enough to startle and excite them tremendously. At the end of his conversation, the pseudo-tramp jumped off his stool.

'In half an hour or so,' he declared to the sergeant, 'three or four cars will arrive with men from headquarters. Do you know the house of a Russian called Voronoff?'

The sergeant nodded.

'Very well, sir.'

'Good. I want you to send someone to point out the way to the Intelligence and Special Branch men. You need only direct them to the gates. They will wait there for me.' He held out his hand, which the other grasped warmly. 'Thanks for the help you have given me, Sergeant, and excuse the dirty paw.'

'It's a privilege to shake it, sir,' was the hearty reply.

'Nice of you,' grinned Cousins, adding with an exaggerated bow: 'Mine is the privilege. "But oh! For the grip of the bobby's hand."' He walked to the door; glanced back. 'There's a car standing nearly outside. Take charge of it, will you? It belongs to an adventurous young man who, by now, probably longs for the existence he left rather abruptly and rudely. He'll claim it later on. And, by the way, it's been left in gear.'

Outside he became aware that dawn was beginning to break. 'Dash it!' he muttered. 'I forgot that, I'll have to hurry.'

The feelings of Sonia Hardinge and Anthony Anstruther can perhaps be much better imagined than described. The agony of that journey from Soho on the floor of a car, their bodies twisted and bent in a manner that would have been painful to a contortionist, well nigh suffocated by the gags over their mouths and the thick rug covering them, and the added indignity of the legs of the men in the car resting none too gently on them, all combined to produce in them a feeling of utter hopelessness. Up to the very moment of their removal from the house in Soho Square they had pinned their faith on the word of the man masquerading as a drunken tramp. It was all they could do. When they were jammed agonisingly into the car, and felt themselves being borne rapidly away, they lost hope completely. Of the two, Anstruther suffered the more, not because of the pain caused by the unnatural position of his body, though, being taller and bigger altogether, he must have endured absolute torture, but on account of his mental anguish. He blamed himself entirely for the fact that the girl he loved was undergoing such a terrible ordeal. He would have gladly welcomed even greater torment, or death itself, if he could have bargained for her release and security. But he had not even been given the opportunity of making a proposal by which she could be ransomed.

Sonia was desperately frightened, but she did her utmost to fight against the dread tormenting her that at the end of all the suffering, all the humiliation and insults, she and Tony would only be murdered. She, for her part, took all the responsibility for the desperate position to which her desire for something out of the ordinary had condemned them. *She* had accepted Karen's invitation to enter the house. Tony had concurred, it was true, but she could not blame him for a foolish impulse which had primarily influenced her. During the journey she fainted, due to the pain and the suffocating atmosphere, but recovered consciousness when they were carried into the house near Loughton. Neither, of course, had the slightest idea where they were. They did not care much. Their minds were too troubled and their bodies too racked with agony for them to be concerned with their whereabouts just then. It was a wonderful relief when they were deposited on a bed, and could lie at full length, even though their bonds and gags were not removed. The cords cutting into their wrists and ankles were forgotten for a while in the luxury of feeling their limbs and bodies in natural positions.

The repulsive man with the horrible, lashless eyes, and hairless head left to watch over them, sat looking at them until Sonia wanted to scream from very loathing. It was a relief when he rose and searched them, even though he subjected the girl to the most insulting indignities. He pocketed her rings, Anstruther's watch, ring, and pocket case. When Gortschakoff entered the room and took him away, she felt intensely grateful. She and Tony turned on their sides, and lay facing each other, their eyes expressing all their lips were unable to utter.

In that time, her indecision about marrying him evaporated completely. She longed with all her soul for the event that she felt now would never take place. They had both become suddenly changed, from two rather bored, light-hearted, gay, and irresponsible young people to a man and a woman who desperately wanted to live – just for each other. All this they read in each other's eyes which contained the promise that, if they ever escaped from their terrible predicament, they would devote themselves to that ideal.

Karen entered the room; gazed mockingly at them.

'Like the lovebirds you look,' he commented. 'It is so pretty picture. I am ver' sorry I am compel to leave you like this so tied. But soon, when the cheque has been sign, you will be free. I will come back at eight of the clock. Goodnight, Mademoiselle – and Monsieur. I hope you have the good sleep.'

With a laugh that sounded diabolical to them, he switched off the light, and left the room. The door closed behind him. Then commenced desperate attempts by both to remove their bonds or, at least, to loosen them, but they were tied too skilfully, apart from which their arms and legs were by then completely numb and incapable of action. Forced to desist from their useless efforts, they lay close together, seeking the consolation of their nearness to each other. To them both there was an infinite amount of happiness in this. Time passed with dreadful slowness. They longed for and yet feared the coming of daylight. Neither of them believed Karen's assertion that, when the cheque was signed, they would be free. A monster who could treat them as he had done would not stop at that. Also, would he not fear to let them go now, because of their information they could give the police regarding him and his associates? Anstruther would give the cheque, but only in the desperate and forlorn hope that it would, at least, save Sonia.

Neither, of course, could sleep. Their minds, for one thing, were in too much of a ferment, while their bodies, particularly the cruelly-bound wrists and ankles, hurt abominably. A faint light began to steal through the uncurtained lattice window. Dawn was breaking. It was then that Sonia caught a slight sound. She held her breath in order to listen better. For some time she heard nothing further then it came again. She was lying facing the door, and presently, although it was still far too dark to see much, was certain it was gradually opening. Before long she had no doubt at all. Her fear became greater than ever. What was going to happen now? All kinds of terrible fancies flitted through her mind. Mentally she visualised the faces of the five loathsome men in whose power she and Tony were and, in none of them, could she remember a spark of anything but cruelty, wickedness, and lust.

A form entered the room; the door began to close again. In her utter distraction, Sonia nudged Tony desperately, realising at the same time that he could do nothing. They were both entirely at the mercy of the 'thing' that was in the room now with them. She wondered if her lover had heard. He could not have seen, because he was lying with his back to the door. Straining her eyes and ears she was unable to find out where the creature was, yet she knew he was there. Silence, utter and complete, reigned in that little chamber. It was to her, the most terrible, nerve-racking moment of all that horrible night. Then, all at once, the most tremendous joy possessed her. She almost fainted with relief.

'Don't be startled,' whispered a voice close to their ears. 'It is only I – the tramp. I am going to cut the cords and move your wretched gags, but before I do so, I must warn you. For God's sake, don't groan, give vent to your relief, or make any sound whatever. Now, here goes!'

Skilful fingers started working at the gag over Anstruther's mouth. Quickly it was unfastened, the cords round his wrists were cut through by a knife – the same broken and rusty implement that Turgenev had ignored – those binding his ankles suffered the same fate. Anstruther was free. A similar service was rapidly performed for Sonia. Cousins then commenced gently and soothingly to massage the girl's aching wrists and ankles.

'Excuse the liberty, miss,' he whispered with a soft little chuckle. 'It isn't a habit of mine to caress a lady's ankles.' She could have laughed and cried together in her wonderful relief. It took all her resolution to obey his injunction. 'There, how's that?' he asked after some time. 'Better?'

'Much, thank you,' she breathed, taking for granted he expected an answer, despite his warning.

He turned his attention to Anstruther, who had already been engaged in performing a like office to his own wrists and ankles but without the skilful touch that Cousins now applied to them. It was not long before the young man indicated that feeling had completely returned. The Secret Service man sat himself quietly on the bed.

'Listen carefully,' he exhorted them. 'It's not going to be an easy job getting you out of the house. I thought at first of releasing you and concealing you somewhere inside, until the raid takes place, but that's impracticable. Besides, there's no knowing what might happen, if they are alarmed. Bullets and what not will be flying all over the show. So I've got to get you out. First of all, take off your shoes, both of you.' They obeyed. 'Outside, to the right,' he went on, 'is a steepish staircase, descending to a corridor. Several rooms open on to that, and I believe are occupied by the owner of the house and the men who brought you here. We shall have to pass three doors before we reach the main staircase to the hall. Once there, things should be easy enough. The trouble will be getting there. Fellows like Karen generally sleep with one eye open. You'll have to move like ghosts. A little way along the passage outside is another attic, and I strongly suspect Voronoff's henchmen are slumbering within.'

'Who is Voronoff?' whispered Anstruther.

'He is the owner or renter of this desirable country residence – a fat little fellow, but whether with or without his mammy's eyes, I can't say.'

'How on earth did you get here?' pursued the young man.

'S'sh,' warned Sonia, 'there'll be time enough for questions afterwards, Tony. We were told to make no sound.'

Cousins smiled in the darkness.

'As Vaughan in *The Provoked Husband* put in,' he murmured, '"The flat simplicity of that reply was admirable." Are you ready? Then let us go.'

They stood up. Sonia found and clasped Tony's hand. Gone was all her terror. She only felt now a tremendous sense of thrill and also deep gratitude to the little man who, she realised, must have risked his life to reach them. They crept silently to the door. Cousins had hold of the handle; was about to pull it open.

Instead, he suddenly pushed them back, muttering an order to return to the bed and lie down. They obeyed, their pulses racing madly. The little man must have possessed acute hearing; neither of them had heard a sound. Straining their eyes through the gloom, they could just discern his form posed rigidly by the door. A cry almost broke from Sonia's lips; she only succeeded in stifling it with a great effort of will. The door was opening by slow degrees. As slowly, a short round figure insinuated itself into the room; began to creep towards the bed. It had almost reached its objective, when Cousins, from behind, hit it skilfully and scientifically upon the head with the butt of his heavy automatic. It collapsed with a grunt; was caught as it fell, and eased softly to the floor.

"'I am as poor as Job, my Lord, but not so patient,'" quoted the little man. 'You asked,' he added to Anstruther, 'who was Voronoff. This is he. A nasty piece of work with a foul mind. If the road to hell is paved with good intentions as Dr Johnson is reported to have said, I should like to know where he thought the bad ones lead to.' There was no mistaking his interpretation of Voronoff's stealthy appearance, and Sonia shuddered, while Tony's teeth snapped together angrily with a distinct click. 'We'd better tie him up and gag him before we go,' decided Cousins. 'He won't be unconscious long.'

With the help of Anstruther, the fellow was lifted on to the bed, tied securely with the ropes that had bound the young man and girl, and gagged. Tony took a vicious pleasure in assuring himself that ropes and gag were as tight as he could make them. 'I hope this chokes the swine,' he muttered, referring to the latter.

'It probably will when he comes to, and finds what has happened to him,' commented the Secret Service man. 'He looks an apopletic subject. If he'd had more sense we'd be in queer street now. Either he was too intent on what he meant to do, or lacks grey matter, otherwise his suspicions would have been roused by the fact that the door was unlocked. Anyhow, we'll lock him in. It was fortunate the key was left there. Unintentional kindness on Fish-eyes part. Now, come on. If we're waylaid, Miss Hardinge, run down the stairs, get out of the house somehow, and make for the gate. You'll find a dozen or so men there – send 'em along. Anstruther and I will hold the fort until they arrive, won't we?' he added to Tony.

'Rather,' whispered that young man enthusiastically.

'"But when the blast of war blows in our ears,"' quoted Cousins. '"Let us be tigers in our fierce deportment."'

His companions, rendered calm and without qualms on account of his supreme coolness, were greatly amused at his proclivity for quotations. They were, more than ever, burning to know who he really was.

By now, it was getting quite light, and they had little difficulty in seeing their way. This time they managed to get out of the attic without any further alarms, Tony and Sonia carrying their shoes in their hands. Cousins locked the door; stood listening intently for a few moments then, with great caution, led them down the narrow, rather steep stairs to the corridor below. Again he stood straining his ears, but nothing of an alarming nature reached them, and presently on he went, the other two creeping along behind him. Sonia marvelled at the easy manner in which he moved, without making the slightest sound, despite the fact that he had not removed his dilapidated footwear. She and Tony found the going extremely difficult, even in their stockinged feet. They discovered how hard it is to move without sound; were in agony all the time lest they caused a board to creak or made any other noise. They reached the broad, well-carpeted, main staircase, descended in Indian file; had almost reached the hall when, in a moment of carelessness, Anstruther allowed the shoes he was carrying to hit against the banisters with a distinct clatter. To their ears the noise was almost deafening. Sonia came to an abrupt halt, frozen with dismay; Anstruther felt himself go hot and cold all over; he knew his face was scarlet with shame and self-mortification. Cousins quickly brought them to the realisation that standing still on the stairs was hardly wise in the light of that which had happened.

'Come on,' he whispered urgently. 'Not lingering in the hope of being invited to a game of Noughts and Crosses, are you?'

Anstruther felt grateful to him for his kindly humour and non-reproachful manner, and hurried after Sonia down the remaining stairs. Unfortunately, however, the damage had been done. They heard a hasty and heavy step in the corridor above. Cousins guessed, from the nature of the sound, that it was the hunchback on the prowl. He was right. A flood of light suddenly illumined the staircase as they reached the bottom and sped for the darkness of the hall, but Karen had caught a glimpse of them. A cry of fury broke from his lips. It was animal-like in its timbre, and Sonia shivered involuntarily. Cousins caught her by the arm, hurried her into a room, and pointed to an open window.

'No time to fool about with a door,' he muttered. 'I forced the catch of that window; left it open in case. Out you go, and follow instructions. Put your shoes on in the garden.' He bundled her out of the window. 'Now, back we go,' he shot at Anstruther. 'I want to help them in this house – must bag the lot.'

He raced back into the hall, which was now blazing with light, followed by Tony. Shouts and cries of alarm were resounding throughout the house. Karen was coming down the stairs in his lop-sided manner, but extraordinarily swiftly; behind him crowded Turgenev and Gortschakoff. All were in various stages of undress. They pulled up suddenly in rank amazement as they recognised the little tramp. For one stupefied moment the hunchback stared unbelievingly at him; then from between his lips came the most fiendish cry Cousins or Anstruther had ever heard. It contained fury, hatred, the very essence of satanic viciousness and yet, at the same time, the Secret Service man thought to recognise in it the plaintive note that might be inspired by disappointment, as though some part of Karen was regretting the discovery that the man who had given him such pleasure at his beloved game was an enemy. But that note was not recognisable in his subsequent invective. Foaming at the mouth, his eyes gleaming with the utmost evil, he poured forth filthy obscenities at the two men below in a mixture of Russian and English. Anstruther wondered why he and his followers did not attack, but Cousins guessed the reason. They were not armed, while he was. Karen was not madman enough to throw himself forward in face of the automatic held so steadily pointed at him. Panting furiously the hunchback paused for breath. Cousins was about to speak, when from above sounded Vogel's voice. Apparently he had been sent to the attic in which the prisoners had been confined.

'They have gone.' The Russian words tumbled over themselves in the man's alarm. 'Voronoff was there, gagged and bound – in their place. He was just recovering consciousness – I have released him.'

Vogel came into view; was as dumbfounded as the others had been by sight of the tramp below. His repulsive face was the picture of utter and blank – not to mention dismayed – astonishment. Cousins gave them a further shock by addressing Karen in perfect Russian.

'The game is up,' he stated calmly. 'I know exactly why you and those others are in this country. You blundered badly by conceiving the idea of kidnapping Mr Anstruther and Miss Hardinge, Nicholas Karen; you blundered more badly by being taken in by a tramp who played Noughts and Crosses. The best thing all of you can do is to surrender quietly.'

'Who are you?' screamed the hunchback. 'What have you done with the girl?'

'She is safe, you vile murderer. By now—'

He never finished the sentence. There was the crack of a revolver, a bullet imbedded itself in the door behind him. At the turning in the staircase, he caught sight of two men, both armed. They were obviously Voronoff's servants. A glimpse was enough for Cousins. Like lightning he fired. There was a sharp cry. One of the fellows pitched forward, slid down a few steps, and lay still. The other disappeared. Vogel, Turgenev and Gortschakoff followed his example, turning, and running up the stairs like startled rabbits. Karen alone held his ground. He stood where he was, snarling like an animal at bay. Repeated cries from above failed to influence him, until something was said which Cousins did not catch. Even then there was no haste about his movements. He turned and walked up the stairs in the most leisurely manner.

'It is useless you retreating like that,' called out the Englishman. 'You may as well surrender at once. I have examined the house, and know exactly what possibilities it offers of escape from above. By now it is surrounded.'

The latter was sheer bluff. He certainly was confident that men of the Secret Service and Special Branch had arrived by then at the gates but, even if Sonia had reached them, there had been no time for them to arrive at the house. His words had an effect that he hardly expected. A fusillade of shots rang out from the turning on the stairs. All the Russians were now apparently armed, and they were bent on killing him and Anstruther, and perhaps fighting their way out. However, in their anxiety to avoid exposing themselves too much to his undoubted skill as a marksman, their aim was badly directed, and their bullets hummed harmlessly by.

'Get out through the window and see if the others are coming,' ordered Cousins in a whisper to Anstruther. 'Bring half in the same way. Tell the other half to watch the windows above.'

'Hadn't I better stay with you?' began Tony. 'You will be—'

'Do what you're told,' snapped the little man. 'I'm in charge here. What do you expect to do? Charge them with your bare fists?'

Anstruther went without another word. Cousins drew up a heavy chair with a tall, solid back, and crouched behind it. Another fusillade came, the bullets a good deal nearer this time. Cousins caught a glimpse of a pair of fish-like eyes; again his deadly automatic barked, and the long, gaunt body of Vogel came sliding sickeningly down the stairs to land with a crash at the bottom. It lay grotesquely still, and the Secret Service man regarded it grimly.

"'There's a divinity shapes our ends, rough-hew them as we will,'" he murmured.

A chorus of execrations from above told him how the other Russians had taken the death of their comrade, for there was no doubt he was dead. It is impossible merely to wound a man who shows only his eyes. With a sense of relief, Cousins heard the coming of several men, and knew his friends were at hand.

'How goes it, Jerry?' asked the voice of Cartright.

'I've got two out of seven, another's locked up. Don't stick that lantern jaw of yours in the way. They're shooting prettily.'

'You leave my face alone.'

'My dear chap, I wouldn't touch it. Have you got men watching those upper windows?'

'Yes; eight of 'em – another six are behind me. By the way, who are the cubs?'

'Tell you about them later on. What do you think this is – a conversazione? I think we'll mop up. Bring your men—'

He stopped. From above came a confused medley of cries. It sounded as though the Russians were quarrelling, though it was impossible to distinguish anything that was being said. Suddenly Karen appeared, walking down the stairs in the most nonchalant manner. He was unarmed. Cousins rose to his feet, ranged himself by the side of the long and lanky Cartright, and watched. The men behind, all with revolvers aimed, stared with curiosity. The hunchback's eyes gleamed madly, his sallow face was ghastly. Reaching the bottom he stood, for a few moments, surveying the group of Englishmen. The voices above had become suddenly hushed, except for a sound that suggested someone up there was sobbing. Cousins' wrinkled face creased in perplexity. There was something very sinister about this move of Karen's, of that he felt sure, but could not fathom it.

'So, my frien',' remarked the hunchback in English, 'you are of the police – yes? Well, I am ver' glad to welcome these gentlemen. They will have mooch amusement.'

With amazing speed, he suddenly darted for a door at the right of the hall. As he pulled it open, Cousins fired. Karen gave a sharp cry, stumbled through. He was hit, but obviously not killed. The door slammed behind him. Cartright and the other men heard the key turn in the lock as they dashed forward. At the same time, with a shriek of mortal terror, the rotund form of Voronoff, his face white as death, came into view running headlong down the stairs.

'He have to the cellar gone,' he cried. 'He mus' be stop. It is—'

Two revolvers barked viciously from above. Voronoff screamed hideously, swayed and pitched forward on his face. With a flash of horrified enlightenment, Cousins knew what Karen had gone to do.

'Out of the house, all of you,' he yelled. 'Jump out, fall out, anything, but get out, and as far away as you can.'

Cartright and his men did not stop to ask why. They had been trained in a school where rigid discipline holds complete mastery. Rapidly they retreated the way they had come. Cousins brought up the rear and, as he scrambled through the window, shouted:

'Every man among the bushes, and throw yourselves flat.'

Those who had been watching outside obeyed the order as promptly as the others. Cousins caught sight of Anstruther standing in the drive, the picture of astonishment. Without ceremony, he grabbed him by the arm; pulled him on to the lawn, and forced him down flat on his face. He threw himself by his side. They were only just in time.

A tremendous sheet of flame seemed to shoot through the very centre of the building. There came a devastating roar and concussion that shook the earth and was heard miles away. The house appeared to rise giddily into the air; then burst assunder in a cataclysm of pyrotechnic ferocity. For several minutes after this ravaging upheaval a rain of masonry, glass, lead piping; fragments of furniture fittings, and other more horrifying remnants. What had once been an attractive country house had been utterly demolished; the remains of it blazed furiously.

Cousins and Cartright escaped uninjured; were the first on their feet; went among their men anxiously to ascertain if there were any casualties. Several had been hit by flying splinters, but none very badly. There was not a soul there, however, who was not shaken.

'Well, that's that,' commented Cousins to his colleague. 'Having recognised that they had failed in the object that had brought them to England, Karen tried to blow us sky-high as well as his own party. Can't help thinking there was something heroic in those fellows waiting upstairs for their shocking end, knowing what he was going to do. Only Voronoff funked it. And thank the Lord he did. I doubt if I should have guessed his intentions in time otherwise.' He eyed the flames, and quoted: "'Fierce Phlegethon, whose waves of torrent fire inflame with rage.'"

'Great Scott!' ejaculated Cartright disgustedly; 'must you break out at such a time.'

'Peace!' ordered Cousins. 'And for God's sake give me a cigarette.'

He was greatly relieved to hear that Sonia Hardinge had been left with the men in charge of the car at the gates. Anstruther was sent to keep her company, a duty which he was not slow to carry out. He was trembling like a leaf with shock. The fire brigades from Loughton and Epping arrived and quickly extinguished the conflagration, after which the men of the Secret Service and Special Branch searched carefully among the ruins. They found little worth salving, however. Karen's body was discovered intact, though burnt almost to a cinder. Only gruesome fragments here and there were found of the others. The whole official party eventually drove to the Loughton Police Station taking Sonia and Anstruther along. Ivan Keremsky was told of the destruction of his comrades and, under stern interrogation, collapsed, giving away the names of the two men at Deptford, who had been selected by Karen for a hideous deed that would have horrified the world. They were apprehended later in the day.

At the express invitation of Anstruther and Sonia Hardinge, Cousins travelled back to town in the Bentley, much to the disgust of Cartright, who had anticipated hearing all details of his colleague's adventures on the way up. He was told to wait until later.

'There are a few words of fatherly counsel,' Cousins informed him, 'I feel it my duty to impart to the young people you so inelegantly described as cubs.'

The three sat together on the front seat of the Bentley, Cousins between Sonia and Tony. The curious sight of a young man and a pretty girl in evening dress – very much the worse for wear it is true – consorting with an incredibly tattered and grimy tramp, must have greatly intrigued the people who saw the ill-matched trio.

In the light of a glorious June morning, Sonia was able to regard the events of the night as nothing more than a hideous and fantastic dream. It seemed impossible then that she and Tony could have passed through an ordeal so terrifying and terrible. They were both exceedingly inquisitive regarding their companion.

'Of course,' confided Anstruther, 'I know now you are a prominent member of the Secret Service, sir, and that your name is Cousins.'

'Ah, you've been asking questions. *Ergo propter hoc*, I'd better satisfy that curiosity of yours. A branch of a particularly virulent gang of anarchists,' he related, 'was suspected of operating in London. Detectives of the Special Branch and men of my own department searched for weeks for a clue to its whereabouts, without results. Then our agent in a certain country abroad got hold of a useful item of information; namely, that the leader in England was a hunchback called Karen with a childish passion for the game of Noughts and Crosses. It was believed he was domiciled somewhere in Soho, and was planning something big. The general search went on with renewed zest, but I became a tramp with no fixed abode, haunting Soho, and possessing a harmless love for Noughts and Crosses. In addition, I became known for my violent diatribes against law and order, royalty, aristocracy, and so on. I called you two "dir'y aris'crats", if you remember.'

He grinned, and Sonia who, despite her terrible experience, had recovered marvellously all her spirits, gurgled with delight to see his face wrinkle into myriads of little laughing creases.

'I played that wretched game,' went on Cousins, 'until I was sick, sad, and sorry of it. I played it for weeks in almost every street in Soho – on the pavements, on shop windows, on doors, on carts, on cars, every conceivable place I could think of, in fact. Several times I was arrested, but was released, of course, with apologies, when the police knew who I was. Last night I selected your car, Anstruther, for my operations. You both know the result. Is there anything more you'd like to be told?'

'Lots,' intimated the girl. 'What was the plot Karen was engineering?'

Cousins' face grew grim.

'He had planned an assassination,' he replied 'an assassination that would have shaken the Empire to its foundations that might have caused chaos and disruption. I believe there was a certain country, antagonistic to England, behind it. But the proof of that – if proof existed – was destroyed with the house. Two men were selected to throw the bombs; others, Turgenev, Gortschakoff, Vogel, and Keremsky, were to be standing by to see there was no failure. You had practical experience of the terrific power of those bombs. There is no need for me to say more, is there?'

His words were followed by a horrified silence, which lasted until the car was threading its way through the London traffic; then:

'What a great debt the Empire owes to you, Mr Cousins,' observed the girl softly.

The little Secret Service man adroitly changed the subject.

'I owe you two a debt for the use of your car,' he chuckled. 'In a way, you were responsible for my finding Karen. All the same, you deserve a wigging for behaving like a couple of idiots. I know I looked a disreputable scarecrow but, thinking I was drunk, you should have had sense to realise there was something in the wind, when I spoke to you in a perfectly sober voice. I guessed Karen wasn't taking you into that house through sheer good nature, and I took a risk in warning you. It might have spoilt my game completely. Why, in heaven's name, didn't you do what I advised, and get out while the going was good?'

They were very contrite. Tony explained their – particularly his – anxiety to find a thrill, to experience something out of the ordinary. He told how he had wandered round London, searching for the romance and adventure that never came.

'Well, you got all the thrills you wanted last night, I should imagine,' commented Cousins, 'and a bit over.'

'By Jove! You're right, sir; we did.' His eyes glistened. 'I suppose there's not a vacancy in the Secret Service for a fellow like me?'

Cousins laughed heartily.

'There may be for a fellow like you,' he replied, 'but not for *you*. Your methods of going about things are not exactly calculated to be successful in intelligence work. For instance, rattling a pair of shoes on banisters in sheer exuberance of spirits, when the need is for dead silence, is not good pidgin, as my Chinese boy would say.'

Tony looked crestfallen.

'I'm damn sorry about that, sir,' he apologised. 'I suppose I was really the cause of—'

'We'll think no more about it,' interrupted Cousins in kindly tones. 'Drop me at Lancaster Gate, will you, please? I'm looking forward to becoming a respectable human being once more. By the way, you two will have to do some explaining to Miss Hardinge's relations, won't you? Refer to me, if you need any help. Oh, that reminds me!' he fished out a pound note from his rags, and handed it to Sonia. 'I'm afraid all your valuables went to glory with Karen, but he took this pound from your purse, Miss Hardinge, when we were at Soho, and pushed it into one of my apologies for pockets. Queer fellow, Karen. Even he, I suppose, had some sort of good in him somewhere.'

Sonia took the note with a little word of thanks, but rather as though the sight of it was repugnant to her. Cousins was not surprised, when he saw her surreptitiously drop it over the side. He understood.

The car stopped, and the Secret Service man ascended to the pavement. A most elegant individual stepped away from him with a grimace of mingled surprise and disgust. The little man chuckled. He shook hands with Sonia and Tony.

'Take my advice,' he urged, 'give up searching for thrills and excitement. There's a tremendous lot to be said for a humdrum, commonplace mode of existence, you know.'

'We've found that out,' admitted Tony ruefully. 'No more aching for adventures for me. Sonia and I are to be married as soon as possible. That will be my biggest thrill.'

'We are going to settle down like sensible people,' added the girl, 'and just be wonderfully content with life as we find it.'

'Splendid,' approved Cousins. '"Content is wealth, the riches of the mind; And happy he who can such riches find." Goodbye!'

They drove away amidst a duet of gratitude. He stood watching the car until it had passed from sight. Then, with a little sigh, he set off for home.

# THAT BLOODY AFGHAN

## Part One

Major-General Sir Leslie Hastings, General Officer Commanding Peshawar Command, entered his headquarters, and marched to his office, perfunctorily returning the salutes of the sentries. A young staff officer, catching sight of him, beat a hasty retreat into the room of Captain Charteris, the general's secretary.

'Look out for squalls, Topknot,' he warned the latter, 'Jumbo's got 'em badly this morning. His breakfast curry's disagreed with him, or Mrs Jumbo's sent him a cholera belt or something. His face is like a beetroot fresh from the boil.'

'It always is,' commented Charteris who, due to a tuft of hair that would stick up, was affectionately known as Topknot. 'What can you expect when he weighs twenty stone if an ounce and has a tummy like Rashid's bullock?'

'Oh, it's worse than usual. It's not only beetroot red, it's vermilion, magenta, cerise, purple and crimson by turns. The old boy has definitely got the needle.'

Charteris looked concerned.

'Oh, damn!' he exclaimed. 'He'll keep me fussing about all the morning with his blasted orders and counter-orders. I have a date to go riding with Phyllis Goddard, too. It's infernal heat, I expect, that's got him. Why the devil he can't run the show from Murree or somewhere less like Hades, I can't fathom.'

'What's Phyllis doing down here? When did she come from the Hills?'

Charteris was about to reply, when an orderly entered the room; came smartly to attention.

'General's compliments, sir,' he snapped like an automaton. 'Will you step along to his room?'

'Very well, Barley.' The orderly departed as smartly as he had arrived. 'He hasn't wasted much time,' grunted Topknot. He rose from his desk. 'I'm damned if I don't think I'll ask for leave.'

'Don't ask him this morning, old son,' grinned the other. 'Shall I go a-riding with little Phyllis in your place?'

'Go to the devil!' grunted Charteris.

General Hastings hardly merited his secretary's uncomplimentary description. He was certainly stoutish, but not unpleasantly so, and his weight was probably not more than thirteen stone, if that. Perhaps the fact that he was rather short caused him to appear more rotund than he actually was. Despite these physical drawbacks, he contrived to look thoroughly military. His closely cut, crisp grey hair and small moustache aided in producing this – Charteris called it 'delusional' – effect. Somebody had, back in the distant past, labelled him 'Jumbo'. The nickname had stuck, and was so well known throughout the army that wonder had been expressed on occasions, by disrespectful brother officers, at his name not appearing in the army list as Major-General Sir Leslie (Jumbo) Hastings. He possessed a face that was invariably a deep red. It was almost round and, from it, glared a fierce pair of blue eyes under bushy eyebrows that, like his hair and moustache, were grey.

Charteris found him running a large handkerchief round between his collar and bull-like neck, and muttering to himself. The young officer saluted, stood respectfully watching the operation from the other side of the huge desk.

'Morning, Charteris,' grunted the general. 'Why the devil can't those idiots at the War Office, who are always messing about with uniforms, devise something for the tropics without a collar. This heat's damnable. Twenty past ten only, and it's a hundred and seventeen in the shade already.'

Charteris felt inclined to remind him that, although it might be, and probably was, that temperature elsewhere, it certainly was not as high in that large, airy office, with the windows shuttered and the two large, electric fans spinning rapidly above. In fact, the secretary thought it delightfully cool. His room was a good deal warmer. However, Sir Leslie was obviously not in a mood to be corrected on any point, no matter how trivial it might be. As it was, Charteris blundered by making a suggestion.

'Why not go to the Hills, sir?' he remarked. 'You could keep in hourly touch, if necessary, with the situation on the

Frontier, and could return at a moment's notice if—'

'Talk sense, man,' barked the general, suspending the mopping process to glare balefully at his subordinate. 'You know as well as I that the Afridis might swoop at any moment. I'd cut a damn fine figure were I capering round hills when those devils took into their heads to play merry hell down here. I suppose you're thinking of girls, and dances, and all the rest of that damned nonsense. All you young fellows are good for these days is poodle-faking. Can't think what the army's coming to – I'm hanged if I can.'

Charteris reddened a little, but was not greatly concerned. He had heard all that before – not once, but many times. Sir Leslie stuffed the voluminous handkerchief up his sleeve.

'Why the devil did I send for you?' he growled. 'Oh, I know, ring up that Intelligence fellow, and tell him I want him here at once. He's at Dean's, isn't he?'

'He's here, sir,' replied the secretary with a tinge of malice in his tone. 'He's been kicking his heels waiting to see you since half past nine.'

'Why the hell didn't you say so before? Send him in. And see that I'm not disturbed until he's gone.'

Captain Charteris departed with relief. He found the 'Intelligence fellow' hobnobbing with a staff major with whom he had been at Sandhurst.

'So Jumbo's on the warpath, is he?' he commented in reply to the secretary's message, given with the warning that Sir Leslie was extra lavish that morning. 'That don't worry me. I knew him well in Mespot – we had lots of fun and games together. I rather like the old boy.'

'Do you? We don't,' was the emphatic rejoinder of the staff officer. 'Life was apt to move on well-ordered lines before Jumbo took over. He's only been here three months, but – oh, Lord!' Words failed him.

Major Kershaw grinned. He was a spare man of medium height, whose hair, moustache, and eyebrows were of that colour generally described by females as auburn, but which most males are content to call ginger. He was exceedingly freckled, possessed a snub nose, square jaw, and a pair of twinkling blue eyes. From this description, it will be gathered he was not exactly, in the words of the song, lovely to look at, but he was a great favourite, wherever he went, equally at home in male or female society, nursing the baby of a sergeant's wife or hobnobbing with a governor of a province. His whole military career had been spent in India, except for his service in Palestine, Egypt, and Mesopotamia during the Great War. For some time now, designated with the mystic military abbreviation, GSO3, he himself, as was to be expected of an important Intelligence officer, had been somewhat of a mystery man. He rarely wore uniform, disappeared entirely for long periods, and lived in hotels where it was his custom sometimes, to the scandal of the management, to interview, behind closed doors, a weird assortment of individuals of diverse races, creeds and colours.

He sauntered into General Hastings' office as though he was part owner; grinned cheerfully at the choleric man sitting behind the huge desk glaring at him.

'How d'you do, sir?' was his salutation. 'By Jove! You're looking well. It's a long time since we met – fifteen years, isn't it?'

'Eh? What's that? Met?' The general stared at him as though an outburst of fury was imminent then, wonder of wonders! The viate expression faded from his face, to be replaced actually by a smile. 'Good God! Why, Ginger Kershaw!' He rose, and the two shook hands heartily. 'So Major Kershaw, GSO3, and that damned precocious cub, Lieutenant Kershaw, are one and the same.' He resumed his seat, waved his visitor to another. 'I never connected you, but I might have known. Those were grand days, Kershaw, and I've never forgotten what I owed to that impudence of yours. I wonder if I'd have taken the same risks then, if I'd held my present rank. One can do things as a major or lieutenant-colonel that one daren't countenance as a general.' He sounded regretful.

Kershaw's eyes twinkled. He flung his topee across the room where it landed unerringly on a rattan chair similar to the one in which he was sitting.

'Nonsense, sir,' he objected. 'You're not going to persuade me that the spirit has altered. Why, I can see it in your face. Still the same old Jumbo inside – though perhaps not out,' he added, eyeing Hastings' corpulent figure with a grin.

Nobody but he would have dared refer to the general to his face as Jumbo. It was typical of the man. He was no respecter of persons or personalities. He was as liable to speak his mind to the viceroy as to his own servant. Probably that was one of the reasons why he was held in such high regard by all. The general showed no resentment at his remark; on the contrary, he laughed heartily. The sentry on the veranda outside heard it; was so unnerved by the unusual sound that he almost dropped his rifle. Sir Leslie patted his middle.

'I've certainly put on flesh,' he admitted. 'But seriously, Kershaw, this job has got me down. It's not in my line. Why the devil they wanted to send me up here, when little of my service has been in India, and none on the frontier, is beyond me.'

'Because you're a damn fine soldier, sir,' returned Kershaw, and he meant it.

The general grunted. There was no suspicion in his mind that the other was flattering him. He had learnt to understand the ginger-haired man thoroughly in Mesopotamia, where the latter had acted as his adjutant for many months. He knew quite well that it was his habit to speak bluntly. Had Kershaw thought he was 'a damn bad soldier', he would have said so probably in exactly the same tone as he had uttered the reverse.

'That's all very well, but these rumours and counter rumours have got me jumpy. If I could march right in and tackle the blighters, I'd be as happy as a king's cadet. But I've got to wait and watch, wondering all the time what they're going to do next. I know damn well everyone here thinks I ought to migrate to the Hills, and the staff is thoroughly disgruntled. They regard me as a plague spot – and dash it all! I don't blame them.'

Kershaw laughed.

'Take my tip, General,' he advised, 'go to the Hills. You'll be out of this sweltering heat, everybody'll be pleased, and you'll be better tempered. You can take my word for it, you can go quite safely. Nothing's likely to happen – at least not yet anyway.'

Sir Leslie eyed him hopefully, but still doubtfully. He leant across the desk, and some of his old fire returned.

'Look here,' he growled, 'one of my greatest grouses has been lack of adequate intelligence. I was kept informed of a lot of stuff that meant nothing. You had disappeared into the blue shortly before I took command. Since then, we've only had reports from you at rare intervals, most of them as barren as Baluchistan. Yesterday you returned and, by Gad! It was my intention to pulverise you. I came here this morning prepared to work the third degree on you, until I obtained some information from you that I could get my teeth into. What's Intelligence up to, Kershaw? Tell me something I want to know.'

'That's why I'm here, sir,' came from the other. 'I'll tell you enough to make you skip off happily to Lady Hastings at Murree, and forget there are such places as Peshawar or disturbers of the peace like Afridis.'

'Well, get on with it, man, but, for God's sake don't feed me with stories about the Haji of Turangzai. I'm sick to death of him. Hotheaded fanatics, always ready to preach a holy war against Britain, don't matter a hoot. One always knows what they're up to. They broadcast their intentions by their very blatancy, and end by proving their own worst enemies by acting as publicity agents against themselves. I want to know something definite of this Abdul Qadir Khan and what he actually is plotting. The mass of rumours, your own noncommittal reports, and the obviously suppressed excitement of the tribes round about are what have been worrying me. Also, I'm anxious to find out where Afghanistan comes into the affair.' He pushed a box of cigarettes across the table. 'Help yourself, and tell me all you know.'

Major Kershaw accepted the invitation, leant back in his chair, and lazily watched a spiral of smoke being ruthlessly disintegrated by the wind from the fan above.

'For a newcomer to the frontier, General,' he observed, 'you are a boon and a blessing to a poor Intelligence man like me. Ordinarily, I should have had to start my discourse with something like, "This continually seething, rebellious spot within the Empire, the North West Frontier of India, was never more troublesome or ready to revolt than it is today." Thank the Lord, you've saved me all that by wanting to get at the core of the situation. You're quite right about Turangzai and his like, who make a big song and dance about their show. They'll give us heaps of trouble yet, but we'll keep on subduing them, so long as Abdul Qadir's ideas don't bear fruit. He is the most dangerous man who has ever plotted against us and, if he, by any chance, succeeds in the cunning scheme he is weaving, we shall find ourselves plunged into the worst war we've ever had to face up here.

'Abdul Qadir Khan is a Mahsud by birth. He was educated at Islamia College here, where he obtained a Punjab University degree. His family had plenty of money, and they were so tickled at his success, as a scholar, that he was sent to Europe to continue his studies. Thus was added to the stock-in-trade of a naturally subtle rogue with the utmost resource all that Europe could teach him of Western culture, habits, weaknesses, and strength. In addition, he made an investigation of methods of warfare, of offence and defence. In fact, to use an Americanism, he got acquainted with the whole works. On his return to the North West Frontier he commenced to apply his researches to his own schemes. It is his idea to unite the Afridis into one powerful force. While not interfering with their natural methods of warfare, he yet intends imbuing them with a real military sense.

One by one, the tribes are falling into step, and are allowing themselves to be trained as real well-disciplined soldiers by men whom he has personally selected. What is more, they are taking their training very seriously and with great earnestness. You don't need to be told what the finished article is likely to turn out. A natural born fighter, trained in modern military methods, is going to prove a formidable enemy – far more formidable than the Afridi we have been in the habit of facing.

'But Abdul Qadir does not stop at that. He wants to rouse Afghanistan to ally itself with him in a war against Great Britain. He knows very well the amir, his principal advisers, and certain sections of the people are friendly to us and wouldn't consider such an arrangement, but to him they don't count. His agents are swarming through the country, plotting, planning, promising. All he needs is the assistance of an Afghan strong and ambitious enough to rise up at the head of the mass of people, overthrow the king and government, and take possession of the country. You remember what Bacha Saqao did? Well, it can be done again but, of course, from Abdul Qadir's point of view, the man must be one who, once he has Afghanistan under his control, will promptly throw in his lot – and the well-trained Afghan army – with him against Great Britain. Abdul Qadir believes he has found the man.'

'The devil he has,' ejaculated the general. 'Who is he?'

Major Kershaw smiled slightly.

'Have you heard of Aziz Ullah, sir?' he asked.

'What! That bloody Afghan? Certainly I have. Who in India hasn't? His name and his Robin Hood adventures are always in the papers. I don't believe half of them anyway, but he seems to be causing a hell of a lot of trouble. A thorough scoundrel, of course, but a damned elusive one, from all accounts.'

'He's certainly elusive. He has to be, considering he is being sought on all sides by emissaries of the Afghan government who are only too keen to earn the reward offered for his capture.'

'But what help can Abdul Qadir expect to get from the fellow? He's only a bandit, isn't he?'

'You can call him that if you like, sir, but it is hardly true. He has actually done nothing unlawful. That is, he has not been endeavouring to rouse the people against the government. He appears in a district without warning, preaches reform and the betterment of conditions, and disappears as suddenly as he has appeared, only to turn up again somewhere else. He is provided with ample funds, which he is using to help the poor and needy. He has done a great deal of good. The tales of his robberies from the wealthy and attacks on government banks and institutions are fabrications of the ruling classes who fear his growing influence. You call him a scoundrel because you, like everyone else in this country, know only of him through the stories appearing in the Indian papers – stories, which I can assure you, are inspired by the Afghan authorities. As I say, they fear him and, having so far failed to lay their hands on him, are fighting his propaganda by concocting lies and broadcasting them.'

The general stared at him in amazement.

'Damn it all!' he exploded. 'You seem to admire the fellow.'

'I certainly do,' nodded Kershaw. 'I have seldom felt such an intense admiration for anyone. He is running a greater risk than you'll probably ever realise. In less than four months he has obtained such a hold on the minds of the great majority of Afghan people that it is likely they would follow him blindly now in any enterprise he thought fit to conceive. That's where Abdul Qadir Khan comes in. He realises that, if he can persuade Aziz Ullah to rise against the king and government and take possession of the country – he'll offer the help of his own Afridis no doubt – he can then count on him, once the Afghan army is on his side, to assist him against us. The cunning of the fellow will be quite apparent to you without any long effort at explanation on my part. The Afghan army is well trained, well equipped, and efficient. Were it thrown into the scale with a different, better disciplined, and more united Afridi force you will gather the great danger that would threaten us. It hardly bears contemplation.'

Sir Leslie considered his words thoughtfully and, like a good soldier put his finger on the weak spot.

'I can see what we would be up against, if Abdul Qadir *had* the Afghan army with him,' he grunted, 'but your very argument concerning its strength and efficiency seems to me to be a safeguard. Under those circumstances, it is unthinkable that Aziz Ullah at the head of a horde of unarmed – except perhaps with home-made weapons – undisciplined fanatics could overpower a government backed by such a fine fighting force.'

Ginger Kershaw smiled.

'There you lose sight, sir, of something upon which Abdul Qadir is counting. I refer to the superstitious native mind. The Afghan army is a splendid fighting machine under ordinary circumstances, but it is recruited from the very people who are almost sanctifying Aziz Ullah. The men are certain to have come under his spell, as their fathers and brothers, uncles and cousins have done. If not, you may be sure that Abdul Qadir's emissaries will see to it that they do. The chances are, therefore, that they would go over to Aziz Ullah without firing a shot against him.'

The general folded his arms before him; frowned portentously at the smiling Kershaw.

'Damn it, man!' he growled. 'This is a far more serious state of affairs than even I contemplated. And you airily tell me to run away to the Hills and – and play.'

At that the Intelligence officer laughed outright.

'Why not, sir?' he asked. 'The Afridis are going to be very quiet for a long time. In the first place, it will take Abdul Qadir several months before he considers they are trained, disciplined, and united sufficiently for his purpose. It would take several months for Aziz Ullah to gain control of Afghanistan and be prepared to join with him in a war against India; that is, if Aziz Ullah were to allow himself to be thus influenced.'

'Well, he will, won't he? It stands to reason the infernal Afghan is playing a mighty cunning game in which his own ambitions take first place. It's all very well your trying to persuade me he's a fellow to be admired. Naturally, he's engaged in feathering his own nest. He's not attempting to gain influence over the people for their good – that's all rot! Altruism is a word in the dictionary, and it stops there. It isn't used in real life.'

Kershaw pretended to look shocked.

'The Jumbo I used to know wasn't a cynic,' he commented.

This time Sir Leslie frowned at the nickname. He felt he

was discussing matters in which levity had no place.

'It isn't a case of cynicism,' he snapped. 'It's common sense. People all the world over are only altruistic when it pays them to be so.'

'Well, you're wrong concerning Aziz Ullah,' Kershaw told him. 'But Abdul Qadir probably thinks the same as you. What is more, Aziz Ullah has no intention of allowing him to think otherwise. Had he not appeared suddenly, and obtained his present influence over the Afghans, Abdul Qadir would himself before long, have found an ambitious Afghan with a personality who could gain the same ascendancy. Only the man our Mahsud friend would have backed would have been utterly unscrupulous. Aziz Ullah is not, despite what you have said about him. He has no more intention of wresting the throne from the present amir and overthrowing the government than you have.'

The general looked thoroughly puzzled.

'How the devil do you know that?' he demanded.

'Because Aziz is by way of being a friend of mine.'

'A friend of yours!' echoed the astonished GOC.

Kershaw nodded.

'I've been in Afghanistan for the last two months,' he told the general calmly, 'ostensibly as representative of a southern India steelworks. I've moved about the country quite a lot, and have been in the company of Aziz Ullah on many occasions. That is why I can tell you that the stories of his robberies and depredations have been fabricated, mostly by the people who fear his sudden influence. He has also, whimsically you may think, circulated quite a number himself. He knows all about

Abdul Qadir, and it is his intention to allow the Mahsud to believe the worst of him and find him apparently eager to fall in with his plans. Up to now he has been elusive even with the wily Abdul, but one of these days, when it suits him, he will allow a meeting to be arranged, the result of which will appear entirely satisfactory to Abdul Qadir. But you can take my word for it, sir, that far from joining hands with the Afridis, he is Great Britain's trump card in this present very interesting game.'

Sir Leslie had listened with amazement and the greatest interest. He leant forward and eyed Kershaw eagerly; quite forgot, for the moment, their difference in rank.

'Are you absolutely certain of this, Ginger?' he urged. 'You're sure you haven't somehow fallen under the spell the fellow seems able to weave?'

'I am so sure,' returned the Intelligence officer solemnly, 'that I would bet every penny I have in the world and every penny you have also,' he added with a smile, 'if I could lay my hands on it. Aziz Ullah means no harm to the king, government, or any Afghan authority. He is all for helping the people, but that means no disrespect or antagonism to the powers that be. But, for reasons of his own, it tickles him to be classified in the same category as Bacha Saqao. You'll find out why one day, sir. Anyway, it all boils down to this, and I give you my word it is absolutely authentic: Aziz Ullah has no intention whatever of being a cat's paw or falling in with Abdul Qadir's plans. He is going to lead him on, which will be of immense help to us – will probably, like most Orientals, plead for time, and more time, to make up his mind. But you can leave Abdul Qadir and his machinations to him – and to me, sir. The only thing that worries me is that there may be a slip or a betrayal by some dastard, which will enable the authorities to pounce on him. That thought, I admit, gives me nightmares.'

General Hastings gave vent to a great sigh of relief.

'You Intelligence fellows certainly do things sometimes,' he conceded. 'I take my hat off to you, Ginger. I've read about that beggar, and thought he was just a—'

'Bloody Afghan,' supplied the other with a grin.

'Exactly,' went on Hastings unperturbed. 'The notion that you had made an ally of him against Abdul Qadir Khan would have struck me as fantastic.' He rose. 'Come and have a drink in the mess. You've taken a great load off my shoulders.' They left the office, and walked along the corridor together. They were passing the office of Captain Charteris, when the general stopped, opened the door, and glanced in. His secretary sprang to his feet. 'I'm off to the Hills tonight, Charteris,' Sir Leslie astonished that young man by saying. 'Make all arrangements for my HQ to be established at Murree until further orders.' He shut the door before the secretary had recovered sufficiently to murmur a formal 'Very well, sir,' and walked on. 'That took the wind out of his sails,' chuckled Jumbo. 'By now the young jackanapes is performing cartwheels.' He became serious again. 'You see the load I am putting on your shoulders, Kershaw. Gad! If that Aziz fellow has deceived you—!'

'He hasn't – and won't, sir. I know.'

'Well, you never made a mistake in the old days. I'm putting my whole trust in you.'

'You can. I'm not a prince.'

'Eh? What's that?'

'I think the Bible warns us that trust should not be placed in princes, sir.'

'Oh, I see. Just your way of backing yourself. Well, it sounds confident. But, listen to me, mystery man: I expect you to keep me posted while I'm in Murree. I loathe being kept in the dark.'

'You shall have a full report of how things are progressing directly I get back, sir.'

'Why – where are you going?'

'To Afghanistan.'

'The devil you are. Then, for heaven's sake, don't get arrested as a spy or something.'

The entrance of the general into the staff mess room, where his appearances were exceedingly rare, created a profound impression among the officers there. They sprang to attention as duty-bound, then were still further mystified by his geniality, as he made it clear that he wished for no formality.

'Carry on, gentlemen,' he directed, 'and don't mind us. Kershaw and I are old brothers-in-arms.'

The mess room orderly quickly supplied them with cold drinks in which ice tinkled pleasantly.

'Here's a toast, sir,' murmured Kershaw with a mischievous twinkle in his blue eyes. 'To that bloody Afghan!'

Sir Leslie laughed, and responded with hearty goodwill. 'To that bloody Afghan!'

# Part Two

At about the time Sir Leslie Hastings and Major Kershaw were drinking their toast to him, the man, to whom the general had referred in such uncomplimentary terms, was lying flat on his back resting after an arduous climb. A short distance away, squatted a score or so of wild-looking Afghans, men who had attached themselves to him and now refused to leave him. Armed to the teeth, they formed an impressive-looking bodyguard and, were the truth revealed, he was glad to have their company. When he had commenced on his strange enterprise four months previously, alone and unknown, he had faced enormous difficulties; on every side, was beset by dangers. Somehow he had overcome all obstacles gradually gaining the confidence of those among whom he appeared so mysteriously and to whom he lectured with such deep earnestness. His works of charity, his kindliness, his great knowledge, as it appeared to the untutored, ignorant masses, of the power of healing, which he was always prepared to exercise, worked wonders. His terrific strength, for he was a man with enormous shoulders and a great depth of chest, alone won him hundreds of admirers, for all Afghans love physical power, and he was never backward in displaying his. Above all, a most engaging and magnetic personality, gained for him a following that grew with bewildering rapidity, until he knew quite well there were thousands upon thousands ready and eager to follow him were he only to raise a finger.

He would probably have been the first to admit that superstition was responsible for this to a great extent. He was an utter mystery and anything apparently beyond understanding or explanation exercises a profound influence on the untutored mind. Nobody knew actually whence he came, who he was or, in fact, anything about him. In consequence, wild and impossible stories arose concerning his origin. This added to the fact that his mission was so obviously the establishment of a better ordered state of existence for the downtrodden masses, caused him to be regarded as a saint. Some there were who expressed the belief that he had actually descended from Paradise at the behest of Mohammed himself in order to work a miracle on their behalf. Another and a great factor in his favour was his apparently unlimited control of wealth. At least, to the people, among whom he chose to appear, his financial means seemed boundless. It is true he distributed money generously to the really needy, though seldom more than three or four annas a time to each, but these annas to people, accustomed to living on a few pice a day, came in the nature of a windfall.

It was astonishing how quickly news concerning him circulated throughout Afghanistan, once he had become known, and had swept away the suspicion and distrust he first encountered. Hardly a month had passed since his initial appearance, when his arrival in the various villages he decided to visit began to assume the nature of a triumphant event. He exhibited a great love for children which alone won him most of the women as adherents. He wrestled with the strong men, whom he invariably defeated with ease. He soothed the sufferings of some, cured others, who were ill with fevers and kindred diseases – this, I strongly suspect, was accomplished by the judicious and private use of drugs which he carried secretly about his person. In three months the whole of Afghanistan was talking about him, the great bulk of the population in a spirit little short of adoration. His fame gradually spread beyond the borders of that country and articles concerning him became features of quite a number of newspapers not only in Afghanistan, but in India, Persia, Turkestan and other countries devoted to the Muslim faith.

At first the authorities and the enlightened subjects of Afghanistan regarded his coming with a benevolent eye. When, however, it became obvious that he was teaching the masses that they were unnecessarily downtrodden, that they had the right to demand better conditions, better housing, in short, an altogether improved form of existence to that which they endured so stoically and uncomplainingly, government circles began to grow alarmed. They visualised an uprising, a sudden nationwide revolt that would plunge Afghanistan into a state of anarchy. They now saw in this man, who called himself

Aziz Ullah, but who was known generally as The Master, not a harmless visionary but a definite menace. Steps were taken to apprehend him, but that was easier ordered than accomplished. Partially through the resentment such orders almost generally caused and the consequent help and warning he received, and partially through his own forethought, Aziz Ullah was able to avoid the police or soldiers sent to seize him with ease. None of the local authorities in the villages to which he confined his activities dared touch him. They knew any such attempt would probably be more than their lives were worth; perhaps also they were under his dominating influence. Nevertheless, he had several narrow escapes.

The difficulty of apprehending him became such an acute problem that underhand means were adopted by certain officials in the hope of discrediting him. Every crime almost that took place in the vicinity of districts he visited were attributed to him, and inspired articles, declaring him to be a rogue imposing on a gullible people, were printed in the various government-influenced organs. This appeared to amuse rather than dismay Aziz Ullah. In fact, Major Kershaw stated to General Sir Leslie Hastings, he had even started secretly the circulation of certain stories against himself. It is likely that the ginger-haired Intelligence officer was behind this, for most of them hinted at the possibility of Aziz Ullah desiring to seek power and compared him with Bacha Saqao – the bandit who had seized the country after Amanullah's flight and, for a short span, had reigned as king. They appeared in Indian newspapers, which Kershaw knew Abdul Qadir Khan, the ambitious Mahsud, received and read with keen attention.

Far from undermining Aziz Ullah's hold on the populace, the government propaganda actually did more to strengthen it. The people who had taken him to their hearts were not so easily influenced to cast him out again. The persecution to which he was subjected only attached them more warmly to him, and began to rouse their resentment and authorities. Matters had reached this pass at the time Major Kershaw was interviewing the General Officer Commanding Peshawar.

Aziz Ullah's hiding place was situated in a wonderfully secluded spot in the Hindu Kush Mountains, not far from Kabul itself. He had discovered it when preparing for his enterprise and before he had disclosed himself. Nine thousand feet above sea level, a narrow pass meandered by a couple of hundred feet below. There was no actual track to the place; in fact it would have been inaccessible to any but the hardened natives of the district, athletes, or expert mountaineers. Therein lay its great security. It was a saucer-shaped opening in the mountains surrounded on all but one side by grim towering rocks on which a goat could not have found foothold. There was only one way of approach, and that, as described, was only possible to skilled climbers. A handful of men could have held the place against an army, provided they were well provisioned. Aziz Ullah had stocked it well and every time he and his would-be disciples returned they brought fresh supplies to add to the store. A stream trickling down the mountainside provided all the water needed. A small, almost flat plain covered with coarse grass, dotted here and there with boulders and stunted bushes, mostly of the cactus variety, was Aziz Ullah's recreation ground, his residence one of many caves penetrating far into the frowning and gigantic rock walls.

His followers preferred to herd all together in one of the others.

As he lay on his back apparently asleep, Aziz Ullah was turning several problems over in his mind. One – the reward that had been offered for his apprehension – caused him more interest than concern. He could rely to the hilt on the twenty men who had attached themselves to his person – he had been compelled to choose them from hundreds who had clamoured for the honour – they alone knew where he concealed himself, but wild horses would not have torn the secret from them. His great danger of betrayal lay in the villages and his journeyings from one to another. In every community there is likely to be a Judas. It would be comparatively easy to trap him under some pretext or other and, if the betrayer had companions of the same kidney, spirit him away to a police post. He opened his eyes, and they lighted on the band of stalwarts squatting at a respectful distance from him. Sight of them caused him to smile slightly, and he shook his head a little. No; it would not be easy. It would be most difficult, for the would-be Judas would have to trap that faithful band as well.

A problem that gave him a great deal more thought was the knowledge that the Afridi chieftain, Abdul Qadir Khan, was making earnest attempts to get in touch with him. Emissaries of his were continually endeavouring to arrange a meeting, but always when these men had sidled quietly up to him and whispered their message Aziz Ullah had shaken his head. He chose to let them think he distrusted them – for the present. Sooner or later, he would accept Abdul Qadir's invitation, but the longer he denied him, the more anxious, he knew, the Mahsud would be to make an alliance with him.

The matter which intrigued his mind above all others, however, was a strange communication that had been imparted to him by the headman of three villages in which he had spent the previous two days. It was to the effect that the government was prepared to delegate a mission to meet him and inquire into the reason for his pilgrimage through the villages and small towns. The mission would hear him in Kabul on a date and at an hour to be decided by him, and promised to give sympathetic consideration to all proposals he cared to put forward for the improvement of conditions for the lowly. The only stipulation imposed was that he should cease until then his public speaking, and should reply at once indicating his readiness to meet the government delegation at the earliest possible moment. Safe conduct was promised to him. Was it a trap? Aziz Ullah was unable to decide. The Afghan mind is subtle and cunning, and the turnabout was, to say the least, startling. The attacks on him, the reward for his apprehension, and now – this! If it were a genuine attempt to meet him amicably, with a view to receiving, at first hand, his suggestions for the welfare of the people, Aziz Ullah felt His Majesty the Amir was behind it. He knew the reigning monarch to be an enlightened ruler eager to serve his people to the best of his ability. The fact that he personally had made little attempt at reform, since coming to the throne, was probably due to his cautious character. No doubt, he always had in mind the fate of Amanullah who, after a visit to Europe, had attempted wholesale westernisation in a gigantic hurry, the result of which had been chaos and the loss of his own throne. Possibly the reigning amir welcomed the idea of a man, who had so quickly and so amazingly gained the confidence of the masses, being the instrument by which improvements in conditions could be achieved to everyone's satisfaction. Aziz Ullah had been accepted by the mullahs, whose opinions still carried the greatest weight and who exercised tremendous influence in the country. It was possible they had persuaded the amir to command that he should be given a hearing.

On the whole, Aziz Ullah was disposed to accept the invitation. He thought little of the risk. After all, his whole enterprise had been most hazardous from the beginning. Its success had astonished him. He had expected much greater opposition; had been prepared for complete failure. The manner in which he had carried the people with him had been something of which he had not dreamt in his most optimistic moments. Many times of late, he had found himself lost in admiration of the brilliance of the mind behind that had conceived the project. It was typical of the man that his innate modesty caused him to be utterly unconscious of his own great part in the undertaking and to give all the credit elsewhere. It did not occur to him that, had his own personality and handling of an intensely difficult task not risen triumphant, the thought devoted to the idea, the anticipation of native reactions, the whole conception, in fact, of events as they had actually occurred by a clever, subtle brain would have been useless.

He rose from his resting place in the coarse grass and sauntered towards his followers who sprang to their feet at his approach. In his loose native garb, his great depth of chest seemed perhaps more herculean than it actually was, but no one could doubt that he was an immensely powerful man. He stood over six feet in height, possessed the light brown skin typical of the Afghan and grey eyes not unusual in that part of the globe. His glossy black hair and beard were well-kept, and offered a striking contrast to the wild hirsute appendages of his twenty doughty disciples. On the whole, he was a strikingly attractive man. Addressing one whom he had chosen to be leader of the others, a gigantic fellow who stood inches taller than he, he directed him to partake of a meal at once, and prepare for a journey.

'I have considered,' he declared in his deep, musical voice, 'the invitation which has been conveyed to me to meet a mission selected by government. It is my wish that my reply shall reach the minister, upon whom may Allah shed light, by the morning hour of prayer. You will tell him, Yusuf, that I will appear before the delegates on the day of the full moon at the tenth hour.'

'But, master,' cried Yusuf, 'is it not unwise? May not the unholy ones have planned this as a trap? Great sorrow should overshadow all who love you, were harm to befall you.'

'I am in the hands of Allah, the All-merciful, the All-seeing. Great is His Name,' came in sonorous tones. Every head was bent reverently. 'You will go, Yusuf!'

The giant Afghan raised no further objections, but set about his preparations at once, assisted by his companions. When he had had a meal, he appeared before Aziz Ullah, who had seated himself on a boulder, and was gazing into space as though in deep meditation. Yusuf stood behind him as though fearful of disturbing these profound thoughts. Aziz, however, had heard him approach and, without turning his head:

'You are ready to depart, Yusuf?' he asked.

'I am ready, master.'

'It is well. You have committed the message to memory — repeat it.'

The Afghan did so.

'Is it not your wish,' he added, 'that I carry writings with me, master?'

'It is not my wish. I use only word of mouth. You are my messenger. In you I have implicit trust.' He rose, and turned smilingly to the man. 'Go, Yusuf, and may Allah go with you.'

The giant seized his hand, conveyed it to his forehead; then, without another word, departed on his mission.

It was not Aziz Ullah's way to hold himself entirely aloof from his men who had elected to form themselves into his personal bodyguard. When in their mountain retreat, he encouraged them to engage in games and sports, and even joined with them sometimes. Many were the wrestling bouts held there in that great mountain range which forms the western part of the grim, towering Himalayan wall round northern India. At first, the men had been shy and embarrassed at indulging in their simple pastimes before or with him, but he displayed such hearty, good-humoured enjoyment that they quickly forgot any restraint; laughed and shouted like excited children, and entered into everything with the utmost zest. It was hard to realise when watching them at play, that these simple, unsophisticated creatures could be the fierce, cruel, sometimes brutally vicious men they were by nature, even though their appearance indicated it.

Yusuf returned after an absence of thirty-six hours to report that he had delivered the message. The date and time fixed for the meeting, he announced, had met with the approval of the minister. The members of the mission would at once be selected, and Aziz Ullah would be expected to arrive punctually. He thanked Yusuf, and informed the men that he would remain in the mountains until the day of the appointment drew near. It was his intention to respect the stipulation imposed, principally in order to give not the slightest excuse for treachery, also to prepare the matters which he would put before the officials chosen to hear him. It was necessary to get his ideas in order. His orations to the people, in which he had exhorted them to claim improved conditions, reduced taxation, better housing, organised training for the young, and satisfactory scales of wages, to mention but a few of their needs, had been delivered without much idea as to how these reforms were to be carried out. That rested with the government, but the delegation would naturally expect something in the nature of suggestions or plans. He had six clear days in which to prepare them, and he spent a considerable amount of thought on them. It was an extremely difficult task, for they had to be of such a nature that they would mean no violent clash with the extremely conservative temperament of the people they were intended to benefit and, at the same time, be well within the power and financial resource of the government to provide.

He smiled to himself many times as he laboriously drilled his ideas into shape. He had little thought, when commencing on his enterprise, that he would actually appear before an official mission to plead for the oppressed thousands. However, he eventually satisfied himself that he had prepared a well-ordered and concise harangue which should meet with the approval of all. He provided himself with no documents, everything being committed to memory, and repeated over and over again in the seclusion of his cave, until he was word perfect.

Yusuf and his other followers were not at all sanguine concerning the visit to Kabul. Like the majority of Afghans of their class, they utterly distrusted everything connected with officialdom. They saw in this invitation to The Master nothing but a treacherous bid by the government to get him into its power, because all other means had failed. They dared make no further attempt to dissuade Aziz Ullah from going; they were too much in awe of him for that, but they formed plans among themselves for his protection. If Aziz guessed anything of this, he gave no indication. It was noticed, however, that a smile was on his face and no hint of surprise, when, on the day before the appointed meeting, on descending from his retreat, he found a vast crowd, entirely composed of men, awaiting his coming. Almost all were armed in some sort of fashion, while the absence of women and children was a significant factor that was not lost on him. As a matter of fact, he had expected something of the sort. He had not been blind to the absence of three of his disciples during the preceding three days; neither did he fail to notice the unobtrusive manner in which they now attached themselves to him again.

He was greeted by the throng as a saviour, and was greatly embarrassed by the men who strove to kneel before him and place his foot upon their heads. True to his determination to refrain from any public speaking, in accordance with the condition imposed, he merely contented himself with a sonorous, '*Salaam alaikum*', and proceeded on his way. The crowd fell in behind, and he made no attempt to stop them. It would be as well, he thought, if the government did purpose treachery, that its intentions should be restrained by actual evidence of that with which it had to contend. On the road, more and more men fell in behind The Master. When, towards evening, Kabul was sighted, there must have been close on ten thousand with him. How they provided themselves with the means of satisfying hunger and thirst, Aziz Ullah did not inquire, but obviously they had done so. On deciding to camp for the night outside the walls of the city, hundreds of fires sprang up in a remarkably short space of time, pots and pans appeared miraculously from bundles, and the smell of cooking quickly permeated the air. Aziz Ullah's own necessities were provided by the faithful twenty.

A white man riding a native pony, followed by a servant on another, leading a pack mule, approached Kabul shortly after the horde had settled down. He gazed at it in astonishment, then rubbed his eyes. Darkness was not due to fall for some time, and the light was perfect. He could not be mistaken. Reining in his animal, he turned to the bearer.

'Do you see what I see, Rashid?' he asked in Urdu.

'Indeed I do, sahib,' was the reply. 'It is a camp, and there are many men.'

'You are right. For a little while I thought perhaps the sun had blinded my eyes and put visions into my sight that did not exist. It is strange that such a concourse should gather outside Kabul.'

'Very strange, sahib. It is my mind that The Master has been apprehended and these have come to demand his release.'

Mahommed Rashid was actually a havildar in a Punjabi

regiment; had been for some time on Intelligence service and had proved his value. Major Kershaw – he was the white man – vowed he would not change him for a dozen officers of the political branch of the police.

'By Jove!' exclaimed Ginger in English and in a somewhat perturbed tone. 'I hope to God you're wrong.' Mahommed Rashid understood English passably well, but he was a poor hand at speaking it. He waited, and presently his companion reverted to Hindustani. 'Ride over and find out, Rashid. Leave the mule with me. Be judicious in your questioning. I know there is a Persian saying, much quoted in this country, that he who remains silent questions easily, but I must know if harm has befallen Aziz Ullah.'

The havildar, garbed as a bearer and wearing nothing that might indicate the soldier, galloped his pony across the rough ground, until he reached a group of wild-looking peasants, squatting solemnly round a hookah. Their fierce eyes regarded him questioningly, but they responded civilly enough to his salutation.

'I am the servant of the English lord over yonder,' he announced. 'Many times a year he comes to Kabul, where he has friends and does much business. His eyes have fallen on this mighty gathering, and it is in his mind that there is trouble. If that is so, he will return to India. Speak, therefore, friends, that I may tell him whether or not he should proceed.'

They laughed. One, whose shaggy locks hung untidily round his face and mingled with his ragged beard, spat somewhat contemptuously.

'Does the unbeliever fear danger to himself?' he asked.

'Nay. It is only that he likes not to be present at matters that concern him not. Truly he is a brave man, and a kind and considerate master.'

'Then tell him we have come hither in peace. Have you heard tell of The Master, stranger?'

'I have heard many wonders concerning that great one, the peace of Allah be with him.'

He bowed his head respectfully. The Afghan's eyes showed their approval, as they responded reverently to his pious wish.

'Then know,' went on the spokesman, 'that tomorrow The Master enters Kabul to have speech with the government regarding our many wrongs. These,' he waved his hand round him to indicate the lounging multitude, 'have accompanied him without desire of his, because it is feared that danger may threaten him. We do not trust the great ones of government. Many lies have they spread regarding his works, many times have they wished to take possession of him, and throw him into prison. If they intend to respect him, and listen with peace to his words, all will be well. But if they purpose harm; then shall we rise in our anger to his aid.'

'You are indeed men,' returned Rashid approvingly. 'May the blessings of Allah descend on you and on your children, and may He prosper you. *Salaam!*'

He wheeled his pony; galloped back to Major Kershaw who awaited his coming a trifle impatiently. The havildar retailed that which he had been told, whereupon the Intelligence officer became deeply thoughtful.

'I like it not, Rashid,' he declared presently. 'It is in my mind that treachery is intended. The present Afghan government is half composed of men of corrupt ideas, who fear reform lest it rob them of their ill-gotten gains, make impossible for the future any profits by fraud, and even force them from office. It is difficult to believe they will be prepared to meet Aziz Ullah with honest purpose in their hearts.'

The havildar had a similar thought to that which had some days before occurred to The Master.

'It may be, sahib,' he observed, 'that the amir has ordered that he be heard.'

'I wonder. Hark you! Ride again to those men with whom you had speech. Say that I have heard much of the greatness of him they call The Master, and if they think he will not scorn to meet an unbeliever, who yet has much respect for the Muslim faith, I have a desire to send him my *salaam*s and to be received by him.'

Rashid's heavy black brows met together in a frown.

'You would be seen in public with him, sahib?' he asked.

Kershaw nodded.

'There will not be the time to meet in the usual way before he goes before the government officials; also the risk would now be too great. Go, Rashid!'

Like a good soldier, the havildar obeyed orders although he nursed a feeling that Kershaw sahib was not behaving with his usual wisdom. The Englishman watched him gallop across the uneven ground to the men from whom he had obtained his information. This time he dismounted; joined the circle round the hookah, which was pushed towards him as a sign of good fellowship. Kershaw sat his pony patiently, smiling to himself a little at the realisation that his request was apparently causing a good deal of argument. At last one of the men rose, and went off through the camp. There was another long period of waiting before he returned, accompanied by a giant of a man who seemed to be literally bristling with arms. The latter spoke to Rashid, who promptly sprang to his feet and, taking his pony by the bridle, led the fellow to Kershaw. The major thought he had never seen a dirtier or fiercer-looking Afghan. His greasy locks, unkempt beard, and dark, glittering eyes gave him a wilder aspect than most; yet he carried himself with a dignity that was rather impressive. There was a good deal of insolent contempt in the stare he directed at the slight, freckled Englishman.

'The Master has bidden this man take you to him, sahib,' announced Rashid.

'I feel it a very great honour,' replied Kershaw.

Yusuf, for it was he, looked questioningly at the havildar. Apparently he did not understand Urdu. The Englishman promptly repeated his remark in Persian, receiving a grunt from the other.

'Come!' he directed.

Without waiting to ascertain whether he was being followed at once or not, he turned, and strode back towards the camp. Kershaw dismounted, threw the reins to Rashid, and set off after him. He found it difficult to keep pace, since Yusuf took long and rapid strides. It was a considerable distance to the spot, under a group of trees, where Aziz Ullah was reclining. The Master was in the very centre of the camp, the thousands who had joined him having placed themselves round him in a huge circle, obviously with the intention of guarding him.

Those comprising the inner circle had remained at a respectful distance, however, his own immediate followers being the only men actually in his vicinity.

Kershaw's progress through the camp was an ordeal from which a good many Englishmen would have shrunk. The Afghans stood to watch him pass, and there were not many present who did not openly show they regarded him with the utmost suspicion. They were a fierce, unruly-looking lot, few of whom gave any indication that they were of other than the lowest order of Afghan society. The Englishman, however, seemed actually to enjoy the sensation he created. He nodded and smiled, as he progressed through their ranks, appearing completely at ease, which indeed he was. Few people had ever seen Kershaw out of countenance. He had the wonderful faculty of being at home under all circumstances and in any company; could adapt himself to everything, no matter what it happened to be.

Aziz Ullah rose, as he entered the clearing behind the giant Yusuf. There was not a flicker of recognition in the eyes of either, as they looked at each other. Aziz bowed low. Kershaw followed suit, standing a few yards from the man he had come to see as though he thought it might be disrespectful to approach too close. This attitude on the part of an Englishman greatly impressed the many who viewed the meeting. The stock of Kershaw rose very much.

'It is to me a great privilege,' he observed in his flawless Persian, 'to be permitted to meet Your Holiness. I have heard—'

A slight smile crossed the face of The Master, as he held up a powerful, shapely hand in protest.

'I do not claim,' he objected, 'neither do I permit a designation so exalted to be applied to me. I am but a man, no greater than these among whom and for whom I work. You have come to meet me. You are not prompted by idle curiosity, but by real interest and, for that, I am glad. Will you recline here for a little while with me, and tell me of your great country?'

Kershaw thanked him, but declared he wished rather to learn all about the great work on which his host was engaged.

'I have been told so much,' he added, 'that has kindled my admiration. If I can hear from your lips something of your ideals, it will give me much happiness. It will also enable me, from my own knowledge, to dispute the false and lying rumours that have been circulated by your enemies.'

There was a hearty murmur of approval at this from the hearers. Suspicion of Kershaw was rapidly evaporating. When he and Aziz Ullah sank amicably side by side to the rug spread on the ground, the latter's twenty disciples turned contentedly away, while the others in the vicinity, who had been watching and listening, once again occupied themselves with their own affairs.

'Was this wise, think you?' asked Aziz Ullah softly.

'It was necessary,' was the reply spoken as quietly. 'I should not have taken the risk had it not been that I learnt of that which is to take place on the morrow. Surely you do not trust these officials?'

'No; I do not trust them.' He smiled. 'But there is a chance that their purpose is honest, and while that chance exists I must not hesitate. These people, and others like them, have placed great reliance in me. I feel it my duty not to betray their trust.

He – you know whom I mean?' Kershaw nodded. 'He would not have me do otherwise.'

'But what if there is an assassin or assassins in waiting to murder you?'

Aziz Ullah shrugged his shoulders slightly.

'I am in the hands of Allah,' he remarked with a smile.

Kershaw smiled also, and there was an expression of affection on his face.

'You are a brave man,' he murmured.

'That is woman's talk,' returned the other in a tone of disgust. 'Listen! I will not only be salving my conscience to a great extent by doing all I can to get consideration shown to these poor people, but I believe firmly that this meeting and the consequent recognition shown to me – that is, presuming treachery is not intended – will force Abdul Qadir Khan to become more insistent than ever. That is the chief reason why I think you have been unwise to come here. He will have been informed of the action of government and my acceptance. It is in my mind that he himself may come to Kabul. Is it not likely, my friend, that his agents are even among this multitude? They will report to him concerning your having speech with me. Will that not rouse the Khan's suspicions, and perhaps undo all our plans?'

Kershaw was looking distinctly uneasy by this time. He quickly forced the momentary expression of alarm from his face, however, and smiled lest anyone should notice and wonder what it was perturbed him.

'You are right,' he admitted. 'I have been thoughtless. I was alarmed for you, though. You see, I have brought something with me from Peshawar which will act as a safeguard against murderous attacks and, when I heard of your appointment for tomorrow, I wanted you to have it at once.'

Aziz Ullah looked questioningly at him.

'What is it?' he asked.

'A jacket of mail to wear close to your skin. It is light and of the finest mesh. I guarantee it will resist bullets or daggers.'

'That was thoughtful of you. Where is it?'

'I have it under my coat. Presently, when I am certain I am unobserved, I will slip the parcel down and push it under the rug.'

'Thank you. Now I think you had better go. The time is nearly ripe for our scheme against Abdul Qadir. I will be back in the retreat in two days from now. At this hour I will meet you in the cave of the witch and we can make our final plans. Be cautious on entering Kabul. Abdul Qadir may be there, and he also may know who you are. You are not of a type regarded without interest in these parts, my friend. Your hair, your eyebrows, and your moustache are of a colour too distinct to pass unnoticed.'

'That is a sore point with me,' confessed Kershaw. 'My work would be a great deal easier were I dark. But it is of no use railing against Fate. On the rare occasions I disguise myself I am all the time worried lest the colour shines through the dye. Roots of red hair refuse to be suppressed . . . The parcel is well under the rug. For the love of Allah use it. You promise?'

'I promise. It would be ungracious as well as ungrateful of me not to wear it. Besides, I have no wish to die – yet. You have relieved my mind greatly.'

'Good.' Kershaw rose to his feet. 'I am obliged,' he observed in a louder voice, 'for the exposition you have given me of your ideals. As an Englishman, I am in entire sympathy, and wish you success in all your endeavours.'

Aziz Ullah had also risen. He bowed courteously.

'It is indeed a pleasure to hear such words from your lips,' he acknowledged. 'I am happy to have had the opportunity of explaining to one whose understanding is so great. Go, and the peace of Allah be with you.'

He summoned Yusuf, bade him escort the Englishman from the camp. The two conspirators bowed to each other with solemn politeness, after which Kershaw followed his giant guide back to Mahommed Rashid and his pony. This time he observed no suspicious or hostile looks on the contrary, men eyed him approvingly, many called out *salaam* to him. His initial words on meeting The Master as well as a report of the latter's friendly reception of him had been circulated. He of the hair that is red left an excellent impression behind him.

# Part Three

News of the vast concourse of men that had accompanied Aziz Ullah to Kabul had, of course, reached the high officers of government. Directly after the hour of prayer on the following morning, the self-constituted sentries observed issue from the city a troop of military horsemen. News was at once conveyed to Aziz Ullah who, despite objections, went to meet them. He was not permitted to go alone, however; well over a hundred fierce-eyed peasants insisted on keeping in close touch, for fear harm was intended to his person. A gleam of approval showed fleetingly in The Master's eyes as he gazed at the smart habiliments and equipment of the cavalrymen. At a command, the troopers halted, their captain riding forward alone to meet Aziz Ullah. He was a handsome young man, whose modern and very serviceable uniform suited him to perfection. There was a look of undisguised contempt on his face as he looked at the wild, ragged crowd forming a semicircle round their leader, but obviously he was impressed by the latter's appearance, for his eyes showed unmistakable admiration as they met. Saluting smartly, as Aziz Ullah bowed, he announced that he had been sent to inquire into the reason for the display of force.

'Do you come in peace?' he demanded.

'I come in peace,' replied the other simply.

'Then why are these with you?'

Aziz Ullah smiled.

'They come of their own will. It is they I represent, for whom I work. Is it not natural that they should wish to be on hand at the time when matters so gravely affecting them are discussed?'

The officer eyed him narrowly.

'Is there no other reason for their presence?' he asked doubtfully.

'Not in my knowledge. They are not with me by my command.'

'It is well, though I like not their warlike appearance. I am ordered to escort you into Kabul, but these men cannot be admitted. The police could not cope with such a rabble and riots might result. You will understand the difficulty.'

Aziz Ullah understood well enough that the authorities feared the consequences, should harm overtake him, with ten thousand devoted but fierce followers loose inside the city walls. It also proved to him that they were either planning treachery or were not certain that the safe conduct promised him could be respected. He gave no indiction of his thoughts, however, merely pointing out that the men who had elected to follow him had as much right in Kabul as anyone else. He also delivered a friendly homily on the impropriety of the officer's contemptuous use of the word 'rabble'.

'It is only because they have been downtrodden and denied the privileges of decent citizenship,' he pointed out, 'that you dare designate them by such a term. Are not we all true believers? Does it matter whether we are of peasant or gentle birth? All are alike in the eyes of Allah, the Beneficent, the Merciful. "Those who strive hard for Us, We will most certainly guide them in Our Ways. Allah is most surely with the doers of good."'

This quotation from the Koran was received with bowed heads and murmured responses from all who heard it. The officer appeared somewhat ashamed of himself. He muttered a half-hearted apology. The news spread quickly throughout the camp that The Master was expected to enter Kabul alone, whereupon there was a great outcry. For a time matters looked ugly. Scores of angry men surged threateningly round the officer, with no other thought in their minds but that evil was intended to their leader. The second-in-command of the troop of cavalry became alarmed; ordered his men to advance with drawn swords. Such an action was calculated more to precipitate a riot than to protect the captain. Aziz Ullah quickly recognised the danger.

'Halt those soldiers,' he snapped peremptorily to the other. 'I cannot be answerable for the consequences should they continue to approach in such a manner.'

Fortunately the officer was a man of common sense. He swung his horse round; galloped back to his men with hand upraised; ordered them to halt, and sheathe their swords. It could be seen that he was speaking angrily to his subordinate. Presently he came trotting back. In the meantime, Aziz Ullah was loudly haranguing his followers or rather those in his vicinity. He pointed out that there was a good deal to be said for the reluctance of the authorities to permit the entrance of so vast a multitude into the city, as congestion might be caused and traffic arrangements dislocated. Had it been expected, preparations could have been made to cope with it, but there was no time for that now. He also declared that any display of aggression would only prove a serious obstacle in the way of obtaining that in which his hopes were centred. Finally he adjured the men to remain patiently where they were, and await with confidence his return. He would enter the city with his twenty immediate followers and no others. The captain of cavalry arrived back some time before he concluded his exhortation; sat his horse listening with approval. He saw no objection to Aziz Ullah being accompanied by a mere score of men. There were many in The Master's party however, who shook their heads dubiously, and muttered to each other. They put no trust in promises of safe conduct; remembered only the efforts that had been made to discredit and apprehend the man most of them regarded as a new prophet. However, Aziz Ullah had his way. He set off at the head of the twenty, the captain of the cavalry riding by his side.

When the troop was reached, half of it wheeled and went ahead; the other half fell in behind. Thus they proceeded towards the city. Aziz Ullah could not help reflecting somewhat grimly that the arrangement gave the appearance more of a guard conducting a prisoner than of an honoured person being escorted. This feeling was intensified by the fact that no courtesies had been extended to him. At least, a horse might have been provided, in order that he could have ridden with the captain on terms of equality. Not a word was exchanged between the two as they went along, and it seemed to the men walking by his side that the officer was a trifle uneasy.

On entering Kabul, Aziz Ullah was not surprised to find the streets lined by jostling crowds anxious to catch a glimpse of him. Occasionally cheers were raised but, on the whole, the people regarded him with silent curiosity. His campaign on behalf of the downtrodden peasants of the countryside made no particular appeal to the inhabitants of Kabul. He walked along watchfully, feeling that, at any moment, an attack might be launched by a body of assassins engaged for the purpose. It will be gathered that he had scarcely more faith in the promised safe conduct than had his followers. Once he glanced behind him, to notice Yusuf and the other men glowering suspiciously from side to side. Their attitude was comforting. At least, were an attack to come, they would not be caught unprepared.

Aziz Ullah also obtained a measure of consolation when, passing the British Legation, he caught sight of the Union Jack above, floating lazily in the breeze. There was something about that not very attractive flag that caused the thought of stabs in the back or other treacherous actions to appear ridiculous and imaginative. Among a group of people standing at the gate, he observed a slight man with freckled complexion and red hair. The ghost of a smile flitted across his face as he passed on.

The small procession reached the very imposing modern government buildings, but instead of being escorted inside, Aziz Ullah was led into the well-kept grounds. Here a *shamiana* had been erected. Apparently the government had ordained that the meeting should be held in the open. Aziz Ullah wondered why. Although early, it was already very hot. Kabul is close on seven thousand feet above sea level; nevertheless, the heat can be intense there, and that particular June morning gave promise of a high temperature before many hours had passed. It would have been cooler and altogether more comfortable inside a building than in the close confines of a marquee. Possibly the government expected the meeting to be of short duration or else considered Aziz Ullah, whom it had outlawed, to be unworthy of such entrance into halls devoted to legislation. There were few people in the grounds and not a sign of a police officer which, he thought, was strange.

He was kept waiting in the open for nearly an hour before an usher arrived to escort him into the *shamiana*. At once the escort of cavalry trotted away. Yusuf and his men were about to follow into the tent but were ordered to remain outside. They obeyed reluctantly, and only when their leader had signified his wish that they should do so. Inside, on a rostrum, was a long table, behind which were fifteen chairs, the one in the centre being a large, ornate affair above which hung a shield bearing the arms of Afghanistan. A solitary stool was placed on the nearer side of the table alone. This Aziz Ullah concluded was for him, and his brows met in a little frown at the thought that even the courtesy of a chair was denied him. Below the platform, squatted half a dozen clerks, who gazed at him with deep curiosity as he appeared, but did not rise to their feet.

Again there was a period of waiting. At last, however, the curtains at the entrance were thrown back with a flourish. The fifteen members of the commission, headed by the Minister of the Interior, walked solemnly to the rostrum. All, except two, affected the sober morning attire fashionable in Europe. The couple dressed in picturesque native garb were obviously mullahs. None of them took any notice of Aziz Ullah, until they were seated, and the usher had led him to his stool. Then all eyes were focused on him and, in most, he read antagonism. The Minister of the Interior, a black-bearded, sharp-featured man, sitting below the national coat of arms, spent several moments staring at him as though endeavouring to probe into his very soul. Aziz underwent the scrutiny without discomfort; in fact, he appeared to be entirely at ease, and forced the minister, by his own return gaze, presently to drop his eyes to the papers on the table before him.

Lack of space does not permit me to report in detail the proceedings of that historic meeting. It is necessary to be brief as, although vastly interesting, the discussion and arguments are not actually of importance to this narrative.

Aziz Ullah was at first subjected to a veritable inquisition concerning his origin and family. He replied simply and with assurance, stating that he was born at Herat, moving to the holy city of Mesched in Persia with his family at an early age. There he had sat at the feet of learned doctors of divinity and inculcated the principles which had eventually led to his returning to Afghanistan, in the hope of being able to do something to improve the lot of the suffering thousands in that country. The announcement that he had studied in the city of Imam Riza, which is visited annually by thousands of Muslim pilgrims, made an impression on his hearers. They proved their antagonism, however, in demanding by what right he constituted himself the champion of the people of Afghanistan, stating that everything possible was being accomplished for their welfare. The Minister of the Interior pointed out that improvements are expensive, that the process must necessarily be gradual, and that the government was alive to requirements without the ill-considered intervention of a fanatic whose methods were calculated to cause unrest.

In reply, Aziz Ullah used quotations from the Koran in support of his right to make himself champion of the people. He managed this so adroitly that he silenced many arguments against him. He also reminded the commission that a promise had been publicly made that sympathetic consideration would be given to any proposals he put forward for the welfare of the lowly, and stated vehemently that he had not come there to be pilloried, neither was he on trial. His firmness of tone and apparent sincerity had their influence. The members of the commission spoke together for some time, then he was bidden deliver himself of the suggestions he had in mind. He, at once, plunged into a well-prepared oration, in which housing, employment, wages, education, child and maternity welfare, as well as a host of other important matters, had their part. Not only did he point out the necessity of all these, but he also showed how improvements could be accomplished by the government with the greatest thoroughness and least expense; proved how the outcome of capital expended would be interest gained, the building of a finer, healthier, more peaceful, more united people and a sure road opened to national progress and contentment.

During his discourse he took care to ascertain that every word he said was being taken down by the clerks. He had no intention of finding afterwards that no record had been made and that all had been wasted. He spoke at great length eagerly, clearly, and with the keenness of a zealot. His enthusiasm and power of oratory carried most of his hearers with him; even those who had feared his rising influence, lest their well-feathered nests be affected, now saw little in the plans suggested whereby their greed might be checked. On the contrary, they wondered if they were not opening up other paths by which they could eventually enrich themselves. Nevertheless, they resented still the coming of this unauthorised reformer. An attempt was made by some to cast doubt and discredit on his altruism, but it was half-hearted, and was quickly and smartly combated by the astute Aziz. He saw at once that it had been the intention to prove him an impostor, a man working for his own ends, and thus to confound him utterly in the eyes of all. But his clear enunciation of proposals and the manner in which they could be carried out, in which not an atom of self-interest could possibly be involved, defeated them entirely. Aziz Ullah won a great victory.

During the discussion that followed, he became aware that many of the members wore uneasy expressions as though they were anticipating something they wished now they could avoid. This caused Aziz to think deeply. When, from outside, rose an angry murmur that presently increased to a roar, in which he caught such expletives as 'betrayer', 'unholy one', 'false prophet', and others of a like nature, his mind became suddenly illumined. He gritted his teeth with anger. The reason for the *shamiana* was now manifest. He was marked as the victim of a vile plot. It was not difficult to understand the whole treacherous scheme. While the government commission granted him an apparently sympathetic hearing, arrangements had been made for an attack by hooligans which would end in his destruction and, at the same time, be made to appear entirely beyond the control of the authorities. Everything would have been engineered in such a manner that suspicion could not fall on them as the perpetrators. The members of the commission would doubtless act in a way to prove afterwards they had done all in their power to save him. But Aziz Ullah was not a fool. Such an attack by a rabble would have been impossible inside the government buildings, thus the *shamiana*; the absence of police in the grounds had puzzled him; the departure of the troop of cavalry, after the usher had taken charge of him, had been significant. He knew now he stood practically alone. Yusuf and the other nineteen men being his only protection against, perhaps, a couple of hundred or more savage ruffians.

Even at that moment, however, as the yells outside grew more threatening, he was able to smile a little. Matters had not worked out quite as the plotters expected. They did not desire his destruction now; in fact, being favourably disposed towards his schemes, they would rather he lived, in order that he could show how anxious they were to do good for the people and how quickly and eagerly they had fallen in with the proposals. But how were they to stem the flood they had caused? It was probable the ringleaders of the rabble had been told the officials would cry out in protest and command, but no notice was to be taken of their pleas. Perturbation showed on every face; they whispered and gestured together, careless of how their actions might be construed by the man they had betrayed. Obviously the clerks knew nothing of the plot; every one of them was on his feet, stark fear showing plainly in all faces. The noise outside grew more vicious; there came now the sound of blows and groans. Aziz Ullah knew the faithful twenty were barring the way. He stood and regarded the commission with the utmost contempt.

'What of the safe conduct promised me?' he demanded. 'Is it thus the government of Afghanistan fulfils its pledges?'

Turning his back, he stepped from the rostrum, and strode towards the entrance. Someone shouted to him to come back, that a way of escape would be found, but he took no notice. He had no intention of allowing his handful of loyal disciples to be butchered. Drawing the curtains aside, he looked out. An astounding sight met his eyes. His twenty men had spread themselves across the entrance; were fighting desperately, shoulder to shoulder, against a horde of filthy ruffians, even more fierce-looking than themselves. Fortunately the fight had only just commenced and, except for a few blows and cuts, from which the blood was streaming, none of Yusuf's men had, up to then, been seriously hurt. It was only a matter of time, however, before they would be overwhelmed unless something was done to stop the fight. Aziz Ullah's appearance was the signal for a deafening uproar. A chorus of execrations greeted him, and it seemed as though pandemonium had broken loose. Yusuf's bloodstained face was turned momentarily to him in frantic appeal.

'Go back, Master,' he cried. 'They would murder you.'

For answer Aziz Ullah strode forward, pushed two of his disciples to one side, and stood exposed to the attacks of the rabble. For a few moments his action gave the fierce-looking mob pause. The men in the forefront were visibly discontented. Then, with a roar of triumph, a great, hulking brute of a fellow flung himself forward, knife upraised to strike. Down it flashed, glittering balefully in the brilliant sunlight. Aziz Ullah stood without making the slightest attempt to defend himself. He was counting upon superstition to turn imminent assassination into victory. Everything depended on the jacket of mail he was wearing. If it failed in its purpose, the end was come. He admitted afterwards that it was one of the most nerve-racking moments of his life. The dagger struck him with terrific force just over the heart. But the finely tempered steel withstood the thrust. Aziz Ullah hardly moved. He had braced himself for the shock, not wishing to give his assailants even the satisfaction of seeing him stagger.

A great cry of wonder rose on all sides as it was observed that he remained unharmed. The fellow who had struck dropped the dagger from suddenly nerveless fingers; shrank back, an arm before his face, as though protecting himself from a blow. The twenty disciples stood for a few seconds dumbfounded; then gave vent to shouts of joy and praise; threw themselves on their knees before Aziz Ullah. Yusuf raised one of his feet and placed it upon his head, whereupon great shouts of acclaim rent the air from the very ruffians who, shortly before, had been bent on murder. Aziz Ullah gently bade the faithful twenty rise; thanked them for their gallant efforts to defend him.

'Allah will reward you,' he declared. Then, turning to the ragged crowd of hired assassins, he delivered a vehement speech in which he exhorted them to mend their ways, to forsake evil, and walk in the path of Allah. '"And do not kill whom Allah has forbidden except for a just cause,"' he quoted from the Koran. '"Whoever is slain unjustly We have indeed given to his heir authority." Go in peace!' he concluded in ringing tones.

They slunk away like a lot of bewildered cattle. The miracle they believed they had witnessed had completely flabbergasted them. They would spread the story throughout the bazaars and, although Aziz Ullah was not complacent enough to think everyone would believe a miracle had been worked – Afghanistan was not a country in which mail armour was unknown – he felt himself safe for the time being. At least, untutored minds would be influenced as those of his assailants and his followers had been. He waited until all but Yusuf and his men remained; then, stooping first to pick up the dagger that might have so easily transfixed his heart, walked back to the *shamiana*.

At the entrance stood a group of stupefied ministers of state. The sudden change in tone of the shouts, from execration to wonder and adulation, had brought them rushing from the seats in which they had been sitting so uneasily with undignified haste, in their anxiety to discover the reason for the surprising volte-face of the mob. They had heard the latter part of Aziz Ullah's address, had watched the men who were intended to murder him creep away bemused and shaken, but had been unable to learn how he had accomplished the feat. He had no intention of enlightening them. They stood aside meekly now to let him pass, then followed in to the *shamiana*. This time he took supreme control. Standing on the rostrum, with them grouped below him, and his followers waiting watchfully in the background, he delivered what amounted to an ultimatum. It was artfully wrapped in the flowery language of Persia, liberally flavoured with the proverbs and sayings with which that tongue is adorned, but he knew no doubt would linger in their minds that he was aware they were the instigators of the treacherous attack on him. One or two proved this by uttering protests, but he paid no attention to them. He demanded and received an assurance signed by all that his proposals would be placed not only before government but also before His Majesty the Amir. They were left with the knowledge that failure to comply would result in his rounding up the men who had taken part in the attack and forcing them to disclose every detail of the plot.

Eager declarations were made that not only would their assurances be faithfully carried out, but they would guarantee acceptance of the proposals he had elaborated. Aziz Ullah knew he could safely rely on this. They were probably delighted, after witnessing his extraordinary ability to tame a crowd of assassins, to be spared unfortunate consequences to themselves.

Their treatment of him at his departure was the very opposite to that which they had accorded him on arrival. He refused all their eager offers of hospitality but permitted them to escort him to the government buildings, where he and his men were accommodated with carriages to convey them back to their camp. A whole regiment of cavalry, despite his objections, was hastily ordered from the barracks. Thus he returned in great triumph. Crowds watched him go by, but not this time in comparative silence. On all sides rose deafening cheers, for the news of the supposed miracle of his escape from death had already preceded him. He was not deaf to the note of awe and reverence which could easily be detected in the acclamations. Perhaps Aziz Ullah felt rather a hypocrite as he reflected that hereafter, unless unforeseen events took place to confound him, he would be regarded as a saint by the majority of people in Afghanistan.

Major Kershaw watched the procession go by; smiled with satisfaction as well as a deep sense of relief. He had been gnawed with anxiety. The regiment of cavalry, the carriages, above all the person of Aziz Ullah, safe and sound, now apparently a national hero as well as a champion of the oppressed was complete answer to all his doubts and fears.

The cavalcade arrived at the camp to receive another uproarious welcome. At first the thousand waiting there thought the troops were coming to attack and disperse them, but when the carriages were observed in the midst of the escort and, in them, could be seen The Master and his disciples joy knew no bounds. Of course Yusuf and his men quickly circulated the story of the 'miracle' with the result that awe, very nearly approaching adoration, was added to the pride and admiration of the peasants in their leader.

Gifts of various kinds, from a richly damascened sword to baskets of fruit, arrived for The Master from admirers in Kabul. They came in such abundance that he decided to break camp instead of resting for the remainder of the day, as had been his first intention. The sword only he retained for himself, everything else was distributed among his followers. He has kept the beautiful weapon as a treasured reminder of Kabul, but it takes second place to a very ordinary Afghan dagger, which is badly blunted at its point.

Before the departure could be made, there approached the camp, from the direction of the city, a string of ornately caparisoned camels, the riders of which, with the exception of the first, were finely-built, bearded men who sat their mounts with impressive dignity. Aziz Ullah happened to see them coming; recognised them at once as Afridis. Not a flicker of interest showed in his face, but inwardly he felt a deep sense of satisfaction. Before the strangers were announced to him, he knew the leader must be Abdul Qadir, the Mahsud whose advances he had previously rejected. It was no longer his intention to hold him aloof, however; he had been hoping for his appearance, or that of an emissary, ever since returning to his camp. The time was at hand for which he and Major Kershaw of Indian Intelligence had schemed.

Abdul Qadir Khan sent a message begging humbly to be received. With an appearance of reluctance, Aziz Ullah bade Yusuf bring the Afridi to him. Unlike the men in his train, Abdul Qadir was neither very tall nor broad. Also, except for a slight moustache, he was clean-shaven. He was not unhandsome, though his thin, hooked nose, tightly-drawn lips and rather small, restless eyes gave him a somewhat sinister appearance. A broad forehead, and powerful, finely-moulded jaw, however, suggested keen intellect and strength of character. Like his followers, he was attired in pyjamas and flowing shirt of spotless white, this cleanliness being a rather rare virtue in an Afridi. Their puggarees were also of white material, but his was green, denoting that he had made the pilgrimage to Mecca. Aziz Ullah, whose unkempt appearance compared unfavourably with the smartness of his guest, greeted him courteously. They squatted together on a Persian rug out of earshot of the other men. Yusuf placed a hookah between them.

'It has been my wish, O Holy One, to meet you,' began Abdul Qadir in silky, flattering tones. 'My happiness is now very great and my mind at rest.'

'I do not deserve the title of "Holy One",' Aziz reproved him. 'We will speak as man to man. What want you with me?'

Like all natives of that part of the world, the Afridi took some time to get to the point, but he did not delay it longer than usual. Aziz Ullah's previous refusals to meet him had aggravated him greatly; had made him all the keener to put the proposal he had been nursing for so long before this man who had obtained such power in Afghanistan. The events of that day, of which he was well-informed, had increased his eagerness to the point of a burning fervour. It did not require a great deal of imagination to realise that, had he wished, Aziz Ullah could take command of the country, which was exactly what Abdul Qadir wished him to do. He got over the preliminaries, therefore, as quickly as Oriental procedure permitted. Then commenced an exposition of subtle craftiness that Aziz Ullah afterwards declared was positively classic. The Mahsud flattered but not fulsomely; his praise and admiration was neither overdone nor prolonged. By gradual and admirably reasoned stages he progressed discursively from the benefit the coming of Aziz Ullah had proved to the peasant classes to the wonderful advantage it would be to the whole of Afghanistan were he dictator or had been born to reign as amir. He spoke as though he had no intention whatever of suggesting that the man listening to him should aspire to such greatness. But all the time he was cunningly engaged in attempting to insinuate the ambition in the other's mind, desiring that the temptation should be firmly rooted there, without the fact of his playing the part of tempter becoming apparent. He dwelt regretfully on the happiness and contentment that would be the people's, the greatness and prosperity that would be Afghanistan's had Aziz Ullah been amir instead of the man who was ruling. It was only when he felt, from observation of Aziz Ullah's reactions to his remarks, that the poison he was instilling was beginning to work that he emerged into the open, so to speak, and then only momentarily.

'There is no need,' he declared half-laughingly, 'to speak of that which would be were you amir. It is evident you could ascend the throne at any time, if it was your wish.' He rose to his feet. 'I fear I have wearied you. In my enthusiasm, I have allowed my admiration of you perhaps to outweigh my discretion. You must forgive me.'

Aziz Ullah had let it appear that, from merely polite interest and grateful acknowledgment of the compliments, his imagination, and later his ambition, had been stirred by the other's words. He rose now, giving the impression of a man deep in thoughts of a nature that were attractive to him. His eyes sparkled; there was a half smile on his lips. He walked with his guest to the place where the camels were tethered. Neither of them spoke on the way but, ever and anon, Abdul Qadir stole a look at his companion, and was well satisfied. Visions of the splendid Afghan army fighting side by side against the hated English began to assume a reality. He pictured Peshawar, Nowshera, Kohat, Campbellpur, Attock, even Rawalpindi razed to the ground, in flames; saw a beaten British army falling back before his victorious forces, leaving the Punjab in his power. Mentally he shook hands with himself. He had been very clever. Aziz Ullah would rise to the bait, and he (Abdul Qadir) would prove to the old men of the Afridi villages, who had shaken their heads and named him mad, that the days of petty warfare on the frontier were indeed over, that he, Abdul Qadir Khan, had risen to destroy utterly and for ever all English claims to the territory that belonged to the Afridis, to the Pathan, perhaps even that of the Punjabis.

As the Mahsud chieftain was about to mount his obediently kneeling camel, Aziz Ullah uttered the words which completed the plotter's joy and proved conclusively that the intended cat's paw was not above ambition or beyond temptation.

'Your words have given me much thought,' he admitted. 'The welfare of this country is dear to me, and I would shoulder any responsibility, however great, in order to raise the people to prosperity. We will speak again, O Khan.'

Abdul Qadir tried not to appear too eager, but could not repress the gleam in his eyes.

'It will give me much happiness,' he returned almost casually. 'Where and when shall our meeting take place? I am wholly at your disposal.'

Aziz Ullah's eyes became fixed on the ground apparently in deep reflection. At last he looked up.

'Go alone to the village of Gharat in two days at the hour of noon,' he bade Abdul Qadir. 'It is not far from my retreat. Say nothing of your intentions to any man. It would be unwise. Yusuf,' he indicated that faithful shadow, standing a few yards behind him, 'will conduct you to me. *Salaam alaikum*. The peace of Allah go with you.'

Abdul Qadir, triumphant, though showing little of it in his attitude, responded suitably, and mounted his camel. The ungainly animal rose and presently the Mahsud and his followers were heading once more for Kabul. Aziz Ullah stood for some time watching them, and there was a smile on his face. In fact, there was something so happy and mischievous about it that it would be more aptly described as a broad grin.

Towards evening on the following day, Aziz Ullah climbed down from his secluded retreat in the mountains and reached the pass a couple of hundred feet below. He was not accompanied, having indicated to his disciples that he wished to be alone. There was nothing unusual about such a desire; he had often before wandered by himself about the mountains, which he was understood to love. Nobody but he and Major Kershaw knew that these excursions invariably led him to a cave high up and well hidden, though easily accessible. It was their rendezvous; a place utterly safe, because it possessed a bad reputation. Known as the cave of the witch, it was believed to be inhabited by a wicked old woman many hundreds of years old, who held intercourse with satan and other evil spirits. No Afghans of that district would approach anywhere near. It was Kershaw who had first thought of it as an ideal spot in which he and Aziz Ullah could meet. Ginger's knowledge of eastern Afghanistan and the North West Frontier of India was probably unique. He also possessed an amazing acquaintance with all the local folklore and superstitions.

It took Aziz Ullah the best part of an hour to reach the cave from his retreat. It was a gloomy place, running an incredible distance into the mountain – neither Kershaw nor Aziz Ullah had discovered how far it penetrated; it hardly invited exploration. The entrance, a little over eight feet high by perhaps six feet wide, was hidden by a large withered tree that looked as though it had come under the witch's spell. Inside, the cave broadened out and was quite roomy, narrowing again farther back.

The Master found Kershaw sitting near the entrance, leaning against a rock, hands clasped round his knees, placidly smoking a pipe. He sprang up with an exclamation of delight, and the two men warmly shook hands. Aziz Ullah sniffed.

'By Jove!' he exclaimed in English, referring to the tobacco, 'that smells good.'

For answer the Intelligence officer took another pipe already filled from his pocket; handed it to his companion who accepted it eagerly. A few seconds later the two were squatting together, smoking with great contentment. Yusuf and his men would probably have had the shock of their lives had they been able to set eyes on their revered leader at that moment. The spectacle of a bearded Afghan smoking a pipe is strange enough in itself. When the Afghan happened to be Aziz Ullah, whom most people in that district now regarded as a saint sent specially for their benefit, the sight would be well nigh devastating. Fortunately for their peace of mind, none of Aziz Ullah's followers were able to see him.

'This is great,' he murmured. 'You're a lifesaver, Bob, which reminds me' – he turned to the other impulsively – 'I owe you my life. If you hadn't thought of that mail jacket, the vultures would have picked my bones clean by now.'

'Heard there'd be an attempt to assassinate you,' nodded Kershaw. 'Rashid went ferreting about and was told excitedly of a miracle. Your stock has soared to the sky, my boy. Tell me about it.'

Aziz Ullah obliged; then plunged into a full account of the proceedings in the *shamiana*. He may surely be pardoned if he displayed a little pride and triumph when speaking of his great success.

'They realised,' he concluded, 'that it would be more to their personal advantage to recommend my proposals than reject them. Anyway, after what happened, and my threat, I don't think they dare break their promise to put them before government and the amir.'

'I can satisfy your mind on that point,' Kershaw told him. 'I made judicious inquiries this morning by making use of the resources of the legation. A memorandum has already been placed before the amir for his approval and government met today to discuss the recommendations – recommendations, mark you! You've done a wonderful job of work for Afghanistan, old son. It must never be known that Aziz Ullah is anybody but – Aziz Ullah. How are you going to manage that?'

'Like an old soldier,' laughed the other, 'I'll simply fade away. I should hate to rob them of their illusions.'

Kershaw nodded.

'It's the only way,' he agreed. 'It won't do any harm if they continue always to think you're a saint sent specially to succour the oppressed, and disappeared in proper saintly manner when your work was accomplished. Shouldn't be surprised if that's how most saints won the label. I wish we could make those blighters suffer who engineered the plot to murder you. Bloody swine!'

Aziz Ullah knocked out the ashes from his pipe, and asked for a refill. Kershaw handed him a bulging pouch. Quickly Aziz stuffed the bowl full, lit the tobacco carefully and, when it was burning evenly, puffed away with deep contentment again. Presently he smiled quizzically at his companion.

'Bob,' he remarked, 'your patience is monumental. You are burning to yell, "What of Abdul Qadir?" Yet not a murmur concerning our *pièce de résistance* has left your lips. Amazing!'

Kershaw grinned.

'I knew you'd out with it when you thought fit,' he returned. 'The ubiquitous Rashid found him, and kept watch on him and his boy friends. He told me they had gone to visit your camp. Well, since you have brought up the subject, what's the news?'

'The very best.' He entered into a detailed account of his conversation with Abdul Qadir Khan, concluding with the arrangements made to continue the discussion on the following day. 'Talk about craftiness,' he declared. 'Abdul Qadir has the cunning of all the monkeys, serpents, and devils that were ever conceived – that is, if a devil is conceived. We'd never have nailed him any other way, but this. Lord! What a brain the chief has!'

'We haven't nailed him yet,' commented Kershaw, but he was tremendously elated, and made no effort to hide his glee. 'The chief's brain,' he went on with frank admiration, 'may have worked out the whole scheme, but what a marvellous job you've done. I take off my hat and boots and any darned thing you care to mention to you.'

'Don't!' begged Aziz Ullah. 'You'll make me blush.'

'Blush away. It'd be a pretty sight. I've never seen a blush on a brown skin before. But seriously, you gave me fits yesterday. If you'd gone and got yourself killed—Hell! I don't want to think about it. What's the scheme for tomorrow?'

'Is Rashid with the ponies in the usual place below?' asked Aziz.

Kershaw nodded. 'He has the pack mule with him.'

'Good. Well, listen! I'll bring Abdul Qadir here on the pretence that it is not safe to talk anywhere else. If he knows of the evil reputation of this cave and won't come up, things will be a trifle difficult. But keep your eyes skinned, Bob. Before you and Rashid do your stuff, I must fool him into telling me where he has all those machine guns and ammunition stored, and I want you to listen in, for you know his country and I don't. I should hate any mistake to arise through my not getting hold of names or directions properly. Taking it for granted I get him to come up here, you and Rashid will be concealed in the cave, and I hope you miss nothing that is said. What signal shall I give when I think it is time for you to act?'

'I think the best thing you can do is to stroll away with him. That will be signal enough.'

'Stroll away with him!' exclaimed Aziz Ullah. 'But—'

'I've been thinking things over,' interrupted Kershaw. 'On no account must he think you're concerned in any way, otherwise he'll take steps afterwards to damn you in Afghanistan. We don't want your pearly white reputation to be soiled, for the sake of the poor beggars who believe in you. It wouldn't be fair. Just walk away with Abdul Qadir and leave it to Rashid and me. We'll appear when he can't possibly suspect that you took him to the cave for any ulterior reason; I know several ways down from here; Rashid and I will circle round, and get ahead of you. Don't worry! He won't see or hear anything suspicious. And don't forget! Directly we appear on the scene like a couple of villains in a Lyceum melodrama, beat it like hell, shouting that you're off to fetch Yusuf and Co. I'll take care afterwards he thinks you and your men are searching for him. Believe me, there won't be a chota suspicion, even in Abdul Qadir's astute mind concerning Aziz Ullah, when I've done with him.'

They sat perfecting their plans for half an hour or so longer; then Aziz Ullah knocked out the ashes of his pipe, and reluctantly gave it back to Kershaw. The two friends shook hands, and parted, descending to the pass by separate ways.

As arranged Yusuf met Abdul Qadir in Gharat at noon on the following day. The Mahsud was conducted towards the retreat in the mountains. He was entirely alone, having fully understood, or so he thought, the reason for Aziz Ullah's warning. He knew quite well that the hiding place was known only to the twenty disciples apart, of course, from Aziz Ullah himself. No doubt he was greatly flattered that so much trust should be placed in him that he was to be taken actually to The Master's home, the whereabouts of which had always been kept a closely-guarded secret. He proved to be wrong in his expectations. He was not conducted to the place after all. Aziz Ullah met him in the pass. Telling Yusuf to join the others and informing him that he would probably bring the Khan up to the little plateau later on for a meal, he led his guest on up the pass.

'It is well that we should be alone,' he explained to Abdul Qadir. 'My followers are entirely trustworthy, but the matters of which we speak should not be heard by other ears than our own.'

He did not think it necessary to mention that he could quite easily have ensured secrecy on the plateau. His present manner of leading Abdul Qadir into the trap prepared for him was least calculated to rouse suspicion in the Afridi's mind. Once the latter had been in the retreat and had noted how easy it was to avoid eavesdroppers there, he would have been bound to wonder why it was considered necessary to take him elsewhere. Abdul Qadir Khan smiled to himself. His words had obviously taken root. Aziz Ullah was no different from other men where ambition was concerned. The Mahsud was riding a hill pony and, out of courtesy to The Master who, of course, was on foot, dismounted. Aziz Ullah told him he was acquainted with a cave where they would be quite secure from interruption. Casually he asked if his companion knew the mountains well; was greatly relieved when Abdul Qadir confessed entire ignorance of that district. They came at last to one of the paths leading to the cave of the witch. The pony was tethered in a clearing, and the two climbed to the ledge where Kershaw and Aziz Ullah had sat the day before. Abdul Qadir shivered a little. He was as superstitious, despite his European training, as most of his race, and the gloomy neighbourhood depressed him.

'Truly this is a lonely and dismal place,' he observed, as he accepted his companion's invitation to sit down. 'It is certain we shall remain undisturbed here. It is in my mind that men would avoid it as a place of the devil.'

Aziz Ullah laughed softly.

'True believers who walk in the ways of Allah need fear no evil,' he reminded the Afridi.

Abdul Qadir eyed him curiously.

'You speak Pashto with an unusual accent, O Master,' he remarked. 'You come not from this part of the country?'

'I was born at Herat,' explained Aziz Ullah, 'and have been, since a child, in the holy city of Meshed. Persian has thus become more my tongue than Pashto.'

For some time they spoke of Persia; of anything, in fact, but the subject upon which Abdul Qadir's mind was centred and which, he believed, was uppermost also in the mind of The Master. To come directly to the point is rarely done in the Orient. Gradually, however, the eager Afridi brought the conversation to the reason for the meeting. Even then they conversed more or less in parables, each knowing perfectly well the hidden meaning contained in the other's words. The longer this went on, the greater became Abdul Qadir's elation. He was certain now that the man squatting by his side yearned to control Afghanistan, would never be satisfied until he was created amir. Whether the reason behind this was a belief that he could do great things for the people or merely personal ambition did not concern the Mahsud. The latter's only interest in helping him ascend the throne was in obtaining him as an ally to fight later against the English. At last, after they had been sitting in that lonely spot for nearly an hour, Abdul Qadir Khan threw aside all subtlety. Suddenly he launched into an enthusiastic discourse, its main theme being Aziz Ullah as amir. He told his intended cat's paw that the time was ripe for him to take possession of the country.

'The people will rally round you with great eagerness,' he declared. 'From your retreat in these mountains, you must issue a proclamation that it has been revealed to you by Divine interposition, that you must rule. I have no doubt,' he added craftily, 'that this is the truth, for the thought would not have entered your mind had it not been put there by Allah. Wait but until I can bring twenty thousand well-armed Afridis across the border ready to back you or fight for you. In three weeks I can rally fighting men of the Yusufzai, Mohmand, Orakzai, Mahsud, Bettani and others into a powerful force. The Shinwaris on this side of the border will join at once, and before long the whole Pathan race will be behind you. The Afghan army will quickly follow the example. I have talked with many of the soldiers, and know they are much impressed by you. The first and most important matter will be to imprison without warning the present amir in his palace at Paghman and to arrest all the members of government as they sit in session. I will undertake all military plans. It will be best for you to remain in the mountains until this is done. Then will come your proclamation. I am wholeheartedly your ally, O Master. Speak that I may know you are agreeable to this, and our compact can be made.'

It was not Aziz Ullah's intention to appear too eager, for fear of rousing suspicion. He showed himself reluctant, therefore, raising many objections. Abdul Qadir had replies for them all and, by slow degrees, the other allowed him to think he was being won over. It was when he was apparently on the point of agreeing that he looked Abdul Qadir full in the face.

'Why,' he asked, 'are you, a Pathan from the land of the Mahsuds, so eager that I should take this step? What advantage would it be to you or your race were I to become king?'

A slow smile spread across Abdul Qadir's crafty face.

'That,' he declared, 'is the question of one of much wisdom. I make no pretence that there would be no advantages; there would be many. You see, I am frank with you. The reigning amir is a timid, cautious man whose intentions are good, but as king he is useless to his people. He is inimical to the great Pathan race that lives beyond the borders of his country, and languishes under the laws of the English. Rather than help us, he would help those hated unbelievers against us. You, O Master, have proved your love for the people. You have shown yourself, in a short while, to possess a great power. With that power you can work wonders. You would not be inimical to the Pathans, for are they not of the same blood as those for whom you are already accomplishing so much? I could speak for many hours about the advantages that would come to us either directly or indirectly, were you King of Afghanistan, but it is not necessary. There is one ambition dear to my heart, however, and you, when amir, could help me accomplish it.'

He paused and Aziz Ullah looked at him questioningly.

'Speak!' commanded The Master when his companion showed no signs of continuing of his own accord.

'Do you know much of the English?' asked Abdul Qadir, and there was a depth of hatred in his voice that even surprised Aziz.

'I know little indeed of them,' he replied.

Thereupon the Mahsud plunged into a condemnation of the British people that was little short of vitriolic. He spoke of wrongs done to tribes of the frontier, of outrages, insults, indignities that, had they been true, would have called for the vengeance of heaven upon the perpetrators. Vastly amused inwardly, Aziz Ullah wore a look of utter indignation on his face as the tale of wrongs, suffered over a long period of years, went on. At last he cried out in a voice of horror, as though he could no longer bear to hear the recital. Delighted at this manifestation of the other's newly-born belief in the wickedness of the English, Abdul Qadir then went on to tell of his ambition to unite all Pathans under one leader – he made no secret of the fact that the leader was to be himself – and to drive the hated white people from the country that was not theirs. He told frankly of the manner in which he was organising the tribes into a properly disciplined fighting machine.

'It will be many moons before they are ready to advance as a united whole to battle,' he admitted. 'I have much prejudice to overcome, much persuasive force to use, and I am working practically alone. The young men are with me, but are hotheaded and slow in becoming disciplined. It is a weary task selecting, from among them, those fit to be officers. The elders are obstinate, and are difficult to influence. But I will win,' his eyes shone with fanatical fervour, 'and then I will throw my army against the English. In the meantime, it will do much to hasten matters and consolidate opinion in my favour if I take steps to put you on the throne of Afghanistan. I can, as I have said, bring to your help twenty thousand fighting men now. If, O Master, I can assure my people that, in return for that service, you will ally yourself with me, when you are amir and, as soon as I am ready to strike, aid me against the enemy with the Afghan army, I shall have the support of all. The great day of vengeance will be brought very near.'

He ceased speaking; glanced from the corners of his eyes at the thoughtful face of Aziz Ullah. Anxiously he awaited the words that would mean elation or keen disappointment for him.

'You have been frank,' murmured Aziz at last, 'and I will be frank with you in return. I like not the idea of plunging the country into a war with the powerful white people, but Allah is always with the oppressed and, perhaps, as the servant and instrument of the Beneficent and Merciful, I am destined to help accomplish that which you have shown me is the great need of a grievously suffering people. I am inclined to make the compact you ask, O Khan, but you must give me time to think. I will tell you this now, that I truly believe my answer will be favourable to you. There is only one question that is causing me some doubt.'

'Ask it!' begged the highly-satisfied Mahsud.

'I have heard these English have many strange and terrifying machines of warfare. Afghanistan is also now, doubtless, well advanced in this manner. But what of the army you are endeavouring to train? What would be the use of one or two or even three hundred thousand men fighting with weapons which are of the past, or rudely constructed against a great army equipped with these terrifying modern instruments of battle?'

'Truly your wisdom is indeed great,' returned Abdul Qadir in admiring tones. 'I will let you into a secret that will resolve all your doubts.'

He then proceeded to tell Aziz Ullah of the manner in which, over a long period, he had been smuggling materials of war into the Afridi country. These included machine guns, rifles of the latest pattern, field guns that had arrived in parts and been assembled, and masses of hand grenades and ammunition. His hearers – Kershaw and the Havildar Rashid were, of course, listening close by – could not help feeling an admiration for the cleverness of the man. Kershaw had known of this smuggling of munitions but, despite his resources, had been up to then unable to fathom how it was done. Aziz Ullah let it appear that this disclosure had practically decided him to agree to the pact proposed. However, he took care to sound a trifle doubtful of the actual existence of such quantities of warlike stores. Thus with a craftiness matching Abdul Qadir's he succeeded in obtaining from the latter the information that the whole stock was hidden in one place. The Mahsud did not trust the tribes sufficiently to equip them fully, until they had completely fallen into line with his plans.

'It is safely concealed in a series of caves difficult of approach,' he told Aziz, 'known only to me and men of my own village, whom I can trust. I alone have a map of the district indicating the caves and the manner of reaching them, and I always carry it with me. It is here.'

He tapped his breast as he spoke, to imply that the precious document reposed in a pocket inside his clothing. Kershaw, hearing all this, felt a desire to give vent to a cry of triumph. He had not anticipated being supplied with a plan depicting the position of this ammunition depot of which, for so long, he had tried to find the whereabouts.

'It is well,' nodded Aziz Ullah. 'I can no longer doubt that you are a man of great resource and possess abundantly the qualities of leadership. I will spend the night in meditation on the proposition you have laid before me. Now we will go to my retreat and partake of refreshments. Will you remain in the mountains as my guest until the morning?'

Abdul Qadir accepted eagerly.

'It will be a great honour,' he assured Aziz Ullah.

'What of your men? Do they know where you are?'

'I have sent them – all but one who is my brother, and awaits my return in Gharat – back to my country. He only knows of my mission.'

'Will your brother grow anxious if you return not tonight?'

Abdul Qadir smiled, and shook his head.

'I told him I might not return until the morrow.'

'It is well. Come! You must be in need of food.'

They rose, and commenced the descent to the pass. Neither spoke again of the subject that had brought them together. On the way down, Aziz Ullah listened somewhat apprehensively for sounds indicative of the movements of Major Kershaw and Mahommed Rashid. But, except for the occasional note of a bird, the flutter of wings, or the rustling made by an animal, all was silent as the tomb. They came at length to the clearing in which Abdul Qadir's pony patiently stood awaiting the return of his master. The Mahsud bent to untie the animal. It was then that Aziz Ullah caught sight of Kershaw and Rashid hurrying towards them. He waited until they were close by, then:

'Look!' he cried in pretended alarm, clutching his companion's arm in a convulsive grip. 'Who are these?'

Abdul Qadir straightened and swung round. A full-blooded oath, which is certainly not in the Koran, broke from his lips but, before he could raise a finger to defend himself, Kershaw had sprung forward, knocked off his turban, and brought the butt of a heavy revolver down with sickening force on his head. Abdul Qadir crashed to the ground without a sound, and lay still.

'What the—?' began Aziz Ullah in surprise.

The red-haired Intelligence officer grinned at him.

'Altered our plans a little,' he confided. 'It occurred to me that the spectacle of you taking to your heels to bring your men to the aid of this bird, might not appear as convincing as we thought. After all, you look as though you could eat both Rashid and me at one gulp. I'm sure this is much the better way. Except for a headache, Abdul Qadir won't be any the worse, when he comes round. Besides, you know how fantastic these beggars are – he might have forced me to shoot him. He'll recover to learn that Rashid administered the same medicine to you as I did to him; you'll both be trussed up, and you personally will be of the opinion that he has betrayed you, or been careless, or something. How's that?'

'Excellent. And what becomes of Aziz Ullah? Is he to be taken along with you as an additional prisoner.'

'Not on your life. I leave you tied to a tree in the hope that we can get safely away before you are discovered and spread the alarm. I also apologise for the inconvenience, pretend I don't know Aziz Ullah from Adam, and explain that the trouble that has befallen you is entirely due to your own fault in being associated with a man so badly wanted by the Indian government.'

Aziz laughed.

'You've certainly worked everything out very neatly,' he admitted. 'Who unties me from the tree?'

'Nobody. You walk away when Abdul Qadir's packed up and we're out of sight. We'll only pretend to tie you. By the way, that brother's a nuisance. We can't leave him in Gharat.'

Rashid had been listening to the conversation with a slight smile on his stern face. Now he broke in in his laboured English.

'Me know him, sahib. Not worry – I get.'

'Good for you, Rashid,' approved Kershaw. 'Now let us truss this beauty up. Oh, boy,' he exulted to Aziz Ullah, 'what a jolly old triumph! The way you got him to talk about that armament dump of his was priceless, and to think he was obliging enough to bring along a map.'

'Yes; that certainly was rather an unexpected piece of luck,' agreed Aziz. 'You'd better take possession of it before he wakes up.'

The luckless Abdul Qadir Khan was carefully searched. Not only was the plan of which he had spoken on him, but various other interesting documents, among which, after a hasty glance through them, Kershaw brought to light a draft treaty which the Mahsud hoped would be approved by Aziz Ullah, and detailed notes concerning the tribesmen under training as a result of his ambitious scheme. There was also a complete list of the arms and ammunition stored ready for the day when he confidently expected to commence driving the British from the Frontier.

The red-haired major was exuberant. Aziz Ullah seemed no less elated. They certainly had achieved a great triumph. All that remained was to accomplish safely the difficult task of conveying the captive through the lawless country between the frontier of Afghanistan and Peshawar. Under the critical eye of the Englishman, Rashid bound Abdul Qadir hand and foot. They debated whether to slip a gag into his mouth also, but decided that could be left till later. Aziz Ullah was also tied, but his thongs were left so loose that he could have shaken them off whenever he wished. Still he gave the appearance of being effectually trussed. Water from a nearby stream was brought in a pannikin and thrown on the Mahsud's face. At first, this had no effect, but eventually he stirred uneasily; then opened his eyes with a groan. As his opened, those of Aziz Ullah, who was lying close by, shut. The result was that, when memory returned and Abdul Qadir realised that he had been attacked, the first sight he saw was The Master stretched out in the vicinity, apparently unconscious and bound with ropes. At the same time he grew aware of his own trussed condition. Then his eyes became fixed on the slim Englishman standing looking down at him. Immediately his face became convulsed with rage and hate; a string of profanities poured from between his lips. Kershaw listened and smiled, made no attempt to interrupt. Eventually Abdul Qadir Khan obtained sufficient control of himself to demand an explanation of the attack, the reason why he and his companion were bound with rope, and the identity of his captor.

'Do you not know me?' returned Kershaw. 'Well, learn, O man of trouble, that for many moons have I been on your track. Now, at last, I have you. You will be conveyed to Peshawar and will have to answer the charge of planning war and outrage against the Indian government. Your activities are well known and I now have these' – he waved before the other's appalled eyes the documents that had been taken from his pockets – 'to condemn you. My task is complete; your dreams of greatness will now have to be replaced by the certainty of years of exile in the Andamans or some other secure retreat where you can do no harm.'

The previous outburst from the Mahsud was nothing compared with the frenzied utterances that were now flung at the white man. He appeared to have gone mad, his eyes burning feverishly, foam collecting at the corners of his lips. At last he stopped, it seemed from sheer exhaustion. After a pause, during which he made great efforts to regain command of himself, he went on more calmly:

'You fool, do you believe you can carry me out of Afghanistan, through my own country to the land groaning under the iron heel of your vicious race? Do you know who he is who lies there?'

He nodded towards the body of Aziz Ullah.

'One of the Afghans you are endeavouring to fool into joining you, I suppose,' replied Kershaw. 'I know you hope to obtain allies from this country.'

Abdul Qadir scowled angrily, but did not comment on his captor's knowledge.

'He is the man they call The Master,' he declared. 'The whole of East Afghanistan is at his feet. The rest will quickly follow. He is worshipped as a saint. You will be torn to pieces, when it is known you have laid impious hands upon him.'

'It is not in my mind to take him with me,' Kershaw replied, 'but you, of a certainty, will come, O Abdul Qadir. Talk is useless. Quickly you will realise how I propose to convey you to Peshawar.'

At this moment, Aziz Ullah chose to recover from his supposed unconsciousness. At first he was apparently confused but, after a few minutes spent in frowning meditation, demanded from Kershaw an explanation of the assault and the position in which he found himself.

'I regret,' replied the Intelligence officer, 'that my man was forced to treat you as I treated Abdul Qadir Khan, but if you will keep bad companions you must expect to suffer. It is possible that I have thus saved you from a great folly, death, even worse. This man is a source of unrest, of sedition, treachery. He plans murder, massacre, wickedness beyond description, because in him are ambitions sown there by the devil. But enough. We must depart. I am sorry we will have to leave you bound to a tree in this place. I cannot risk my undertaking being ruined. Tomorrow perhaps you will be released. In any case, my servant will contrive to leave information regarding your whereabouts once we have crossed the border.'

Aziz Ullah turned his eyes on Abdul Qadir Khan and, in them, was the deepest reproach as well as a tinge of suspicion. At once the Mahsud broke out into explanations, protests, apologies, but received not a word in reply. Aziz Ullah thereafter maintained an offended, albeit dignified, silence. He was raised to his feet by Kershaw and Rashid, and apparently lashed to a tree. During this process a rendezvous was appointed and full directions given him in a whisper by the Intelligence officer. It was arranged that they should meet in ten days at a spot on the bank of the Kabul River near Dakka. Abdul Qadir's pony was to be left for him.

When the pretended fastening of Aziz Ullah to a tree was accomplished, Rashid disappeared. He was away for a quarter of an hour; then returned, leading his and Kershaw's ponies and the pack mule. During his absence, Abdul Qadir had given vent to another fiery outburst. He now saw all his aspirations, all his ambitions, everything, toppling down like a house of cards. It must have been an intensely bitter experience for him. His one remaining hope, that the Englishman would never succeed in getting him through to Peshawar, was more or less destroyed when he realised the manner in which it was to be undertaken. A roll of material was removed from the mule and unwound. A gag was first thrust into his mouth, and firmly fixed beyond all possibility of slipping. That done, he was wrapped in the cloth in such a manner that it presented the appearance merely of a bale of merchandise. He was then bound securely to the mule.

'Frightfully uncomfortable, I am afraid,' commented Kershaw in English, 'but you'll be able to breathe all right. We'll release you for exercise and food at night. It will be some days before we reach our destination, as we'll have to go slowly.' The preparations completed, he strolled across to Aziz Ullah's tree. 'All right, old chap,' he whispered. 'You can't be seen now.'

Aziz Ullah shook himself free of his ropes, which were gathered up by the careful Rashid.

'Poor old Abdul Qadir,' murmured the man who was known

as The Master; 'he's in for a sticky time. I suppose he's clinging to the slender hope that I'll be freed in time to rescue him. Well, good luck, Kershaw. We meet in ten days.'

They shook hands warmly; then the Intelligence officer and the havildar set off for the pass, the latter leading the pack mule. Aziz Ullah watched them until they disappeared from view, after which he set about searching for a spot where Abdul Qadir's pony could find food and water. Rashid had left him rope of sufficient length in order that the animal's movements should not be unnecessarily curtailed. A suitable place, that was also well secluded, was not easy to find, but eventually he came upon an ideal situation. An hour later he arrived back on the little plateau where the faithful twenty awaited him. He informed Yusuf that his visitor had departed, as he was in haste to return to Kabul. That evening he called his disciples to him.

'The work for which I came,' he informed them, 'is about to be accomplished. I must go from you for a time. Perhaps again I will come. I wish you all to return to your village now. May Allah the Beneficent, the Merciful, pour on you and your people all His blessings.'

There was utter consternation at this announcement. They cried out in protest; threw themselves on their knees before him, and begged him to let them stay with him. Aziz Ullah experienced perhaps the most difficult half hour of his life, before his commands at last prevailed. Then he presented each with a sum of money that, considering their frugal method of existence, would probably mean affluence to them for a very long time. Gathering their meagre belongings together, and imploring him to return to them soon, they departed. It was a very sad little band that left the retreat and turned its steps homeward. He himself felt a pang of regret at parting from them. They had shown themselves such grand fellows. At the same time, he reflected, they would have proved very much the opposite, had they discovered he was an entirely different person from the man they supposed him to be.

He gave them half an hour in which to get well away; then, feeling assured none of them would be returning, climbed to a secret hiding place in a tiny cave, high up above the little plateau. From there he took a bundle, returned to his own sleeping quarters and, with the help of a small mirror and an electric torch, set to work to make certain alterations in his appearance. That done, he changed his clothing, piling those he removed into a compact package. A last look round, and he descended cautiously from the plateau, stopping every now and again to ascertain whether there was any sign of another human being in the vicinity. The chances were against this in such a lonely spot, but he did not intend to take any risks. At length he reached the pass, and set off for the place where the pony had been left.

It is certain nobody would have recognised in the individual, laboriously walking along that narrow track among those vast mountains, the man who had become such a familiar figure to thousands. His hair and beard were grey, there were lines of age on his face into which the grime had deeply sunk, his eyelids hung heavily over his eyes, as though weariness prevented him from raising them. He was very bent, his stature thus being considerably reduced; he walked somewhat shakily, suggesting that his legs were weak. His puggaree was badly wound and untidy, his clothing dirty and rather ragged. Altogether, there was nothing indicative of the young, powerful, and dignified Aziz Ullah about him. The bundle he carried seemed to be almost beyond his strength.

It took him a considerable time to reach the pony, which he found patiently standing without movement except for an occasional swish at hordes of flies with his tail. By the light of a brilliant moon, he studied the animal. It was a shaggy creature of a dull grey colour, but far too well groomed to pass without comment as the possession of a homeless wanderer. He set to work at once and, with the help of dirt and water, transformed it before long into a concomitant of his own disreputable self. It shivered during the process, for it was chilly at night in those altitudes, and the mud which he liberally spread on its body and hair was cold and clammy. Satisfied at length that he and the pony were in harmony with each other, he tied on the bundle with the rope that had tethered the animal, mounted, and set off. It was a somewhat perilous undertaking, even though the moonlight was so glorious, to descend a pass by night that, at times, was little better than a track meandering along the sheer edges of a precipice. However, it was accomplished without accident and, in the early hours of the morning, he reached the security of the lower levels. He continued to travel until daylight, skirting one or two villages en route; then rested for a few hours by the side of a stream which he knew eventually ran into the Kabul River. Thought of the river made his rendezvous with Kershaw seem very near, but he had a hundred and eighty miles to travel over difficult ground, with the necessity of avoiding the usual routes, and he knew ten days were by no means overgenerous for such a journey on a pony.

Day by day went by. Country people, with the generosity of their race, supplied him with food, either for nothing or on payment of a few pice. He told a tale in which he figured as a farmer of a small holding north of Lataband. Having fallen into debt, he had been ruthlessly evicted and, with the pony, all that remained to him of his possessions, was on his way to seek shelter with a brother who lived near Dakka. People of the type with whom he took care to come into contact were mostly those who had suffered or were likely to suffer, in the same way. Their pity for the 'poor old man' was consequently very great and he was the recipient of many favours, as he travelled on. Several times he found himself in touch with caravans, but was careful to avoid those going his way. He was confident enough of his disguise, but did not feel inclined to risk sustained scrutiny when the necessity of touching it up meant that it might appear slightly different from one day to another.

He had traversed the same route, or rather in the vicinity of it, several years before, but under vastly different circumstances. Still he found his knowledge useful. At first, he was greatly interested in the wild scenery as he rode up and away from the direction of Kabul, then down again towards Jalalabad. But, having laboriously skirted that city, and while riding on towards Dakka, he began to find the journey monotonous. He had lived in the wilds of Afghanistan too long to feel any continued pleasure in the country round him. Most of the way now he was climbing, with the rare comfort of descents. He found most interest in the historic associations conjured up on the route, particularly when passing through the Jagdalak Pass where a British force was destroyed in 1842. At length he came within sight of Dakka, and turned off to the spot on the Kabul River selected as a rendezvous. He arrived on the evening before the day appointed, and was not surprised to find he was there before Kershaw. This caused him no misgivings. The Intelligence officer and Mahommed Rashid would, of necessity, have to travel slower than he, on account of Abdul Qadir Khan. There was also the possibility that they had with them the man whom the Mahsud had said was his brother. Nevertheless, he was relieved when, at noon on the next day, they appeared. He chuckled softly to himself as he became aware they had two well-loaded pack mules with them instead of one. The animals were relieved of their burdens which were laid down carefully on the ground some distance from the shady nook Kershaw selected for himself.

Aziz was a little puzzled when no effort was made to communicate with him. In fact, they appeared to take no notice of him at all. Wondering if Kershaw was being watched, and was taking precautions lest his joining an old man, who appeared more of a beggar than anything else, might give rise to comment and suspicion, he remained where he was, and gave no signal. At the same time, he was a trifle surprised. The place selected was very secluded and lonely, actually on the dry bed of the river and well hidden by a bluff. He had had a good deal of difficulty in finding it, despite Kershaw's careful and excellent directions.

The day wore on towards nightfall, and Aziz noticed that

Rashid disappeared several times, was away once for a long period. At length it dawned on him that the havildar was on the lookout for him, that he had not been recognised. He had not told Kershaw of the manner in which he would disguise himself and, as the pony was hidden from them, they had probably not connected the old fellow, fifty or sixty yards away, with him. He chuckled softly to himself and, rising, walked in the bent and shaky fashion he had adopted across to Kershaw. As he approached, he noticed that the latter appeared worried, and decided that he had guessed rightly. However, in case there was any other reason why the Intelligence officer had not communicated with him, he continued to sustain his role. Speaking in the usual whine of a beggar, he asked for food. Kershaw called over Rashid; ordered the havildar to supply the old man's wants.

'What do you here, old man?' he asked in Pashto.

'I have no home, master. My farm was taken from me, my wife is dead, my children are scattered. I go to join my brother. It is Allah's will.' He bent forward until he was very close to the other. 'What game do you think you're playing, you son of a gun?' he whispered in English.

'Good God!' Kershaw shot to his feet as though a scorpion had attacked him. Then he laughed. 'You!' he exclaimed. 'Damn it all! We've been wondering what was keeping you, and getting more anxious every hour. It never occurred to either of us that the old chap sitting over yonder was you. By Jove! What a disguise! I'd never have recognised you. But why in heaven's name, didn't you come across before?' Aziz Ullah explained, and Kershaw laughed again. 'Well, thank God you are here. Perhaps you'd better keep up the character, just in case, although we're safe enough at present.'

'I intend to,' replied the other; 'at least, until it's dark, when I'd better be transformed into a second bearer.'

Rashid came up with some food; was no less astonished than Kershaw had been when he discovered who the old man was. His stern face relaxed into a broad smile, and he made no secret of his relief that Aziz Ullah was safe.

'It was in our minds, sahib,' he declared in Punjabi, 'that harm had befallen you.'

'I have not even been in peril,' replied Aziz in the same language and in a tone that suggested regret. 'My journey has been monotonous and uneventful.' He described how he had parted from his faithful followers and the sorrow they had shown, when he told them he was going away. 'The real Aziz Ullah in Meshed,' he observed, 'will have a shock, if it ever reaches his ears that he has been in Afghanistan and championed the oppressed.'

Kershaw chuckled.

'He will probably believe he made the journey in a state of religious ecstasy. Is he not an imam?'

Aziz nodded. Rashid cast a reproachful glance at the Intelligence officer.

'It is not well to speak lightly of holy men, sahib,' he protested.

Kershaw actually blushed, and bit his lip. He realised he had blundered, and apologised earnestly.

'I intended no offence, Rashid,' he declared. 'It was thoughtless of me. As you know, few Christians have greater respect for the Muslim faith than I.'

Rashid smiled.

'That I do know, sahib,' he admitted. 'I understand the remark was not meant to be irreverent. It is forgotten. I will bring the sahib food that he will like and take these away,' he indicated the chapatis he held in his hands. 'It must be long since he ate as he would wish.'

Aziz Ullah thanked him, whereupon he stalked away with the dignity of bearing so typical of soldiers of his race. The others watched him go.

'Touchy beggars these Mohammedans,' commented Kershaw. 'Still it was damned tactless of me. I could have kicked myself. Let us take a stroll. If we keep well under the bluff we won't be seen, even if there's anyone to see us. Abdul Qadir and his brother can't hear. Still, I'd like to stretch my legs a bit.'

They set off presenting a strange contrast – the apparently old, bent Afghan beside the slight, upright Englishman.

'So you got the brother?' remarked the former.

'Yes; or rather Rashid did. He's the second package over there. Poor blighters! I can't help feeling sorry for them, but there was no other way. Rashid went to Gharat, while I waited a couple of miles from the village. It didn't take him long to find the whereabouts of the fellow – Gharat's a tiny place, as you know. He told him he had been sent from the mountains by Abdul Qadir Khan at the request of Aziz Ullah with orders to conduct him to the retreat. He fell into the trap without question, which isn't to be wondered at, as only he and his brother knew anything about the meeting with you. Rashid brought him to me. Of course I was waiting in a carefully selected spot. I administered the same medicine as Abdul Qadir had received. We bound and gagged him, rolled him up in another bale, and there you are. Of course Rashid had to buy a second mule. It was too much to ask one animal to carry both. The fresh acquisition is a poor flea-bitten sort of creature, but it meets requirements.'

Suddenly from afar off came the cry of a muezzin: '*La Illah ha il Illah ho, O Muhammad Rasul il Illah.*'

Aziz looked sharply at his companion.

'We're nearer humanity than I thought,' he observed. 'There must be a mosque quite close.'

'Not particularly. A cry like that carries a long distance in this still air. Anyhow, nobody bothers to come down here, where the river's practically dried up. Don't worry. I know the country like a book and the habits of the people almost as well.'

But always there is the unexpected element to be feared. That evening, some time after the sun had set and darkness had fallen with its usual abruptness, there appeared with startling suddenness a body of mounted troops under the command of an officer with a ferret-like face and small, shifty eyes. Where they had come from or what they were doing on the dried-up bed of the river puzzled Kershaw and his companions exceedingly. Rashid was just about to unwrap the material binding Abdul Qadir and his brother, preparatory to giving the two exercise, fresh air, and a meal. Fortunately he became aware of the newcomers, and desisted from his occupation in time.

They might have passed by without noticing the little encampment, had there not been a fire burning. The moon was not due to rise for some time, consequently it was darker than it would be later on. Kershaw muttered something that sounded like a curse on the campfire, rose hastily from the rug upon which he had been sitting, and went across to meet the officer who had halted his men. Aziz Ullah crept out of view. As yet he had made no alteration to his appearance. It would not do for an old man of the type he represented to be seen in the company of an English merchant. The officer dismounted as Kershaw reached him; peered suspiciously at him through the gloom. It was not too dark for him to see that he was facing a white man, one who appeared rather well groomed. He grunted.

'It is strange to find one of your race in such a place,' he commented. 'Who are you and what are you doing here?'

Kershaw explained that he was the representative of an English firm and was travelling from Kabul to Peshawar. Purposely he spoke in halting Pashto, to give the impression that his knowledge of the language was not very great.

'The heat was so intense,' he told the other, 'that I preferred to camp for the night rather than enter Dakka. I came to the river, thinking it would be cooler by the side of the water, but alas! There is little water.'

'Of a certainty you know not the Kabul River,' commented the officer. He threw the reins of his horse to an orderly, who had dismounted, and stood by. 'I would look round your camp,' he announced.

That was exactly what Kershaw did not want him to do. However, any sign of reluctance on his part would only cause the other's suspicions to increase, with probably unfortunate results. He avowed himself as delighted, therefore; expressed the hope that the officer would take refreshments with him. The invitation, as he anticipated, caused his companion to become a little warmer in his attitude.

'I fear I cannot stay long,' he remarked. 'I am travelling on an important mission. There is a badly wanted band of outlaws ranging the country. I am in search of them. It is known they are somewhere in this neighbourhood, and when I saw your campfire, I at first thought they were here. It is the kind of place they would choose in which to rest.'

The reason for the appearance of the troop in that out-of-the-way spot was now apparent. It caused Kershaw to reflect, somewhat ruefully, that one can be absolutely certain of remarkably little in this world. He wished to persuade the officer to take a seat on the rug with him, and order Rashid to bring refreshments, but the fellow insisted on walking round, peering at the various bundles on the ground. To Kershaw's dismay, he bestowed particular attention on the long packages containing Abdul Qadir Khan and his brother.

'What have you in these?' he asked.

'Rather a mixture,' confided the Englishman. 'I have collected one or two Persian rugs, some silks, and various other articles, which I hope some day to take to my own country. They are packed like that for easier and more secure transportation.'

The other glanced at him slyly.

'And perhaps to delude the customs,' he observed with a laugh. 'I have heard that people passing into India try often to do so without paying duty on articles they take in.' Suddenly he administered a kick to one of the packages, and Kershaw thought contritely of the Mahsud concealed inside. 'You have something harder than silk or carpets within there,' commented the Afghan. 'Would you mind unrolling this? I am greatly interested to see what it is of my country English people treasure.'

The British Intelligence officer was at his wits' end. Suddenly he saw the scheming, the plotting and planning of months rendered futile, at one unexpected blow, simply because a ferret-faced Afghan cavalry officer was curious. If he refused to unpack the roll, suspicion would immediately become intensified, and he would be forced to divulge the contents to the man, backed by his troop of well-armed soldiers. On the other hand, if he submitted, Abdul Qadir would be freed to continue his subversive activities, all Aziz Ullah's efforts and his own would be ruined. The peril on the frontier would become greater than ever. He did not think of the certainty that he also would suffer, perhaps be thrown into an Afghan prison and left there to die. Personal considerations meant nothing to him.

'I am afraid,' he observed calmly, 'that it will be rather a difficult task to undo these bales. They have been very tightly strapped. However, if you really wish it—'

'I do. I hope you will not think I am too inquisitive.'

He would have been outraged had he known what Kershaw was actually thinking of him at that moment. The Englishman called over Rashid.

'Help me to untie this,' he ordered. 'Untie it, you understand? I know it will be difficult, but the ropes must not be cut. If that is done, we shall never be able to pack it securely again.'

Thus he conveyed to Mahommed Rashid that he was to experience great difficulty in unfastening the knots. Anything to gain time; though Kershaw felt delay would not help. He was becoming convinced that all was up with him and Aziz. The triumph they had accomplished was about to prove barren, to be transformed into utter failure. Working with apparent zeal, the two set to work, while the Afghan officer stood by smoking a cigarette. Ten minutes labour only saw two ropes untied. Kershaw looked up with a smile.

'I am sorry it is taking so long,' he apologised. 'Patience and you will set eyes on that which my people greatly treasure.'

At that moment the clear stillness of the night was shattered by a shot, followed by a cry; then came several in quick succession, a perfect din of yells, more shots, and silence. The Afghan swung round as though he himself had become a victim of the shooting. Kershaw and Rashid ceased their labours, and strained their ears in a futile attempt to pierce the darkness. The firing appeared to have come from the other side of the river. Without a word, the officer ran to his horse; sprang into the saddle, at the same time shouting an order. The troop galloped away, the thunder of the horses' hooves decreasing rapidly as they quickly drew farther and farther from the little camp. Another shot, more cries were heard – this time it appeared the sound came from a much greater distance than before. Then, once again, complete silence was restored to the neighbourhood. Kershaw sat down, and wiped away the beads of perspiration that liberally besprinkled his brow.

'Phew!' he gasped. 'What an escape! If the outlaws, for whom the soldiers are searching, were responsible for that shooting,' he added to Rashid in Punjabi, 'we owe them a deep debt of gratitude.'

In reply the havildar laughed quietly.

'It is in my mind,' he murmured, 'that the shots were

not fired by bandits, but that the sahib came to the rescue.'

Kershaw whistled.

'By Jove!' he muttered in English, more to himself than to his companion. 'I believe you're right. But how did he get over there and where did he get the rifle. He was not armed.'

Rashid disappeared into the darkness; returned silently a few minutes later.

'Your pony and your rifle are gone, sahib,' he announced. 'Allah grant he will receive the good fortune his gallantry deserves. They will shoot him down or hang him if they catch him.'

'For God's sake, don't talk like that, Rashid,' snapped Kershaw. 'Why should he be caught?'

'I believe he will not be satisfied until he has led them so far from us that they will not return here. Your pony is swift, sahib, but it has not the speed of the horses.'

Kershaw knew he was right. Aziz Ullah, in his efforts to prevent Abdul Qadir Khan and his brother from being discovered and released, had taken a step that might well lead to his own death. For a long time he sat, straining his ears for any sounds that might indicate what was happening, even though he realised that it was wasted effort. Once he thought he heard rifle shots again but, if so, they were too far off to be distinguished with any certainty or to convey any clue to his mind concerning the identity of the man or men who had fired them. He decided that he dare not remain in that neighbourhood long. The Afghan officer was far too curious for his peace of mind. Despite Rashid's words, he might return during the night. There was a possibility he would abandon the search sooner than expected or, and the thought caused the Englishman another pang of apprehension, he might quickly overtake Aziz and kill or capture him. No use giving way to morbid thoughts! Kershaw rose and gave orders for the prisoners to be released and fed. That must be done. It was bad enough in all conscience being compelled to make them travel in a manner so unpleasant. He had no intention of starving them, or refusing them fresh air and exercise.

By way of contrast with his and Rashid's laborious efforts to open the rolls while the Afghan officer was present, it was remarkable how quickly the men were now released from their wrappings. Each in turn was allowed to walk about, the strappings being removed from his legs, but his hands were kept pinioned and the gag not removed from his mouth, until he was given food and drink. These precautions, of course, were necessary, but there was little danger to be apprehended from the two now. The manner of their confinement had completely knocked the spirit from them, besides which their bodies had become far too stiff to enable them to make any efforts on their own behalf. At first, Kershaw and the havildar had had considerable trouble from them as well as the most fiery abuse, had been compelled on three occasions to act somewhat severely. For four days they had refused food but nature had conquered that kind of obstinacy. Afterwards they were sullen but utterly quiescent, ate and drank all that was given to them and otherwise submitted. Kershaw intensely disliked forcing them to travel in such discomfort, regretted the necessity of it, but there was no other way. As far as possible, he had lightened things for them, travelling slowly in order that they would not be bumped too much, and in many ways tried to ease their lot.

On this particular night, he was on tenterhooks until the two were packed in their wrappings again. The unexpected appearance of the troop of soldiers had destroyed his faith in the rendezvous he had selected. He had been so sure of it, only to have his confidence shattered. If one body of men appeared there, it was just as likely others might come. Apart from this, he knew it was his duty to get away from the spot as quickly as possible in case the inquisitive Afghan officer returned with his men. Naturally all his instincts rebelled against leaving without Aziz Ullah – he longed almost passionately to wait there for him, at least, until hope that he would return had evaporated. But men in his position, with great issues depending on them, cannot consider personal or comradely inclinations. He compromised with himself by waiting until within an hour of dawn; then reluctantly helped Rashid strap their human and other bundles on to the pack mules, and gave the order to start. He rode the havildar's pony, the latter being astride that of Aziz Ullah. From the time that Abdul Qadir Khan and his brother had been exercised and fed until the departure, Kershaw and Rashid had sat almost motionless waiting for the return of the man whose resource had saved the enterprise from ruin. Both had been afflicted with the keenest anxiety. Kershaw declared afterwards that the suspense was agonising. It can be imagined how they felt when, after waiting until the last possible moment, they were forced to go without Aziz Ullah and in fear that he had been killed or captured.

Their journeyings from then on were fairly uneventful. They crossed the border of Afghanistan safely, but, if anything,

Kershaw's precautions were increased. They were now in the land of the Pathan tribes; in other words, in districts from which Abdul Qadir Khan had hoped to enlist and train the army that he had intended eventually to throw against the British. There was never any certainty that a solitary Englishman would pass unmolested through that lawless country. However, Landi Kotal was reached safely, and there Kershaw obtained an escort of Gurkhas, who marched with him down the Khaibar and on to Peshawar. He had not considered it expedient or wise to travel by train. An inclination had assailed him at Landi Kotal to leave his prisoners there, while he went back to search for Aziz Ullah, but his duty prevented this. He must carry on to Peshawar. Besides, there was very little hope of any success regarding such an undertaking. If Aziz had escaped from the men he had led on such a wild goose chase, it was certain he would now be on his way to Peshawar. The fact that he had not caught them up reduced Kershaw's spirits to the lowest ebb. By the time he reached Peshawar, and Abdul Qadir Khan and his brother had been imprisoned in the Cantonments, he had given up hope for ever of seeing Aziz Ullah alive again.

The two Mahsuds were locked up with the greatest secrecy. It was essential that no whisper of the Khan's capture should leak out. Having handed them over, Kershaw sent a laconic telegram to Major-General Sir Leslie Hastings. Then he was driven to Dean's Hotel. Almost the first person he saw there, squatting on the veranda outside his rooms, was Aziz Ullah!

He barely succeeded in stifling a great cry of joy and relief in time. It would never do for an Englishman to show such tremendous elation at sight of the disreputable old man who rose to greet him. Hurrying the latter inside, he closed the door, and clasped Aziz Ullah's hand in both of his.

'By Jove, old chap!' he cried. 'I have never felt so glad to see anybody in my life before. It is really you, isn't it? I'm not suffering from fever and delusions, am I?'

For answer the other gave him a grip that caused him to howl with the pain of it.

'Certain now?' asked Aziz with a smile.

'Yes; confound you. Was it necessary to break my bones to convince me? Sit down and – no, wait a while. My bearer will be along in a minute or two with a few bottles of iced beer. He's trustworthy enough, but it's just as well that he shouldn't know too much. We'll wait until he's gone.'

'Did you say beer?' asked Aziz Ullah in a tone of ecstasy.

Kershaw laughed.

'A fine Mohammedan you are, O Master. Yes; I said beer, my lad.'

'The blessings of Allah be upon you. I only want five things. Lots of beer – a few bottles will be no good to me – a bath, a shave, decent clothes, and a pipe of baccy.'

'You shall have all. I forgot to mention to you before that your suitcase duly arrived, and has been locked up in the bedroom there for the last six months.'

The bearer put in an appearance as he finished speaking, carrying four large bottles of Allsopp's Lager in an ice pail. He took little notice of the disreputable old man standing before his master. He was used to the queer visitors Kershaw so often had in his rooms. The Intelligence officer sent him to find Havildar Mahommed Rashid.

'That'll keep him out of the way for a bit,' confided the latter when the man had gone. 'Rashid is probably in his quarters some distance from here taking a well-earned rest.'

'Why not let him continue to rest?' queried Aziz. 'Surely you could have got rid of the bearer on some other pretext?'

'Rashid would never forgive me if I didn't let him know at once that you are safe. He's been as anxious as I about you.' He rummaged in a cupboard, produced a couple of pewter tankards, and filled them with the foaming lager. 'Sit down,' he urged, handing one to his guest, 'and tell me all about it.'

Aziz sank into a comfortable cane chair with a sigh of deep satisfaction.

'Do you think I can bear to talk when I have this in my hand?' he asked reproachfully. 'Have a heart! This is the first man's drink I've touched for over six months. Cheer ho!'

Kershaw responded suitably, and the two quaffed the beer in copious draughts. Aziz put down his tankard empty.

'Lord!' he gasped. 'I've always liked my beer, but I've never known it taste quite so good before. Encore please.' Kershaw obliged. His visitor accepted the replenished tankard gratefully. 'I can talk now,' he proclaimed.

Thereupon he plunged into a recital of his adventures since leaving the rendezvous near Dakka. When the Afghan troops had appeared, he had hidden himself by climbing into a tree a short distance away. From there, although he could not see anything but the campfire and the shadowy figures of Kershaw, Rashid, and the Afghan officer, he was able to hear distinctly and thus learnt about the outlaws. Directly he gathered that the officer insisted on seeing what was contained in the large packages, he slipped to earth, and crawled to the animals, picking up Kershaw's sporting rifle on the way. He guessed that the Intelligence officer and Rashid would delay the opening of the rolls as long as they possibly could, and calculated that he would thus have time to get a good distance from the camp. He had been compelled at first to lead the pony he took, in order to make as little sound as possible. But he had mounted as soon as he dared, and had crossed to the other bank of the river. There he had fired a shot and shouted, paused a little, and then fired and yelled again.

'I tried to sound like a crowd,' he remarked.

'You succeeded,' Kershaw assured him. 'I certainly thought the bandits that fellow was after had quite innocently created a diversion. I said so to Rashid, when the Afghans stampeded after you.'

Aziz went on to tell him how he had waited until he heard the thunder of hooves; then had ridden away, firing an occasional shot or two at first, later dropping various things, such as an article of clothing, cartridge cases, and so on.

'They must have wondered what the outlaws were playing at,' he commented, 'but that didn't matter a hoot. They could think what they liked so long as they kept on following me. When I calculated I had covered some miles from you, I stopped, dismounted, and removed the saddle from your beast. It was a particularly English-looking affair, and wouldn't have passed muster as the possession of an Afghan bandit. Then I gave the pony a hearty punch which sent it careering away, hid the saddle, and sat down to wait. I had to wait a jolly long time too, and began to fear the troops had given up the chase and gone back, but, at last, they arrived. They pounced on me with glee. In fact, they seemed so glad to see me that I thought they would pretend I was one of the outlaws, to save themselves trouble, and take me back in triumph to Dakka, saying that they had killed the rest or something. But I suppose I looked too old and feeble to delude anybody into believing I was a tough guy—'

'Phew!' whistled Kershaw softly, admiration showing in his eyes. 'You took an infernal risk. I hate to think what would have happened had they taken you along with them, and washed your face.'

'Well, they didn't. They bombarded the old man – that's me – with questions, and I sent them off quite happily, with a tale that a dozen or so wild-looking fellows had passed by half an hour or so before riding like the wind. They didn't even ask me what I was doing there. I suppose they thought I was just a tramp. That's about all I think. I buried your saddle, and set off to walk to Landi Kotal. It wasn't any use going back to find you. It took me two days pretty steady going to get there. Every time I met anybody, I had to go all bent and feeble and old. I begged or stole food. By that time I was too dilapidated to buy it – it might have roused suspicion had I produced money. Sorry about your pony and saddle, Kershaw, but que voulez vous?'

The red-haired Intelligence officer was sitting as though lost in admiration.

'And they say the old spirit of the adventurers is dead!' he murmured.

'For goodness' sake, don't come all over mushy,' begged the

other. 'By the way,' he went on, 'I managed to hold on to your rifle. I left it with some of the lads at Landi Kotal. They were damned inquisitive to know how I had come into possession of it, and I'm afraid I had to tell a few fibs. Anyhow, you've only to ask for it in the mess next time you're in Landi Kotal.'

'How did you get it over the Frontier in your get-up?' asked the surprised Kershaw. 'And where did you conceal it during your journey?'

Aziz Ullah smiled.

'Rolled it in some of my rags,' he replied. 'As for the Frontier, I crossed where there weren't no bloomin' outposts or prying eyes or nuffin'. As a matter of fact, I travelled to Landi up and down some of the grimmest, most barren-looking precipices I've ever tackled. Talk about mountaineering! If I ever go climbing in Switzerland again, it'll seem like up a staircase, after those I've just negotiated.'

Kershaw gave vent to a deep sigh.

'You're a marvel!' he exclaimed. 'And the general spoke of Aziz Ullah as "That bloody Afghan" in tones of the deepest contempt. He's in for a number one surprise. By the way, how is it you got here before me, when—?'

'Use your brains, my lad. I travelled from Landi Kotal by train; squeezed in among a crowd of smelly Peshawaris, wives, children, family utensils, and whatnots. It was great fun. And now what about your end? You got Abdul Qadir and brother through all right, I hope?'

Kershaw nodded.

'They're lodged secretly and safely in the Cantonments.'

Aziz Ullah drained his tankard.

'Good!' he remarked. 'I can now become human again. Lead me to a bath, Kershaw, where I can soak for some hours. Then for the luxury of a shave, some nice Christian duds, a haircut, more beer, and a succession of pipes. And heigh ho! Farewell to Aziz Ullah. May the peace of Allah be upon him.'

Major-General Sir Leslie Hastings had not heard any news of Major Kershaw for some weeks and had reached the point of exasperation again. The consequence was that his staff, although now in the cool altitudes of Murree, were again in a state of heated resentment. All this was suddenly changed, however, when a telegram arrived from Peshawar. Captain Charteris opened, and read it, gave a single whoop of joy, and actually ran to the general's office, quite oblivious to any scandal this lack of decorum on the part of a staff officer might cause to the orderlies and sentries. He burst into Sir Leslie's room, forgetting to knock, and waved the telegram in the air. The startled general looked at him as though he thought he had gone mad.

'What the devil's the matter with you, Charteris?' he demanded wrathfully.

'A telegram, sir.'

'Confound you! I can see that. What's in it to make you behave like a lunatic?'

'It's from Major Kershaw, sir. He's back in Peshawar with Abdul Qadir Khan!'

'Eh! What's that? What's that?' The general rose from his chair with surprising agility for one of his bulk, leant forward, and almost snatched the telegram from his secretary's hand. "Have brought A. Q. to Peshawar," he read aloud. "If not

coming down, kindly wire instructions." If not coming down!'
he repeated with a sound that was very much like a snort. 'Of
course, I'm going down. Charteris, order a car at once. We'll be
able to reach 'Pindi by dark, and can go on to Peshawar early
in the morning. Send a wire telling Kershaw I'll be there before
noon. Gad! What a man!' he exulted, as the staff officer hurried
from the room.

'Jumbo' was as good as his word. His car, white with dust,
drew up outside command headquarters at ten minutes to
twelve on the following morning. The general found Major
Kershaw awaiting his arrival.

'Glad to see you, Ginger,' he bellowed, as he stepped from
the motor, forgetting for once in a way that such familiarity and
lack of dignity on the part of a general officer was not conducive
to good discipline. As a matter of fact, he was like a schoolboy
on holiday. Captain Charteris who, of course, was with him,
had never seen this side of his character before, and had begun
to form a different opinion of him. 'Come along in,' Sir Leslie
invited the smiling Kershaw. 'Your news sounds so good that
I feel there must be a catch in it somewhere.' When they were
seated alone in the office, with the fans going full speed he leant
eagerly forward. 'Is it actually true? You have brought Abdul
Qadir to Peshawar?'

'Yes; he and a fellow called Sikandar Khan – he says he's
a brother – are under close guard in a part of jail which has
been cleared specially so that the news can't leak out. My
advice to you, sir, if I may presume, is to spirit them away
from this part of the country at once – send them to Delhi
by special train tonight.'

'H'm! Sounds the sensible thing to do. But how the devil did you manage to get him?'

'I did very little, sir. The brain behind the whole scheme was that of Sir Leonard Wallace—'

'What! You mean the Director of the Secret Service?'

'There is only one Sir Leonard Wallace,' returned Kershaw. 'He conceived the scheme, and one of his most brilliant men carried it out marvellously. I assisted in a very chota manner.'

'Who is the man to whom you are referring?'

'Aziz Ullah, sir. The bloke you called "That Bloody Afghan".'

The GOC stared at him incredulously for several seconds; then:

'You'd better start at the beginning and tell me the whole tale,' he decided.

'Right,' assented Kershaw. 'Some months ago, when it was first discovered that this new and very modern menace Abdul Qadir Khan had risen on the Frontier – the news first reached Sir Leonard from an agent of his in Persia – all kinds of traps were laid for him, but he was far too cunning to fall into them. Sir Leonard then conceived a scheme that for sheer subtlety and ingenuity would take a lot of beating. It had been learnt that one of Abdul Qadir's pet ideas was to ally Afghanistan with him. He knew very well the amir and present government were friendly with England, but it isn't so difficult to overthrow kings and governments in Afghanistan, so long as the proper man with the right personality and powers of leadership comes along. From Abdul Qadir's point of view, he must also be one who, for services rendered, would afterwards put the Afghan army at his disposal. He scoured the country for such a man. Sir

Leonard Wallace decided to supply him with one, who would eventually trap him. Now the Chief of the Secret Service is far too clever to create entirely imaginary people. He realised that inquiries might crash the whole scheme. Information was immediately sought concerning Afghans living in Persia. He chose Imam Aziz Ullah of Meshed, who had been born in Herat, and had moved to the Persian city as a boy. There his life has been devoted to religion, he is almost a recluse, and is regarded as a very holy man. Sir Leonard selected one of his most efficient agents, a man who speaks Persian like a native. This man spent some time in Meshed, studying Aziz Ullah; then travelled from Bushire to Karachi, where I met him. I had received orders through the Intelligence Department of the Indian government. The whole scheme was put to me by the new Aziz Ullah, who by then had grown a beard and allowed his hair to lengthen. He dyed his body with a stain that no amount of washing or rubbing would remove, and which wears off slowly, only having to be renewed occasionally. Dressed in native attire, he then departed to commence his work, having had his European belongings packed in a suitcase which was duly forwarded to me at Dean's. He travelled by way of Baluchistan into Afghanistan and spent a couple of months becoming fully acquainted with customs, habits and the part of the country in which he was to operate. From my knowledge, I had been able to give him directions enabling him to find a safe retreat in which to hide and a rendezvous where he and I could meet occasionally.

'Sir Leonard's idea, you see, sir, was that Abdul Qadir Khan could only be trapped by the appearance of somebody who fitted into his schemes, yet was apparently in no way concerned with him. No harm was intended or could possibly come to Afghanistan. If this plot ended in a betterment of conditions for the lower-class Afghans, so much to the good. The poor beggars needed it. It has. Our Aziz has worked wonders for them. Abdul Qadir soon realised, and without any suspicions, that the very man he wanted had arisen. He made attempts to get into communication with him, only to be rebuffed at first. It was part of the game naturally for Aziz to appear reluctant to have anything to do with him.'

Kershaw then went on to give a full account of Aziz Ullah's operations in Afghanistan, the triumph at Kabul, and then the manner in which Abdul Qadir Khan had been trapped and brought to Peshawar. Sir Leslie Hastings sat entranced. At the end of the recital, he seemed to find it difficult to express his feelings.

'Gad!' he exclaimed at last, then again: 'Gad! Kershaw,' he added with a smile, 'I shan't be happy until I shake hands with – that bloody Afghan.'

Ginger laughed, and rose from his chair.

'He's at the hotel, sir. I'll send for him at once.'

When he came back to the room, he described to the general how, for a long time, Abdul Qadir Khan had been smuggling munitions in vast quantities from Russia through Turkestan to a well-selected spot near Shabqadar. He repeated all he had heard Abdul Qadir divulge to Aziz Ullah, and showed Sir Leslie the map and other documents taken from the Mahsud. The general could not read either, as his knowledge of the vernacular was practically non-existent, but his quick mind soon grasped all salient facts. He agreed with Kershaw that he had every excuse for a punitive expedition. The mass of smuggled military stores was more than enough for this. With Sir Leslie, to decide was to act. It may be as well to relate here that two nights later a large force of troops guided by Kershaw, descended suddenly on Shabqadar. The hiding place of the munitions was captured practically without a fight, the surprise was complete. Men of the Sappers and Miners dynamited the caves, wherein the arms and ammunition were stored, and Abdul Qadir Khan's ambitions were destroyed for ever. He himself was sent into exile.

While the two officers were planning the scoop, there came a knock at the door. In response to the general's invitation, a tall, immensely broad individual entered the room. He was immaculately clothed in a well-cut silk suit; was altogether an attractive figure, with his clean-shaven face, clear grey eyes, square jaw and other fine features. His skin, however, was a light brown. Smiling broadly at Kershaw, he stood stiffly to attention, as the general rose to greet him.

'You sent for me, sir?' he asked.

'This, General,' introduced Ginger Kershaw, 'is Aziz Ullah who has done so much for Afghanistan and incidentally for Great Britain. In other words, he is your bloody Afghan – Captain Hugh Shannon of the British Secret Service.'